Pampered

Pampered

Germaine Solomon

www.urbanbooks.net

Urban Books, LLC
300 Farmingdale Road, NY-Route 109
Farmingdale, NY 11735

ISBN 13: 978-1-945855-31-3
ISBN 10: 1-945855-31-2

First Trade Paperback Printing July 2018
Printed in the United States of America

10 9 8 7 6 5 4 3 2 1

This is a work of fiction. Any references or similarities to actual events, real people, living or dead, or to real locales are intended to give the novel a sense of reality. Any similarity in other names, characters, places, and incidents is entirely coincidental.

Distributed by Kensington Publishing Corp.
Submit Orders to:
Customer Service
400 Hahn Road
Westminster, MD 21157-4627
Phone: 1-800-733-3000
Fax: 1-800-659-2436

Pampered

by

Germaine Solomon

Book Dedication

This book is dedicated to my only child, my smart and handsome son, Solomon. Mommy loves you, baby! I also dedicate this book to the two people who gave me life. Mama and Daddy, you are the world's greatest parents. Thank you for everything.

Acknowledgments

To God be the glory for the many things He has done. Thank you, Father, for the gift of creative writing. This book was a project of faith. No one knows that better than my family and my crew. This story would never have come to fruition without your love, support, and encouragement. Thank you, Little Solomon and Big Solomon for putting up with my eccentric self day in and day out. You make me a better wife and mother because of your unwavering support. I love you two to the moon and back. I love you, Mama and Daddy for being the foundation upon which I rise. Words can't describe how much you mean to me. My oldest sister, Dawn, and my youngest sister, Nikki, hold me down in every aspect of my life. But they are deep into my writing career, and I appreciate it with all my heart, ladies. I love y'all crazy heifers. LOL! Andra, you do so much for me, so I don't have time or space to list it all. I'll just sum it up like this: You are there when no one else is, and you give it to me straight all the time whether I like it or not. Everyone needs a ride or die like you in their life. I couldn't do what I do without you. Thank you for everything. I owe a shout out to Jeff and Shirley for supporting me. My family of birth, as well as the family I married into, have been very instrumental in my career, and I am grateful to have each of you in my life. To the best screen team on the planet, I offer sincere appreciation even though y'all can be cruel sometimes. Thank you, Dawn, Nikki, Andra, Deborah

Acknowledgments

Anne, Cherell, Christan, Katanga, and Geisel for taking the ride with me. I listen to everything y'all tell me. Thank you, my sistahs in this cut-throat industry who support me. I'm talking about fellow authors, Perri Forrest, Jasmine Williams, Bianca Harrison, and Phoenix Rayne. I've got nothing but love for you, ladies. I must especially thank Perri Forrest for designing my super amazing book cover. It is fabulous, girl! Thank you a thousand times from the bottom of my heart. Sabrina Diamond Lewis of Diamond Voiceovers, you gave 150% on my book trailer. You are the best who's ever done it, boo! I love you to pieces. Saxton Nyle Keitt, Gerald Alexander Lawson, and Allison Randall Berewa, I appreciate you for lending your voices and talents to the video production. It turned out great because of you three. Thanks to everyone who will purchase this book. It came directly from my heart, and I hope it will be received in the same manner. Finally, thank you, Mr. Blake Karrington for noticing my gift and blessing me with an opportunity to shine.

Prologue

"Aaaggghhh, fuck, nah!" A deep and demonic voice shattered the calmness in the courtroom.

The first gunshot elicited blood-curdling screams from the slowly dispersing crowd all around me. Mama yanked me by my hand, trying to pull me down to the floor along with her. But before I lowered my head all the way down, I looked toward the front of the courtroom. Satchel had a gun in his hand, firing shots in rapid succession toward the prosecutor's table where Eli, Marlon, and Sergio were standing talking to Assistant District Attorney Dunbar. A bailiff was trying his best to get the gun away from Satchel and restrain him, but he was throwing punches with one arm and shooting aimlessly like a deranged terrorist with the other. My heart dropped, and I screamed from deep down in my belly when I saw my husband's body jerk violently as Sergio lunged to cover him. They both collapsed to the floor seconds after Marlon dropped down low.

One last shot crackled above the screams and sound of bodies scrambling in all directions. Women were crying and pleading for mercy, and I saw men crawling around on the floor attempting to comfort them. The scene was insane and chaotic. I raised my head slightly with my heart pounding like a jackhammer in my chest. I saw a group of bailiffs huddled above someone lying on the floor where Satchel had stood firing off shots.

I struggled to my feet when I saw Sergio walking stiffly toward me with blood oozing from his left shoulder, drenching his beige suit coat. I hurried in his direction even though a bailiff tried to hold me back.

"Where is Eli?" I asked, already knowing the answer to my question. I could feel it in my gut. My man had been hit with at least one bullet. Otherwise, I would've been in his protective arms instead of facing Sergio.

"He's been shot, Mrs. Jamieson. I'm so sorry. I tried my damnedest to protect him, but it happened too fast. Stay calm, though. An ambulance is on its way."

I pushed past him and forced my way through the crowd. I didn't stop until I reached my husband. I kneeled down and touched his pale face. He looked at me and attempted to smile. He must've been shot in the stomach because his lower body was saturated with bright red blood.

"Eli, please don't leave me. You promised me fifty more years."

He tried to speak, but blood bubbled from his throat and spilled from his mouth before his eyes rolled to the back of his head and closed. This was not supposed to be happening! Had God suddenly forsaken me? And if He had, I wanted to know why. No, I *demanded* to know why as a seizure ripped through every muscle in Eli's anatomy.

"Noooo, Eliiii, noooo!"

Eight Months Earlier . . .

Chapter One

Eli and Radiance

I took the seat behind my desk as my students filed by to submit their midterm marketing analysis reports. I braced myself as the lovely Ms. Alexander drew closer to me. Everything about the young woman put all of my masculine senses on high alert. In addition to being one of my brightest students, she was the *sexiest* of all. It fascinated me how she seemed to have no knowledge of how gorgeous she was. Her beauty, natural and mesmerizing, was impossible for any virile, warm-blooded male to ignore. Quite honestly, I often found the ebony goddess to be a major distraction.

The sight of Radiance Alexander caused my cock to stand at full attention like a decorated soldier at some of the most inopportune times. For instance, right before my lecture on international mass marketing campaigns last Friday, she arrived ten minutes ahead of the other students, as usual. Her heavenly scent and raw femininity, adorned in an orange strapless sundress splattered with big white flowers, interrupted my concentration and took me prisoner. As she flipped casually through the pages of a book, I studied her intensely from her long, silky mane down to her toenails glossed over with creamy white polish. The young woman was an exquisite female creature. Her deep, rich, sun-kissed complexion was flawless. It reminded me of smooth, sweet Godiva chocolate. Damn! My taste buds and salivary glands betrayed me every time I imagined bathing every inch of her flesh with my tongue. I swallowed deeply to keep from embarrassing myself by drooling like an infant.

My fingertips tingled as I envisioned kneading and caressing her body in its most intimate places until she submitted to my every sexual wish and command. Her ass and set of firm, perfectly round knockers would receive an abundance of my attention. I penetrated her with my gaze as a young man separated us in distance. I disregarded his ramblings about the work he'd put into his marketing report as he placed it on the pile of others on top of my desk. I only had eyes and interest for the charming Ms. Alexander. I smiled at her the instant the young male student stepped away from my desk. She was now in my unobstructed view. And that damn butterfly tattoo on the upper right part of her back, close to her shoulder, caused my blood to simmer and rush to my penis every damn time I saw it. A wave of pure hot lust washed over me, just thinking about it, and I scolded myself inwardly. I was her professor, and she was my student. My thoughts and desires of the things I wanted to do to her were totally inappropriate.

I cleared my throat and attempted to will my immoral thoughts away. "Ms. Alexander, I look forward to evaluating your report. I hope you didn't find the assignment too difficult."

She offered me a faint smile before replying, "The graphs were a little tricky in the beginning, but I think I finally got the gist of them."

When she smiled and walked away, I saw that seductive tattoo. I had to fight my caveman instincts with every fiber of my being. I wanted to hoist Ms. Alexander over my shoulder and kidnap her to make her my captive on a deserted island someplace far away from civilization. I would show her no mercy with the exceptions of nourishment, shelter, and proper hygienic care. She would never wear clothes. As the prisoner of my personal pleasure, all garments would be forbidden. I would feast on her naked body daily, branding her as mine with my manhood, hands, and tongue until she became overcome with exhaustion and needed to sleep. Then I would count down the hours until rest and a decent meal would allow me to take her again and again and . . .

"Somebody's mind is a million miles away today."

I blinked a few times and shook my head, snatching my mind away from my erotic fantasy. "Dean Schlesinger, how are you, sir?" I offered my hand in a friendly shake.

"Apparently, I'm not doing as well as *you* are. There was fire in your eyes while you were daydreaming, Eli. The woman you were thinking about must be a *pistol*. I think I even heard you moan a couple of times." He chuckled at the expense of my embarrassment.

"I . . . um . . . was pondering over a few business matters. Teaching this class while running a global corporation at the same time isn't easy, sir."

"That's why I decided to stop by. I wanted to offer you a little treat for all of your hard work here at the university. Hadassah and I would love to have you over for dinner this evening. Our eldest son, Lennox, and his family are in town visiting us from Portland, Oregon. He's quite the businessman. I'd like you two to meet. I'm sure you could give him a few tips on how to build a money-making empire from the ground up."

I checked my watch and noted the time. If I were to leave campus in the next ten minutes, I would have enough time to complete all of my best man duties, shower, and change before the bachelor party tonight.

"I would love to meet your son, sir, but unfortunately, it can't be this evening. I have a previous engagement."

"Oh my," he said, grinning mischievously as his eyes danced knowingly. "Pardon me from trying to steal you away from your love interest. I understand the primitive call of nature, Eli. I haven't had this gray hair or receding hairline all of my life. I used to be quite frisky."

I nearly gagged at the thought of his last statement, but I recovered quickly. "I don't have a date, Dean Schlesinger. In fact, there's presently no woman in my life," I lied while cringing on the inside when an image of Pandora floated through my mind.

"Well, I may have to do something about that."

"Oh, no thank you, sir. I'm enjoying my life as a single man just fine."

"Very well then. I'll see you at the department meeting Monday morning."

"Of course, sir."

I frowned when Cassidy, the entertainment coordinator at my job, waved me over to the other side of the club. The chick didn't like me, and I couldn't stand her tacky ass. She wasn't my supervisor. Hell, she didn't even work in my department. I wondered what the hell she wanted with me. It was too busy at the Pleasure Palace tonight for any bullshit. I took my time crossing the floor, headed in her direction.

"What's up, Cassidy?"

"I need a favor, doll."

I looked at her like she was a stinky dog turd on the floor. I didn't owe her a damn thing. "I'm listening."

"Magic got arrested earlier today. She can't find anyone to put up her bail."

"*And*?"

"She was supposed to work this bachelor party booked in the Paradise Room tonight." She leaned in and whispered, "These are some highfalutin rich men. They ain't no thugs. They're wealthy, *white*, successful gentlemen. And they're legitimate too."

"What does any of that have to do with *me*?" I folded my arms across my chest. There were plenty of rich legitimate *brothahs* who frequented the Pleasure Palace. How come she felt the need to stress the fact that these men were *white*? Did that somehow make them superior to other men?

"Don't you see? This is an opportunity for you to make some serious cash tonight, Ray. I'm looking out for you, being that you're a grad student raising Croix all by yourself since his daddy is in prison and all. I figured you could use the money."

"I ain't no stripper, Cassidy. I'm a *hostess*. I may dress risqué and put a little extra hip action in my walk around here, but I don't strip."

"Here's the thing," she said, touching my shoulder lightly. "Capri has agreed to get naked and do all of the bumping and grinding. All I need you to do is *one* harmless lap dance. It's a special treat for the groom and best man."

"What the fuck?"

"Hold up now. You've done it before."

"Yeah, I did, but that was at my homeboy's CD release party. I knew most of those guys in the room. Yolo wasn't about to let anything happen to me anyway."

"These men won't hurt you either. They know the rules. There'll be no touching. All you're expected to do is sit down on *one* millionaire's lap and wiggle and purr for a while. By the night's end, you'll have enough dough tucked in your garter to pay rent and buy groceries. What do you say, Ray?"

Chapter Two

Radiance

"You take the best man, Ray. I'm about to dance so good for that sexy-ass groom until he cums in his pants. Then I'm gonna whisper a whole bunch of nasty shit in his ear to make his *wallet* cum too." Capri burst into laughter, the sound of her raspy smoker's voice irritating my ears. "Whatever happens after that is all up to the universe."

I gave the best man a thorough once over, and immediately, my vajayjay got hot and creamy. The man was fine as hell! White men had never gotten any love from me before. I had pledged lifelong allegiance to brothahs. But the super sexy vanilla best man was drop-dead gorgeous. He had me thinking about crossing over. His long, black, wavy hair, cascading over his broad shoulders caused me to envision Sampson in the Bible. I'd always pictured him as a good-looking hunk of a man since he was so strong and powerful. And a Neanderthal of such great strength had to be huge.

Mr. Best Man, who was sitting next to the groom, didn't appear to be a giant like my visualization of Sampson, but he was tall enough. And he owned a chiseled body as far as I could make out. His five o'clock shadow gave him raw and rugged sex appeal that had my kitty cat meowing. I was going to have to change my thong before the night was over because his firm pectoral muscles were torturing my feminine senses. I had an urge to get butt-ass naked and beg him to end my three-year sex drought. He was just that damn tempting in a pair of well-worn, faded jeans with a tear at each knee and a simple black t-shirt. There was a tiny tattoo on his right forearm, but I couldn't make out the words or the symbol. It could've been Big Bird or Captain Crunch for all I cared. The man's mere presence had my body heat spiking off of the thermometer.

"Come, playmates," I heard Cassidy say to Capri and me. "These gentlemen are looking forward to a little bit of *private* entertainment." She turned to the groom and best man, waving her arm in our direction. "Gentlemen, meet Capri and Mysteria."

I licked my lips and squared my shoulders when Kelis' "Milkshake" started blaring through the speakers in the small and dimly-lit space. I saw two flashes of light—one on each side of the best man's face. And when he smiled, I almost stumbled from deliria. Those gold hoops in his earlobes had put the icing on the cake. I was about to enjoy myself while I made some extra money. My car was going to get out of Big Al's shop sooner than I'd planned.

Capri grabbed my arm. "It's show time, boo. Let's stack this paper."

I was as nervous as I'd been the morning the police raided my small campus apartment three years ago, but I wasn't about to show it. There was cheddar to be cut, and I needed every damn slice. As if on cue, Capri and I wiggled our bodies to the beat of the music as we sauntered slowly across the room toward the two men. They smiled appreciatively as we closed the distance, moving in their direction. With each step I took, the best man began to look more and more familiar to me. I was sure that I had seen him before, but I didn't know where. If we had crossed paths previously, I couldn't put my finger on the time or location. And luckily for me, I was unrecognizable behind my black cat mask covered with rhinestones.

My hair was different too. I never wore it straight to work. It was my ritual to wet it each night before I left home so that it would curl up as it air dried on the train commute. My life as a single mother and grad student was never to overlap with my job as a hostess at the Pleasure Palace.

The groom reached out and grabbed Capri's hips, slamming her ass forcefully onto his lap. She threw her head back and giggled like a dumb blonde when he rubbed her inner thigh and eased his hand higher toward her pussy. She didn't have any *performance boundaries* when it came to making money, but *I* did. I swallowed hard as I looked at the best man's large hand reaching out to me.

"I don't bite, babe . . . unless you *want* me to." He winked, and a rich and throaty laugh rumbled from his lips.

I trembled when his arms snaked around my bare midriff and spun me around. In a split second, he pulled me gently to sit on his lap. I felt his warm breath blowing through my hair and across the back of my neck. I also felt a hard bulge pressing against my ass, and it wasn't small by any woman's standards. I shifted my bottom away from it. But he gripped my hips and positioned me directly on top of it again.

"He wants you to dance for him, babe," he whispered in my ear, causing my entire body to shudder. "Go ahead now. Be a good little girl and dance for *him*." He leaned back in the chair and waited while his full erection continued to press and thump against my ass.

I *was* there to dance, and so far, he seemed like a half-decent guy. So I closed my eyes and cleared my mind to concentrate on the music. My body found its groove, and my hips started doing their thing. I rotated, bounced, and bucked while popping my fingers in coordination. My smooth snake-like motions earned me a few deep moans and growls of appreciation seconds before he reached around and dangled a crisp Benjamin in my face. Of course I snatched it quickly and secured it in my cleavage. That C-note motivated a poor struggling sistah.

I bent all the way over until I was almost able to plant my palms on the floor. I twerked like crazy, clapping my butt cheeks together against his dick rhythmically. Then I snatched myself upright again and did a bouncing centipede against his crotch, grinding into it.

"Ah yeah, I like that, sweet babe." He pushed my hair to the left side of my neck and kissed my right shoulder.

"You like that, bad boy?" I asked in an airy voice meant to add fuel to his already blazing fire. I rotated my ass against his stiff dick and felt it jump underneath me.

He did an upward thrust in response. "Yeah, I like it. Do it again, damn it." He kissed my shoulder a second time.

I did exactly what he'd demanded, and he ran his fingertips across my back and shoulder in response.

"*Ms. Alexander?*" he barked.

I bolted from his lap and turned around to stare in his face. The voice sounded familiar, but it couldn't have been who I thought it was. It wasn't possible. But the dark piercing eyes glaring back at me with red speckles of rage flashing through them assured me that all impossibilities in the moment had been defied.

"Oh my God! *Professor Jamieson?*"

I had every intention of running to escape the terribly embarrassing scene, but I must've been too slow. His hand grabbed my wrist with unbelievable strength and yanked my body around to face him again. Everything happened so fast that my mind had no time to comprehend actions, time, or space. Then someone suddenly pushed the slow motion button on the world as it turned.

My feet left the floor, and I felt my body being lifted into the air. My midsection connected with hard muscular flesh. Capri screamed as distance slowly began to grow between us. I was leaving the Paradise Room, but not on my own accord. I was being carried away *fast*. He actually started running.

"Put me down, Professor Jamieson!" I screamed the moment we got outside in the crowded parking lot. "Put me down *now*!"

He growled into the late night air like an uncivilized man from the Stone Age, but he didn't utter a single word. My request went completely unacknowledged. My captor continued his trek through the rows of cars with me dangling over his shoulder like my name was Jane and his was Tarzan. I was beyond humiliated. I was kind of afraid too.

"Yo, Ray, I'm about to call the police! Don't worry, baby girl!"

I looked up and saw Sammy, the club's chief security guard. He was surrounded by a group of Pleasure Palace employees and nosy-ass patrons who all looked horrified. Roscoe, the bouncer, was stomping toward the scene in the distance with his fat, slow ass. I shook my head. "Don't call the police! Please don't do that, Roscoe! I'm not down with the police!"

Moments later, Professor Jamieson stopped walking when we reached the passenger's side door of a sports car with a make and model I couldn't identify. It was black and very shiny. He pressed his thumb against a flat metal circle near the door's handle, and I almost pissed my thong when both doors spread wide and lifted like butterfly wings. My mouth was still wide open as I was tossed onto the soft leather seat and belted in securely.

"What the hell do you think you're doing?" I screamed before he slammed the door, rounded the sleek two-seater, and hopped inside. "Where are you taking me, Professor Jamieson?"

He fired the engine and peeled out of the parking lot like a mad man, ignoring me yet again. I was nervous, but not necessarily afraid at this point. Dozens of people had seen him carry me out of the club like a caveman on a mission, and a car like his would be easily spotted by the authorities. My only concern at the moment was the reckless speed at which he was driving his fancy automobile. My heart raced as he whipped around curves and darted in and out of lanes of traffic, fleeing the Buckhead section of the city of Atlanta.

As we headed toward the downtown area, my mind conjured up a few questions that needed to be asked. But at the same time, visions of the flat-tempered, conservative man who taught me advanced strategies of business marketing every Wednesday and Friday flashed through my mind's eye. He looked nothing like the hot stud sitting next to me, maneuvering the black sports car like a champion NASCAR driver. Professor Jamieson wore blazers, bowties, and nerdy loafers religiously. And where the hell were his round wire-framed glasses and neatly braided ponytail that hung to the center of his back? I felt like I had been cast in a modern-day adaptation of Invasion of the Body Snatchers because some wild barbarian had definitely occupied my professor's body and transformed him into a dangerous and irresistible male sex god.

He pulled into a popular twenty-four-hour diner downtown ATL. My eyes followed him when he exited the car and popped the trunk. I sat quietly in my seat, watching him carefully through the rearview mirror. He

removed something from the trunk and hurried to my
door. He snatched it open.

"Put this on," he ordered, dropping a long overcoat on
my lap. Then he reached out and removed the blinged-
out cat mask from my face. He placed it on the dashboard
in front of me. "Hurry up and cover yourself so we can go
inside and talk. If you're hungry, I'll feed you too."

Chapter Three

Radiance

I studied Professor Jamieson's expression for a few seconds while I contemplated whether I should obey him or act a fool. I hated the police, so I didn't want to do anything that would cause someone close by to call them. Ever since my apartment was raided for drugs as I watched in horror with my son in my arms, I promised to stay clear of the badges. My other choice was to haul ass, but my high heels wouldn't allow me to get very far before the crazy caveman could capture me again and drag me back inside his fancy car. So I decided to put on the coat and go inside the diner with him.

Professor Jamieson and I walked through the parking lot side by side in complete silence. He actually had a little bit of swag. I was kind of impressed. How had I missed his good looks and smoothness all this time?

A short and stocky hostess approached us when we entered the diner. "Table or booth?" she asked. She licked her thick lips and smiled at the professor right after she rolled her eyes at me.

"We'll take a table," he said.

We followed the hostess to a table near the back of the restaurant. Professor Jamieson pulled out a chair for me, and I smiled nervously and sat down. I was shocked when he sat next to me instead of taking the chair across from us. I was even more surprised when he moved his chair closer to mine, causing his right thigh to rest against my left one. We were too close for my comfort, but my anxiety held me in place. The man's domineering presence frazzled me, but it kind of turned me on at the same time.

"What is a smart, good-looking girl like you doing working at a place like the Pleasure Palace?"

"There wouldn't be places like the Pleasure Palace if there weren't men like *you*."

"That was my first time there. Faceless naked women aren't my thing. Now answer my damn question. Why do you work there?"

"I need the money," I snapped, irritated to the max.

"You're too intelligent to take off your clothes for strange men for a living."

"I'm not a stripper. I'm a *hostess*. I was filling in for one of the dancers tonight, but I wasn't going to remove a single damn piece of clothing. I was creating an illusion, and you loved it."

He nodded and then grabbed my wrist all of a sudden. I looked at him like he had lost his damn mind, but I didn't speak because something in his eyes robbed me of words. He leaned in so close to me that I could see my reflection in his orbs. "You don't work there anymore. Tonight was your last day on the job, babe."

"You must be crazy. I have a son to feed, clothe, and educate by myself. Plus I have bills to pay. I *need* my job."

"I'll get you a job on campus or somewhere in my company."

I shook my head. "I have to work at night. That's the only way I can study, help Croix with his homework, and spend time with him before he goes to bed."

"Where is your son's father?"

"He's in prison."

"For?"

"You sure do ask a lot of questions."

"Why is the boy's father in prison, Ms. Alexander?"

"He got busted for storing his drug stash in my apartment."

"Where is your apartment?"

"I don't live there anymore. It was property of Clark Atlanta University. I was evicted because of the drugs, although they weren't mine. Hell, I had no idea they were even in my apartment. Thank God they still allowed me to stay in school and graduate."

"Where do you live now?"

"Why do you need to know that?"

"I want to help you and your son. I like you. You're one of my brightest students. I think you and your little boy deserve a better life, and I'm going to give it to you."

I got lost in his mysterious panty-snatching eyes again and saw sincerity. I sighed, deciding to finally surrender to his line of questioning. "I live with my ex's sister and her girlfriend. I didn't have anywhere else to go after I got evicted. My mother lives in an apartment in a retirement village, and my father died six years ago. I'm an only child, and most of my family still lives in Detroit. So when Satchel, my ex, went to prison, his sister, Janelda, took Croix and me in. I pay half of the rent and utilities although there're *three* adults living in the house. But beggars can't complain now, can they? Plus they watch my son for me for free while I work."

A male server came to take our orders.

"I'll have coffee," the professor said.

"Would you like cream and sugar, sir?"

Professor Jamieson gazed at me with a twinkle in his eyes and smiled before he said, "No. I like it *black*."

His words caused my nipples to harden. I had to wrap my arms around my body to keep from shuddering. It took me a moment to recompose myself and tear my eyes away from his.

"Ma'am, what can I get for you?" the server asked.

"Lemonade will be fine."

"You aren't hungry, Ms. Alexander?"

"N-no . . . n-n-o," I stammered, lying straight through my teeth. I was starving like Marvin.

Professor Jamieson dismissed the server with a simple wave of his hand. Then he removed his cell phone from his pocket and scrolled through it. I wasn't certain, but I think he sent a rather lengthy text message to someone. Seconds later, he smiled at the reply.

When our beverages arrived, we thanked the server and sipped as quiet seconds ticked by. I wanted to call my job to let everyone know I was okay and to tell my boss, Enrique, that I would be there tomorrow night ready to work. But I didn't have my cell phone. It was in my locker at work with the rest of my stuff, including my purse.

The professor must've read my mind because he reached over and removed a wayward strand of hair away from my face and said, "I'll take you back to your *former* job so you can get your handbag and anything else you left behind."

I didn't want to argue with the man, so I bit my bottom lip to keep from speaking. Being a hostess at a gentlemen's club wasn't my life's ambition, but it paid the bills for now. I would work at the Pleasure Palace until after I had earned my master's degree in business and secured a loan to open Boutique Elite, my high-fashion style spot for the stars.

With his hand pressed gently in the small of my back, Professor Jamieson guided me through the parking lot to his car. To my surprise, there was a big, tall, muscular man standing with his foot perched on the front bumper of the car when we approached. He was dressed in a dark suit and tie with a huge grin on his face. He was rocking a long black ponytail. If I had to guess, I'd say he was Italian.

"What's up, Sergio?"

"Ain't much going on, boss."

They did the man hug thing before they turned their eyes on me. "Ms. Alexander, this is Sergio, my personal assistant and occasional driver. Sergio, this is the very beautiful Radiance Alexander."

The big burly guy extended his hand, and I placed my hand inside of it. I blushed when he kissed the back of my hand ever so softly. The professor grabbed my hand from Sergio's hold and growled at him with an ugly frown on his face. The man stepped away quickly and opened the passenger's side door to the white Range Rover parked right next to Professor Jamieson's sports car. He smiled and motioned for me to get inside of the vehicle. I looked at the professor for approval.

"Get in," he instructed.

I nodded and allowed Sergio to assist me into the truck. Professor Jamieson tossed him the keys to the sports car before he joined me inside the Range Rover. I laughed hysterically when I looked out the window to watch Sergio stuff himself inside the tiny two-seater. He looked like he was in pain.

The explicit version of Chris Brown's "Sex You Back to Sleep" filled the truck's interior. It had been three years since I had even kissed a man, so the thought of hot and wild sex seemed like a distant memory to me. I crossed my legs against the dampness in my crotch and my hardened clit. I filed a mental memo to buy myself a vibrator on my next payday.

We cruised toward the Pleasure Palace with the music filling in the quietness. I was comfortable in the moment as I sneaked peeks at the professor, bobbing his head to the beat of the music. I couldn't believe the events of the evening that had caused me to be in an SUV with one of my grad school instructors. It was so weird.

The parking lot was jam-packed by the time we arrived at the club. I figured that Porsche, Phoenix, Blaze, and the rest of the crew were turning up right about now. Those girls were serious dancers who had mastered the craft of draining any man's pockets. They took adult entertainment to a whole other level.

When the truck came to a complete stop in front of the flashing neon sign, Professor Jamieson immediately placed his wide palm on my left thigh. My eyes dropped to stare at his hand before they met his serious gaze.

"You have exactly ten minutes to go inside, gather your belongings, and let your boss know you no longer work here. If you're not back in this seat in ten minutes, I'm going to come inside and bring you out the same way I did earlier. Have I made myself clear?"

I nodded before I exited the vehicle.

Thirty minutes later, we arrived at the house I shared with my ex's sister, Janelda, and her lover, Bambi. All of the lights were off. I searched my purse for my keys while Professor Jamieson watched me closely. I became self-conscious as his eyes roamed all over my body.

"Thanks for the lemonade and the ride to my job and home."

"I drove you to your *old* job. You don't work there anymore, Ms. Alexander. Remember?"

Humph, that's what you think. I'm on the schedule tomorrow night, Mr. Professor, I wanted to say to him, but I swallowed my words. "Good night," I said instead.

He reached over and squeezed my thigh *again*. "The routine is the same, my dear. Again, you have just ten minutes to get your son and pack enough clothes for you and him for the next few days. I'll have Sergio bring you back here one day next week to get the rest of your things." He removed his wallet from his back pocket and pulled several crisp bills from it. He dropped the stack on my lap. "Give this to your ex's sister. It should take care of your half of the rent and utilities for the next couple of months."

"*Say what?*"

"You heard me. Go and get your son, some clothes, and your girlie items. Time is ticking." He killed the engine, reclined his seat, and pinned me in place briefly with his eyes.

"I don't know what you're used to, but I don't take orders, Professor Jamieson. You embarrassed me on my job by acting like some kind of savage! And now you expect me to go to some unknown place with you and take my son? You're crazy as hell!"

"Listen," he roared and grabbed my wrist, forcing me toward him. "You are no longer an employee at the Pleasure Palace or a resident of this house! Go and get your son and whatever you two will need over the weekend. Otherwise, I'm going inside to do it myself. It's *your* choice."

Chapter Four

Eli and Radiance

"Wake up, Ms. Alexander. We're here."

I turned around to nudge her from her sleep, but I was captivated by the heart-warming scene in the back seat, so I couldn't move. The sight of her cuddling her five-year-old son to her chest took my breath away. He was a handsome little fellow with flawless dark skin like his mother's and a head full of wild curly hair. He'd awakened for a few seconds and studied my face through sleepy eyes when I removed him from his mother's arms to carry him to the truck from his aunt's front porch. Then he laid his head on my shoulder and returned to a peaceful slumber in his bright red Spider-Man pajamas.

"Ms. Alexander, we're here. Wake up." I squeezed her knee and shook it gently. My fingertips got greedy, wanting very much to touch her perfect body all over. Her skin was so soft. I drew in a long breath and released it slowly to calm myself.

She opened her eyes and sat up. She took in my guest house before she shifted her eyes to me. "Croix and I will share a room."

I laughed. "You and the little guy can sleep wherever and however you'd like, but the *entire* house is yours for as long as you need it. The main house isn't very far away. It's just a few yards up the path. You can take your meals there with me, or Sergio can bring food down here three times a day. It's up to you."

"Is there a stove in there?"

"Yes. The kitchen is fully loaded with all late-model major appliances."

"Good, because I'll be cooking every day, so you won't have to worry about feeding us. I get paid every two weeks, so I can give you the same amount I gave Janelda each—"

"Ms. Alexander, I won't take your money, sweetheart. And you don't have a job anymore anyway, so you can't afford to pay me a dime. You and your son will be my guests until I figure out a permanent living arrangement for the two of you."

"How will I get Croix to school every day? Hell, how will I get to campus? My car is in the shop, and I'm guessing that MARTA doesn't come way out here." She looked around. "Where the hell are we anyway?"

"This is Alpharetta. And no, the MARTA train, nor the bus comes out here in the boonies. I have an entire fleet of cars. You may use any one of them whenever you need to."

"Why are you doing this for me, Professor Jamieson?"

"You're much too pretty and smart of a young lady to work at a strip club just to earn money to pay an unfair amount of rent and other bills in someone else's home. I'd be less of a man if I allowed you to continue to do so." I ran my fingers through the mass of curls atop Croix's head. "Come on. Let's get this little fellow into a warm bed."

"Croix, don't answer that door! I'll get it!"

I ran behind him to stop him, but it was too late. I came face to face with Professor Jamieson, and Lord, have mercy; he was looking all kinds of delicious in a pair of jeans and an Atlanta Hawks t-shirt. His five o'clock shadow was even thicker than the night before, and his hair was still loose and flowing, giving him that feral and dangerous look that caused moisture to pool in the crotch of my panties. And those gold hoops were making me weak and reckless. Thank God my son was there to keep me from doing something stupid.

"Good morning, Croix. My name is Eli. I invited you and your mother to visit me for a spell. Is that okay?"

He looked over his shoulder for my permission to speak to a stranger. I smiled and nodded my head. "It's fine. You can talk to Pro—"

"It's *Eli*. I'd like him to call me Eli. I think you should too."

"I can do that, but only around here."

"Of course," he said, smiling and folding his arms across his broad chest. "And what should I call *you*?"

"Everybody calls me Ray. It's short for Radiance."

"Okay, then I'll call you *Radiance* because I'm not like everybody else. You'll soon learn that." He turned his attention back to Croix. "Little buddy, would you like to take a walk around the compound with me? There's a pool, tennis court, golf course, and a flower garden. I have five dogs and a batting cage too. And my most prized possession is my plane."

"Wow! You have an *airplane*?"

"I sure do, buddy," he answered with a chuckle. "Come on. I'll show it to you."

"Can I go, Mommy?"

I couldn't deny him much of anything because of those copper puppy dog eyes. "You sure can, but Mommy's coming with you."

After an hour or so of exploring the territory known as Diamond Estate, we ended up in front of the main house.

"Wow! It's a *castle*! Can we go inside, Mommy? *Pleeease*?"

"I'm afraid not, baby. I'm sure Eli has more important things to do today than to show us around his big pretty house."

"Actually, I don't have anything important to do until much later today. It's breakfast time, and I'm sure Mama Sadie has cooked something delicious for us to eat. Do you like pancakes with maple syrup?"

"Yeah!" Croix shouted.

"What about crispy country bacon and cheese eggs?"

"Yeah!"

"Well, I think you and your mom are at the right place. Come on."

Croix took off running into the house behind Eli before I had a chance to protest. It was kind of the professor to offer us a place to stay for a while, but I had no intention of living in his guest house for an extended period of time. And I refused to eat his food every day. I didn't have a plan yet, but I was working on one inside my head.

I entered the house and was immediately awestruck. The foyer was bigger than Janelda's entire house. The platinum marble floors and the teardrop chandelier hanging from the dome ceiling totally fascinated me. I walked slowly through the massive wide open space, admiring the artwork. I heard Croix talking five miles a minute and laughing close by. I also smelled some good ole Southern food cooking, so I hurried in the direction of my son's voice and the mouth-watering aroma.

I smiled when I saw my baby boy sitting on the off-white granite countertop talking to an elderly African-American woman while Eli looked on. "Good morning, ma'am. My name is Radiance."

The woman tore her eyes away from Croix and grinned at me. "Hey there, sugar. I'm Mama Sadie. I'm the boss around here. Everything I say goes. Ain't that right, Eli?"

"Yes, Mama Sadie, you're the queen of this kingdom, but *I* pay all of the bills."

"You better pay the bills, or I'll put you out. You told me when you were ten years old that you were gonna take care of me when you grew up and became rich. Well, you're a grown man now, and your pockets are deep, so you've gotta take care of me until I leave this life for glory."

"Don't worry, Mama Sadie. I will take care of you until death do us part." Eli lifted Croix from the countertop and took hold of my hand. "Let's go and wash up for breakfast, you two."

"Breakfast was amazing. Thanks again, Pro—"

He shook his head. "It's *Eli*."

"I'll work on that."

"Please do." He turned away briefly before he looked into my eyes and said, "I have a wedding this afternoon. I'm the best man."

"I hope you'll enjoy yourself."

"I probably won't. I doubt that I'll hang around past my reception toast. I'm not into formal affairs. And besides, I have house guests. It'll be rude of me to stay and shut the place down."

"Don't hurry back because of Croix and me. We'll be fine. I have to study and start on an outline for a term paper. I wasn't able to bring many of Croix's toys last night, but you have cable, so he'll be able to watch a movie or two. Plus he has a new book. I'll read it to him later."

"That sounds fine, but if you need to go anywhere feel free to borrow one of my cars. Each one has a GPS system, and Sergio makes sure every gas tank is full at all times.

The keys are lined and labeled on a rack on the wall in the garage. You'll find proof of insurance in the glove compartment of whichever vehicle you choose. Take your pick, madam."

"I'll keep all of that in mind."

"Good. I need to head back to the main house to shave, shower, and put on my penguin suit."

"I'll see you later."

I entered the house and found Croix sitting on the sofa in the den watching the Cartoon Network. He'd had an eventful morning touring Eli's property and playing with his herd of dogs. He wanted to take a dip in the pool, but he didn't have his swimming trunks. He'd enjoyed walking through the flower garden and looking at all of Eli's fancy cars. But sitting in the cockpit of the Cessna 421 eight-seat plane had been the highlight of the tour. I had enjoyed watching my baby pretend to be a pilot, and so had Eli. He promised to take Croix for a ride on his plane someday soon.

Fun moments like that made me happy, but they also reminded me of the lack of male influence in Croix's life. I became overcome with anger at times when I thought about Satchel and how selfish and thoughtless he'd been by selling drugs in our home where we were raising our son. We were both students at Clark Atlanta University back then. I had a part-time job working at Macy's in Lenox Square Mall, and he was *supposed* to have been stocking shelves at night at a nearby Kroger grocery store. Unbeknownst to me, my live-in boyfriend, the father of my son, had entered the drug game. He was only a small-time dealer, selling mainly marijuana. But he also slung crack cocaine and meth on occasion.

I was too busy being a young mother, fulltime student, and part-time sales associate to notice the extra money and new pricey luxury items that were coming into the apartment. I never even questioned how Satchel was paying for the expensive daycare Croix was enrolled in. Caring for my son was my main priority, and finishing school came second. As far as I was concerned, life was as good as it could be for a pair of college students struggling to raise a toddler together.

But that morning when a drug unit from the Atlanta Police Department knocked on my door and shoved a search warrant in my face, my whole world quickly went up in flames. The officers stormed into the small two-bedroom apartment with drug-sniffing canines, screaming, and waving flashlights. I was beyond terrified. I clutched my baby to my chest and cried as he whimpered. And when a female cop appeared from Croix's bedroom with at least a dozen baggies packed with potent marijuana leaves, I nearly fainted. In that moment, I truly believed my life was about to end. I just knew that I was going to lose my son to the child welfare system and my freedom to a jail cell.

Tears streamed down my face as the memory of that dreadful day shook me to my core. My body was shivering like I was standing outside in a blizzard. The devastation I had experienced back then still haunted me today. I didn't even realize my cell phone was ringing until I heard my baby boy's soft angelic voice calling my name.

"Mommy, your phone is ringing. It's Auntie J. Do you want me to answer it?"

"No, baby, I don't," I said, pulling myself from the painful walk down memory lane. "I'll call her later."

I was in no frame of mind to speak with anyone at the moment. I especially couldn't handle a conversation with Satchel's controlling sister. I was sure she wanted to discuss my sudden departure from her home. I'd left her a note, but it didn't entail very many details due to the time restraint. All I told her was that Croix and I had found a new place to live and that we were grateful to her and Bambi for allowing us to stay with them since Satchel's arrest. More importantly, I'd left her the thick stack of bills that Eli had given me. Therefore, I didn't owe her one red cent.

I walked over and looked at my cell phone lying on the coffee table when it stopped ringing. I picked it up and dialed the number to the Pleasure Palace. It was time to talk to Enrique, my boss of nearly three years. I wasn't about to quit my job. I was going to ask for a leave of absence. I was in a weird situation, and I had no idea how it would all play out. A serious conversation with Eli was in order, and I planned to have it soon.

Chapter Five

Eli

I thanked the flirty maid of honor for the dance and hurried out of the ballroom. It was a few minutes past ten, and I was on a mission to get home in a hurry. I had surprised myself by staying at the reception as long as I had. It wasn't like I was having a good time, it was just that a few business associates had managed to pull me into a corner and hold me hostage with a proposition. I entertained them for about an hour while we nursed glasses of Grand Marnier. And as soon as I left the gentlemen at the table with every intention of making an early escape, Amy, the maid of honor, pulled me out on the dance floor for a slow dance. I could smell the lust seeping from her pores. Shamelessly, she'd grinded her cunt against my cock and purred in my ear the entire time I was locked in her arms. I was a successful businessman and not a rocket scientist, but I was smart enough to know when I was being seduced. And the frisky maid of honor had done her damnedest to seduce me.

I smiled and shook my head when I thought about the way she'd blown in my ear and moaned a number of times, trying to pull me into her sex trap. At another time in my life when things weren't so complicated, I would've nailed the cute little redhead and never looked back. I didn't have that luxury at the present. An image of Pandora popped in my mind, but I refused to go there tonight. I preferred to think about *Radiance*. I hopped in my Lamborghini and raced out of the hotel's parking lot when a vision of the tattoo on her back invaded my thoughts. I'd enjoyed kissing it seconds before I made out its familiarity.

That damn tattoo had helped me identify her. The instant I laid eyes on it, I knew it was my sexiest student giving me a lap dance. I was shocked shitless. The mask and the curly hair had hidden her true identity perfectly, but the tattoo gave it away. And I'm glad it did. It may have saved me from doing something unthinkable. And that was the last thing I'd wanted to do. There was something special about Radiance Alexander that made me want to respect and protect her. She didn't belong in a strip club with men gawking and lusting over her. She deserved to be pampered like a queen. And I planned to do just that for as long as she and her son resided at Diamond Estate.

Initially, my intention was to provide Radiance and Croix with a place to stay temporarily and hire her to work for me so she could earn a decent living. I figured that after she'd saved enough money to get on her feet, I would allow her to live in one of my properties for dirt cheap. But my agenda had changed drastically over the past twenty-four hours. I had a brand new interest in her. Now that I had her on my private property, I planned to keep her there for as long as I could. I *wanted* Radiance Alexander. And whatever or *whomever* I, T. Eli Jamieson, wanted, I would damn well have.

I shifted gears and fired my engine. I wanted to see Radiance tonight. There were a few things we needed to discuss right away. I wanted to get to know her better and put her mind at ease about her new living arrangement. And I imagined she had some questions for me. I'm sure that her mind was still reeling from the overnight chain of events. Now, she wasn't just one of my students, she was my house guest, but I wanted her to be so much more. Before long, Radiance Alexander would be my submissive lover.

I realized how befitting her name was the moment she opened the door. Even through the dark hallway, her beauty shined brightly, illuminating the space. She was simply *radiant* in an oversized cotton nightgown in a soft shade of yellow. Her velvety skin looked inviting to my touch against the pastel fabric. It took an insane amount of self-control to keep from reaching out to caress her all over.

"I hope I didn't wake you."

She shook her head. "You didn't. I was reading actually."

"I'm sorry. I didn't mean to interrupt your studies."

"It's okay. I was reading to get ahead."

"Is Croix awake?"

"No. He crashed a long time ago," she said with the brightest smile on her face.

My belly did a double somersault. "May I come in, please? We need to talk."

She stepped aside to give me a clear path into the house. I walked into the sitting area and plopped down on the couch. I patted the space to the right of me. My eyes perused Radiance from head to toe and back up again as she closed the distance between us on bare feet. An erection harder than steel crept up on me the second I realized she wasn't wearing underwear underneath her nightgown. The imprint of her nipples pressed against the cotton, teasing me unmercifully. She stopped directly in front of me, and my cocked jumped and pressed painfully against the zipper of my tuxedo pants.

"May I offer you something to drink? Croix and I went to the supermarket to buy a few things in your Toyota Avalon, the least flashy car in your collection. I bought his favorite cereal, milk, a few snacks, and some other essentials. Teabags made the list too. Would you like a glass with a lemon wedge?"

"No, thank you. Have a seat." I patted the empty space next to me again. My brain went on strike when Radiance sat and crossed one leg over the other, causing the hem of nightgown to crawl up her thigh. I couldn't speak because the only thing I could think about was how much I wanted to be squeezed between her well-toned thighs while my penis slid in and out of hot, wet pussy.

"You said we needed to talk."

"Oh yeah, um . . . I want you to know that you and Croix are welcome to stay here for as long as you need to."

"You told me that already, but thanks for the reminder. Hopefully, we won't be here too long."

"Take all the time you need. To assist you financially, I can offer you a job working at night in my company so you can get on your feet."

"Who'll care for Croix at night while I work?"

I rubbed my hands over my face. "I hadn't thought about that."

"What's the name of your company and what type of work would I be doing if I were to find a reliable babysitter?"

"I own Diamond International. It's a global real estate company. I have five-star hotels and resorts with casinos all over the world. I also own high-end condominiums, apartment buildings, and gated housing communities throughout the country. You've heard of Diamond Hotels and Resorts, right?"

"Of course I have, but I thought an old, bald, white dude with glasses owned the Diamond hotel chain."

"He did, but he died many years ago. I took over the company after his death and expanded it worldwide. We continue to use his image as the face of the company out of respect."

"Were you related to him?"

"Yes. I'm his baby boy."

"I'm sorry about your father's death."

"It's fine. He lived a full and insanely privileged life."

"What is a wealthy and successful businessman like you doing teaching at Georgia State University? I know you don't need the money."

I laughed. "No, I'm not exactly poor. I'm teaching one class at GSU this semester as the result of a golf bet. Dean Schlesinger and I became friends a few years ago, so from time to time, as a favor to him, I would visit the university to speak to the business graduate students. I became a hit after a few lectures, so he offered me a position as an adjunct professor, but I turned him down. So on our next tee time at the country club, he talked me into a wager that I was sure I would win."

"But he beat you, didn't he?" she asked, laughing her pretty little face off.

"Yes. The old man kicked my ass, and now I'm your instructor."

"Do you enjoy teaching?"

I enjoy teaching you, I wanted to tell her, but I was afraid it might scare her. "It has its perks, I guess."

"I bet it does. Anyway, what kind of job do you think I can do at night for you?"

That was a dangerous question that could've been interpreted more than one way. Although I knew exactly what she'd meant, my mind went straight to the gutter and refused to return to decency. There were a million and one things I'd love for Radiance to do for me in my bed every single night, but her question was not of a sexual nature. It was about employment.

"Maybe you could work in the financial or marketing department for one of my hotels. Would you like that?"

"Yeah, I think I would. I just need to find someone reliable and with lots of experience to care for Croix while I'm at work."

"Actually, you don't have to work at all, Radiance. You and your son are welcome to stay here until after you've graduated and found a good job."

"Oh no," she drawled out. "That ain't going to work. I'm used to taking care of Croix and myself. The last time I depended on a man to provide for us, my world got turned upside down. I refuse to do that ever again. I'll find a babysitter, even if I have to ask Janelda and Bambi."

"You will *not* do that. Those two women have taken advantage of you long enough. I won't allow you to go crawling back to them for assistance of any kind. I'll talk to my human resources director. He'll find a job within my company that you can work a few nights a week from a company-issued computer right here." I stood, pleased with how quickly I had solved her dilemma. "It's settled. Come and walk me to the door."

I walked toward the entrance of the house with an obviously stunned Radiance a few steps behind me. I turned abruptly to face her, and our bodies collided. She stumbled backwards, and I reached out in a flash to steady her by wrapping my arms around her narrow waist. The softness of her curves and the alluring scent of her skin caused a stirring in my loins. I wanted to taste her and then bury my hard cock so fucking deep inside of her that her inner walls would mold to the shape of me like a key in a lock. I needed her more than I needed my heart to take its next beat.

The sharp flash in her eyes assured me of her desire to be loved, but I also saw a sliver of apprehension in their depths. Her body quivered in my arms, and all I wanted to do was kiss away her fear. I would never bring harm to her, and I wanted her to know as much. It was my desire to pleasure her in every way possible while enjoying the sexual bliss she would bestow upon me in return. She closed her eyes as I lowered my head to kiss her.

"Mommy, I'm thirsty. May I have a drink of water please?"

I released her and took a backwards step before I looked over her shoulder to see my new little buddy.

"Sure, you may, sweetie," she answered lovingly, rushing toward the child. "I was just saying good night to Eli. He came by to make sure that you and I were doing okay in our new house." She picked him up and rubbed his back.

"Good night. I'll see you two in the morning." I hurried out the door, not trusting myself to maintain my gentlemanly behavior once she'd given Croix a cup of water and tucked him in bed again. I pulled in large gulps of air after the door slammed shut behind me. I waited for the sound of the locks to click into place before I started my trudge up the path leading to the main house. I had parked my car there instead of the garage because I was in such a hurry to see Radiance. After spending time alone with her and almost capturing her lips in a kiss, I expected a long and miserable night without much sleep when I reached my lonely bedroom.

Chapter Six

Radiance

I had purposely stayed off of Eli's radar after our conversation Saturday night. The sexual heat in the room had reached a dangerous level, and I'd felt myself melting away in his arms. I don't know what would've happened if Croix hadn't interrupted us, asking for a drink of water. He'd saved his mommy from being consumed by her own lust. The smoldering flames of fire I'd seen dancing in Eli's dark eyes as he'd held me in his arms were an unmistaken warning sign that I'd been on the verge of becoming devoured prey.

He and I shared undeniable chemistry, and the sexual tension between us was damn near explosive. But I didn't want to cross the line. He was my professor, landlord, and future employer. It would be a major mistake to get twisted up into a messy lust-driven affair with him, yet I'd been seconds away from letting him fuck me into unconsciousness. Maybe I had allowed my gratitude for his kindness to get the best of me. Even now, as I walked toward the lecture hall to take my seat in his class, my heart and mind told me something totally different. I wanted Eli. There was no need for me to even try to play the denial game. My body was thirsty for a man's touch—*his* touch, and there wasn't a damn thing I could do about. I had no control over nature. If I did, why couldn't I command my clit to stand down or stop my juices from saturating my crotch as I got closer to the lecture hall? Hell, my nipples had even gone rogue on me, peaking and pressing against the fabric of my t-shirt. I was a powerless, sex-deprived, passion-hungry wreck.

I entered the lecture hall and was pleasingly surprised that I was alone. Usually, Eli would already be seated behind his desk, preparing for class. But he was nowhere to be found today, and I was glad. I had a moment to breathe and get my shit together. Visions of making love with Eli had my body tingling and humming a horny love song. My craving for him was something serious. What the hell was I going to do with all the lust inside of me?

God must've had mercy on me because I'd managed to stay completely focused throughout class. I was mainly able to relax because Eli had transformed back into the clean-cut, conservative professor that I was used to. He had concealed all of that ruggedness I liked behind his glasses, a blazer, and a plaid bowtie. The five o'clock shadow was gone, and so was the wild and wavy hair that I'd been tempted to run my fingers through the other night. His famous ponytail had returned. And along with the entire physical retransformation came the flat and bland personality. I swear the guy was like Peter Parker and Spider-Man.

The other thing that had helped me maintain my cool in class was Eli's lecture on branding tools and strategies. It was off the chart! The discussion it had sparked among the students was on point. He had racked our brains and plucked ideas out of us like a magician pulling a rabbit from a hat. I couldn't remember the last time I'd taken so many notes. My fingers were tired from typing on my tablet. I smiled and breathed a sigh of relief as I loaded my backpack, preparing to leave.

Eli started passing out our midterm reports that he must've graded sometime over the past few days. I watched some of my classmates as they left his desk and made their way out of the lecture hall. Some faces appeared happy while others bore frowns of disappointment. My palms began to sweat. I had worked my ass off on my report. Any grade under a B+ would not be acceptable. I walked down the steps and got in line to await my turn.

"Ms. Alexander," he said, handing me my report. "Your approach to marketing is unique."

I didn't know if I'd just been complimented or not, but one look at my grade would let me know. So I went for it. *An A-! Yes! Yes! Yes!* I wanted to shout and dance around the room, but I dialed my emotions back. I was cool until I saw the comment written in red ink underneath my satisfactory grade.

I will see you tonight after you've put Croix to bed.

I was too pissed off to be nervous or even flattered that he wanted to spend time with me. Why the hell did he need to see me tonight anyway? And why had he insisted that my child be asleep when he arrived? I'd rather pack up and return to Janelda's house with my tail tucked between my legs and take back my leave of absence request at the Pleasure Palace than to pay my debt to Eli with late-night sex acts. I wasn't a hoe or his charity case! I wanted to punch myself in the face for allowing him to pull me into some sick pussy trap.

I stormed out of the lecture hall with a serious attitude. Radiance Imani Alexander did *not* do booty calls! If

Professor T. Eli Jamieson thought he could make me his
sex slave just because he'd done me an unsolicited favor
or two, he was in for the one shitty surprise.

~♥~

"Come on in," I said softly with a wave of my hand.
    The wheels inside my head were spinning like crazy as
I prepared to teach Eli a lesson. This damsel in distress
didn't appreciate the game he was trying to play. I'd
dressed provocatively on purpose to sweeten the pie.
And my mango-watermelon bath products mixed with
my signature perfume, Rise, by Beyoncé was a lethal
combination for any man's resistance. The professor
didn't stand a chance. He thought he wanted to play with
me, but he would soon regret it. I was about to torture his
libido and then send his ass back to the main house with
blue balls. The return of his edgy appearance would have
no effect on me. *I* was in control.
    I took my time crossing the hallway to join him in the
sitting area. My slow stroll was filled with extra *everything* from the seductive sway of my hips to the inten-
tional bounce in my braless breasts. My lavender cotton
nightgown was so thin that I knew he could make out my
hourglass silhouette underneath. And I wasn't wearing
panties. A bottle of merlot sat chilling in a sterling silver
ice bucket on the coffee table along with two crystal
wineglasses I'd found in the cabinet. The fire blazing in
Eli's eyes as I drew nearer to the couch assured me that
I had him in the palm of my hand just where I wanted
him. He was salivating over this sexy drop of feminine
chocolate. I saw his hard dick, thick and long, bucking
like an untamed beast, trying to burst through the zipper
of his worn, faded jeans. He raked his fingers nervously
through his unruly locks. Yeah, the pompous professor

wanted a piece of the pretty pupil, but he wasn't going to get it . . . not *tonight*. I sat close to him on the couch.

"Why are you here, Eli?"

"You know why."

"Maybe I do, but to be sure, I think you should tell me." I reached for the bottle of wine.

His hand gripped mine in mid motion before I could even touch the damn thing. Within seconds, I was on his lap and in his arms being kissed out of my fucking mind. Bells and whistles started blaring, causing my brain to freeze. I saw flashes of light, and the room began to spin violently. Every teasing twirl of his tongue around mine elicited a moan from deep down in my soul. I was floating, defying gravity, yet I was still in his arms. The hardness of his body against my much softer one robbed me of my senses in the heated moment. I had lost complete control of the situation. The script had been flipped on me.

He raised his head slowly to end the kiss. I hadn't drunk a single sip of wine, but I was intoxicated. I fought to catch my breath while sweet sensations continued to travel throughout my body. To hell with my plan to tease Eli! I wanted him to sex me into insanity.

"I'm a man who knows what he wants, Radiance. I don't like games. Do you understand me?"

Every word in the English language had abandoned me. All I could do was nod my head in understanding and blink.

"There's no need for you to deny that you want me because your eyes are telling me the truth. And you're wetter than the seven seas. I can smell the pungent scent of your pussy floating through the air. It's hot and wet because you want me." He eased his hand underneath my nightgown and fondled my vagina before he entered me with one long finger. "All of this is for me."

I closed my eyes as he slid in and out of my wetness before he circled my clit slowly with his fingertip. I trembled and hummed as he intensified his brand of foreplay by pinching my clit with the perfect amount of pressure while the thumb on his other hand pressed mercilessly against my left nipple. He stopped all movement without warning when I bit my bottom lip and threw my head back. I wanted to scream and curse.

He stood with me in his arms. "Which room?"

"I sleep in the master suite."

"You won't get much sleep tonight, babe."

As soon as we reached the bedroom, he placed me on my feet, snatched the nightgown over my head, and dropped it on the floor. I shivered when I stood before him completely naked. He rushed to the door, closed it, and secured the lock.

"After tonight, we'll never be able to go back to the way things used to be between us, Radiance. Can you handle that?"

I had no idea what he was talking about. How could I agree to something I didn't understand? The only thing I knew for sure at the moment was that I wanted him to make love to me more than I wanted the sun to shine in the morning. And if that meant I had to agree to sleep with him every now and then while I lived in his house, I was down with it.

"Did you hear me, Radiance? Once I make love to you, everything will change. There'll be no turning back. Can you live with that?"

"Yes," I whispered.

In a swift and smooth motion, he lifted me off my feet again and sat me on the edge of the bed. Then he took a step backwards and stripped for me in what seemed like torturing slow motion. If he were to ever grow bored of the real estate business, he could always open a Pleasure Palace lady's club and crown himself the showstopper. I swallowed hard at the sight of his bare erected penis pointed in my direction. It was *beautiful*. The breadth, length, and the size of its mushroom head caused me to question if I could accommodate all of that after three years of celibacy. It was too late now, though. I would just have to do the best that I could.

"Lay back."

I did as I was told. Seconds later, he dropped to his knees, spread my legs apart, and positioned his face between my thighs. My jaw dropped to my chest when he lifted my legs high and threw them over his shoulders with the backs of my knees resting on them. With unhurried torment, he traced the perimeter of my pussy with his tongue while he slid a lone finger in and out of my wet opening.

I tangled my fingers in his silky hair. "Mmm . . . Eli . . . aaahhh . . ."

"You haven't felt anything yet, babe."

And he was right because when his hot wet tongue eased up and down my clit for the first time, my back arched high off the bed. Nothing had ever felt that damn satisfying. "Oh my goodness! My, my, my . . ."

Then he went in for the kill without an ounce of remorse. He covered my clit with his humid mouth and sucked it, twirling his tongue over its sensitive tip. His finger steadily entered and exited my damp center, pushing me beyond oblivion. I didn't mean to hurt him, but I yanked his hair in response to the tongue magic he was working on me. My soul soared and mingled among the stars. Fire and desire flooded every cell of my being. His tongue flicked repeatedly against my hard drenched clit, sending me into a state of euphoria. He sucked, licked, and breathed into my pussy while I rolled my hips and grinded against his face. No experience in my memory could match what I was feeling as I was being devoured like I was Eli's final meal of his lifetime.

"Damn! You're sweeter than sugar, babe. I'm going to eat you every day," he mumbled against my pussy.

I couldn't take it another second. I let go and allowed nature to take its full course. My climax struck my body like an electric current, starting at my core before it rushed like hot lava through my veins. It kissed every inch of my flesh with sweet and powerful shock waves that made me jerk, moan, and snatch Eli's hair again.

He stood up and watched me twitch and whimper through the most amazing orgasm I'd ever experienced. And then he gave me a half smile as the wave of ecstasy subsided, seemingly proud of his oral expertise.

Chapter Seven

Eli

My desire for a woman had never been greater. But although I wanted to fuck Radiance's brains out and relieve us both of our sexual deprivation, I refused to give her what she needed until she begged for it. She deserved to be punished for her attempt to tease me. I wasn't a fool. The moment I crossed the threshold I detected her taunting nature. For some reason, she'd been on a mission to torment me with a sexual fantasy of her beautiful body without allowing me to indulge. But now that I had licked her into the stratosphere, she wanted me to take her even higher into orbit with my cock pounding her pussy until she exploded. But it wasn't going to happen until she suffered with the same anguish she had intended to inflict upon me.

Her moans and heavy breathing assured me that I had the advantage in the situation. She wanted me beyond a shadow of a doubt. She would howl at the moon and fart in public without hesitation if I would demand it just to have me buried inside of her to the hilt. But her wish would not be granted without cost. I wanted to hear her beg for what she wanted. It would teach her to never play games with me again. Tonight I was going to give her a lesson in compliance and submission.

I smiled when she reached both arms out to me. It wasn't easy for me to hold back, but I knew that the reward would be more than worth it in the end. So I shook my head and backed away.

"Eli, *please* . . ."

"Teasing me wasn't very wise, my dear."

"I'm sorry."

"Why did you do it?"

"Your note on my midterm report . . . I felt violated . . . like you expected sex from me as payment for Croix and me living here."

"I didn't ask you for anything, especially not *sex*. You assumed the worst of me, so you decided to punish me by tempting me with your body, but you had no intention of giving me the cookie."

"I'm sorry," she whispered while reaching for me again.

"You want me now, don't you?"

"*Yesss* . . ."

The yearning in her voice caused more warm blood to rush to my thick hard cock. I wanted her fiercely. I joined her on the bed and pulled her into my arms. Her body was warm and damp with tiny beads of perspiration. She was in heat. I eased to the center of the bed, pulling her along with me. I rolled on top of her and stared down into her angelic face. Her eyes were two brown pools overflowing with desire. I kissed her hungrily, and she moaned out her pleasure. I released her lips and planted kisses on her neck before I lowered my head to her breasts. I licked one chocolate erect peak and then the other before I covered the right one with my mouth. I sucked and slithered my tongue across it until she screamed and shuddered.

I continued my assault on her breasts, and she hummed and ran her fingers through my hair. My hands roamed over her hips and thighs, kneading and caressing every inch with passion. Her skin was so soft, and its scent was making me high.

"Eli, I need you." Her words were like lyrics of the sweetest love song.

"Tell me what you need, babe."

She eased her hand between our bodies and grabbed my dick and stroked it slowly.

"*Shit*! Ah, babe . . ."

She had the golden touch. The feel of her soft palm gently clutching my cock, stroking it up and down caused air to rush from my lungs. It stoked my fire. Precum squirted from the tip of my hardness and flowed over Radiance's fingers and palm.

"I need *this*, Eli," she whispered.

I got up and hurried to the find my jeans on the floor near the foot of the bed. I removed the row of condoms from the front pocket and rushed to rejoin Radiance on the bed. I snatched one from the row and tossed the others on the nightstand. I ripped the package open with my teeth and quickly rolled the condom onto my dick. Radiance lay desperately waiting with her legs spread far apart. It amazed me how her plan to tease me had suddenly changed to the urgency to be pleased. I would've laughed and mocked her over her silliness if I wasn't so fucking horny and needed to get inside of her right away.

After I positioned myself between her trembling thighs, I took hold of my cock and rubbed it up and down against the opening of her sweet pussy. The fruity fragrance of her feminine moisture was wreaking havoc on my masculine senses. Lunacy was a few seconds away from pulling me in, but I needed to make sure she was ready to receive what she'd begged me for. I stroked her stiff clit drenched with her sex honey. The flow of it was nonstop.

"Damn, I'm about to drown because you're so fucking wet," I whispered in awe before I entered her goodness.

The warm snug fit inside of her pussy immediately caused my eyes to roll to the back of my head. It was like my entire body had floated to a happy place. I started to pump in and out of her slowly at first, but her cooing and fluid motions encouraged me to move faster. She met each even stroke with a thrust and a roll of her hips. She wiggled and bucked underneath me rhythmically as she hummed and purred. Each time I pulled out and reentered her warm depths, she clenched my dick with her inner muscles tightly without mercy, and my heart paused. Control was gradually slipping away from me. I was on the brink of a massive explosion, but I wanted to satisfy her first. So I slowed my pace, leaned in, and sucked her bottom lip.

"Eli . . . mmm . . . Eli . . ." she mumbled even with our mouths partially joined.

"Talk to me, babe."

"It . . . it . . . feels . . . *sooo* . . . damn . . . good!"

Every muscle in my anatomy tightened at the sated tone of her voice. I was on the edge of my release, threatening to topple over. I fought to hold it back. She had to go first. "Cum, babe. I need you to cum for me," I encouraged her through gritted teeth. "*Cum.*"

Her eyes clamped shut tightly. "*Eliiiiii!*" she sang in an operatic pitch loud enough to shatter glass.

The feel of her soft body jerking under my full weight as I continued stroking her deep, fast, and hard launched me into orbit. My release came forth like an uncontainable eruption. It shook my body down to the bone marrow. But the bliss it brought was more gratifying than anything I'd ever felt.

I couldn't move for several seconds because I was too weak. My heartbeat pounded fast in my chest, causing me to struggle for small snatches of air. I finally mustered up enough strength to roll over onto my back with Radiance in my arms. She stretched her body out fully on top of mine. I could feel the rapid beat of her heart against my chest. I kissed the top of her head.

What the hell just happened? I silently questioned myself. I had slept with dozens of women over my forty years on earth, but never had one pleased me with so much intensity as the one in my arms—not even Pandora. Maybe the student had become the teacher and had taught me a lesson in the game that we'd both played tonight after all. Sure, I'd ended up getting what I had come for despite the fact that she'd had no intention of giving it to me. But the way I saw it, Radiance was still the winner because not only had she received the good loving she'd obviously needed, she had also taken a piece of my heart as a bonus without even knowing it.

It wasn't the sex that had me seeing our situation through brand new eyes, although it *was* mind-blowing. But it was the fact that she'd had the audacity to defend herself against me when she thought I wanted to take advantage of her. And she had put her foot down and demanded my respect. I was impressed, and I wondered what other lessons the lovely Radiance Alexander could teach this professor. That was my last thought before I joined her in a satisfying post-sex slumber.

~♥~

"Radiance, wake up, babe." I ran my hand down the side of her waist and left hip. "Wake up."

"No, not again, Eli. My body can't take it."

I grinned and pulled her back closer to my chest as we lay, cuddling in the spoon position. "I wouldn't dare. Besides, we've run out of condoms."

"Thank God."

"Are you trying to tell me that you didn't enjoy any of the five times I made love to you throughout the night? I don't think I believe that because as I recall, you begged for it the first time. And you initiated the second time, you wild and sexy cowgirl." I laughed and tickled her side. "Then the third time—"

"Has anyone ever told you that you're obnoxious and cocky?"

"I've heard it a time or two. Why?"

"Because it's true. You're full of yourself."

"And *you* were full of *me* five times last night."

Radiance yanked herself out of my embrace and sat up. "Get out of my bed right now!"

I couldn't contain my laughter. I sat up too and smiled at her angry face. "I'll leave, but I'll be back tonight."

"No the hell you won't."

"Of course I will. You haven't had enough of me, babe. And I sure as hell could use another dose of you." I kissed her cheek. "I'll see you this evening around six o'clock. Don't bother to cook. I want to surprise Croix with pizza and wings. I'm sure he'll enjoy that."

Without another word, I got dressed while Radiance sat resting her back against the headboard and shooting imaginary silver bullets at me with her eyes. She was silent as well, which confirmed what I'd expected. She wasn't protesting my return visit because she wanted me to come and spend time with her and Croix. But what she wanted more than that was for me to get her back in that bed and make her scream my name and climb the wall again.

Radiance had no idea what she'd gotten herself into with me, but she would soon find out. I had tasted her and been as far into her body as anatomy and physiology would allow me. I was hooked on her like an addict on his substance of choice, and I didn't want to be clean and sober of my drug. As far as I was concerned, Radiance was *mine* now and there wasn't a damn thing she could do to change it. It was too late for her to renege on the verbal agreement we'd made. I had warned her to expect

changes in our relationship before we'd shared a bed.
Now it was time for me to show her the meaning behind
my words.

I saw Mama Sadie standing on the stoop as soon as
I cleared the tree-lined path leading to the main house.
*Damn it! Why is she here before sunrise? And why is she
staring at me like I'm a common criminal on the run?* I
looked down at my unbuttoned shirt and frowned. I guess
I did look kind of suspicious walking around outside
barefoot with a tennis shoe in each hand this time of the
morning. I was so disheveled that I imagined she had a
couple of questions about me tumbling through her head.

"Good morning, Trapper. It's mighty early for you to be
out here taking a walk. And how come you ain't got no
shoes on? Just because it's springtime, it don't mean you
can't catch a cold."

"Good morning, Mama Sadie." I pecked her sagging
cheek when I reached her. "You only call me by my first
name whenever I'm in trouble. What have I done wrong
this early in the morning? The sun isn't even up yet."

"You tell me. Where have you been and what have you
been doing? And for the love of God, *who* have you been
doing it with?"

"I woke up early and couldn't go back to sleep, so I went
for a walk."

"Mmm . . . hmm . . ." she moaned with her hands on her
narrow hips. "Where did you sleep? Your bed is as neatly
made as I left it yesterday."

"I fell asleep watching a movie in the great room."

"Well, I suggest that you be real careful about your new
late night and early morning activities, Trapper."

"Yes, ma'am, I certainly will."

"And since I got your attention, let me remind you about someone very important: *Pandora*."

Our eyes met and locked briefly before I entered the house and headed straight to my bedroom. I hated that Mama Sadie was so wise. She knew me better than anyone, including my deceased parents, my siblings, Marlon, and yes, *Pandora*. And the old woman was right as usual. Her reminder had indeed been necessary.

Chapter Eight

Radiance

"Mommy, Eli's here! And he's got *pizza*! I can see him through the window. Can I let him in?"

"Go ahead, baby. Open the door."

I held my breath as I watched him cross the threshold carrying two pizza boxes and a container of wings. Those damn jeans that were hanging low on his ripped body made him look delicious enough to eat in a single serving. And the way the simple white t-shirt stretched across his well-toned pecs frazzled me. Although he was completely dressed, my make-believe X-ray vision could see him as he was the night before: naked, hard, and proud.

"Hey, little buddy. Did you miss me?"

"Yeah!"

His mommy did too, but she'll never admit it. I stepped forward and reached for the food. "I'll take that. Thank you." I turned to my baby boy and asked, "What should you say to Eli for bringing dinner for us?"

"Thank you, Eli. I love *pizza*!"

"I didn't know what kind was your favorite, so I took a guess and bought one large cheese pizza, and the other one is pepperoni."

"*Pepperoni*? That's Mommy's favorite! Let's go and wash our hands," he said, pulling Eli by the hand and leading him to the bathroom.

I hurried to the kitchen to set the table and pour glasses of apple juice for everyone. It felt weird seeing Eli after all we'd done to each other last night. I didn't have any regrets about the physical exchange. We were two consenting adults who had mutually given in to our passions. My problem now was the emotions that came along with giving my body to a man who I was attracted to, but barely knew. I wondered what Eli thought of me now. Did he think I was an easy lay or some chick from the hood that got her sex hustle on for money and gifts? He had to know better than that because *he* had insisted that I quit my job and move into his guest house free of charge. I hadn't gone to him begging for a damn thing.

I dreaded it, but it was time for Eli and me to have another conversation to clear up a few important matters. I hated that I had hopped in bed with him *before* we had laid down the rules and made a list of expectations. But where I came from, it was always better late than never. So after dinner and tucking Croix in, I would address my concerns with Eli, and we would come to an understanding about what was going on between us.

~♥~

"Is he asleep?"

"No, not yet, but he will be soon. Thanks for everything, Eli. Croix had a blast eating *three* slices of pizza plus wings and playing all of those games on his new Xbox One. Did you see how his eyes lit up when Sergio walked in here with that thing?"

"I did. He's a good kid, Radiance. He deserves special gifts and treats. Come sit down. We need to talk."

He was absolutely right. We *did* need to talk. I walked over and sat down next to him on the couch. "About last night . . . um . . . I um . . ."

"It was bound to happen sooner or later. I've wanted you since the first day you walked into my class. Of course, I never thought we would end up together because of the obvious conflicting circumstances. But that night when I carried you out of the Pleasure Palace, I knew that fate was on my side."

"How did you know it was me? I was wearing a mask. My back was to you too. And you've never seen my hair in a curly style before."

"Your tattoo . . . It became engraved in my memory the moment I laid eyes on it. I didn't realize that Croix's name was scripted across it until I traced it with my fingertip last night while you were asleep. That damn butterfly has haunted me many nights."

His words caused thousands of imaginary needles to prick me all over on the inside. I wrapped my arms around my body to hold it still. "What do you want from me?"

"*You.*"

"I don't understand."

"Last night we made love because we needed each other *physically.* But tonight and the many nights to come, it'll be different. I thought I'd made myself perfectly clear to you before we shared your bed. We have a binding verbal agreement, Radiance."

I was so confused. I had no idea what the hell Eli was talking about. I was so horny last night that I would've agreed to be his maid if he'd asked me. But now that I was in a stable head space, I realized that I had failed to get the details on the deal before I let him screw me senseless until the break of dawn. I cleared my throat. "What exactly did I agree to?" I asked. "I can't recall."

"You agreed to be mine."

"I never said that!" I shouted, hopping up from the couch.

Eli laughed. "Sure, you did. I told you that we wouldn't be able to maintain a normal student-instructor relationship or even host and house guest agreement once I'd had a taste of you. You said you could handle it. Are you trying to go back on your word now?"

"I didn't understand the terms. How could I have made sense of anything while you were touching me the way you were? I didn't know what I was agreeing to."

"Well, now you do. It's official. You're mine, Radiance Alexander. I wanted you, and now I have you. Come here." He opened his arms and smiled at me.

I wanted to resist, but I wanted to be in his arms at the same time. My body overruled my mind, so I walked into his embrace and sat on his lap. The kiss he placed on my lips was soft and sweet. It only made me hungry for more—a whole lot more.

"You're going to enjoy being mine, Radiance," he whispered against my parted lips.

"What exactly does it mean to be *yours?*"

"I'll make love to you every day. And anything you and Croix want or need will be yours. I'll give you and your son the world and take excellent care of both of you for as long as you're mine. And I intend for that to be a very, very long time. Consider yourself a pampered woman.

"Damn! I don't think I could ever get enough of you, babe."

I collapsed from my straddled position on top of Eli as his dick slid out of my pussy. I stretched out on all of his hard muscles, enjoying the feel of them covered with sweat produced by our vigorous lovemaking. I was exhausted, and every muscle in my body was sore, but I was one satiated woman. "Be careful, old man. I don't want to give you a heart attack."

"Now that you know my age, I guess I can expect senior citizen jokes from here on out, huh?"

"I might crack one every now and then, *Grandpa*."

He smacked me playfully on my ass.

"Ouch! Just because you're old enough to be my daddy, it doesn't give you the right to spank me."

"You're mine, babe. I can do anything I damn well please to you."

"And what would you like to do to me right now?"

"Give this old man thirty minutes to cool off, and then I'll show you."

"Do you promise?"

"Hell yeah."

I placed my cheek on his chest and listened to his heartbeat. I was content in the moment. Eli was an incredible lover and a good listener. He even had a decent sense of humor, I'd learned after our first bump and grind session of the night. We talked a lot as he held me in his arms. He was forthcoming about his family and his company. But I was curious about his love life. Why was a handsome, successful businessman like him unmarried and childless? Surely, he'd come across at least one special woman in his forty years who'd been worthy of becoming Mrs. T. Eli Jamieson.

"Eli?"

"Yeah, babe."

"Have you ever been married before?"

"I-I . . . ugh . . . I . . . have," he stammered out.

I raised my head and looked down into his eyes. "What happened? Why didn't the marriage last?"

"It was doomed before the start, but I don't want to talk about it. I'd rather hear more about the boutique you're going to own one day. You know I would give you the money to get it up and running. All you'd have to do is ask."

"I want to do it on my own. Besides, I can't take anything else from you, Eli. You've already done enough for Croix and me. We live in your house, and I drive your cars free of charge. And it was so nice of you to buy Croix the Xbox One and all of those games. You can't keep giving us things because I can't pay you back."

He flipped over in the bed, reversing our positions. I was nestled underneath him looking into his dark, hypnotizing eyes. My vagina got wet on the spot. For a man fifteen years older than me, Eli had way more stamina than I had. And his sexual appetite seemed never-ending.

"You're about to start paying me back right now, babe."

Chapter Nine

Eli

I had expected for it to be kind of weird and uncomfortable for Radiance and me to see one another in class for the first time since we'd started sleeping together. When she first entered the lecture hall ten minutes before her classmates, she greeted me with a shy smile as if she hadn't just let me fuck her in the most awkward position in the shower of the master bathroom in my guest house a few hours ago. I had an ugly bruise on my lower hip bone to prove that we'd just pulled off an incredible gymnastic stunt while the pounding shower spray turned from steaming hot to icy cold. Our Olympic gold-medal performance had lasted just that long because we'd had fresh afternoon energy and stamina after sharing a late lunch in bed. And I swear Radiance had unbelievable agility and flexibility. I could twist her like a pretzel, and she wouldn't break. My dick got hard just thinking about a few positions I was going to try with her tonight.

I sneaked a peek at her from behind a book I'd been skimming through since I had divided the class into groups of ten. Each group was supposed to have been brainstorming ideas for their oral presentations and graphic displays on global marketing. But there was something different going on in Radiance's group, and it had nothing to do with business, marketing, or the upcoming presentations. A young man with an athletic build and a movie star's smile slid a note to her. Then he had the nerve to wink and flash another flirtatious smile. I almost lost it when she read the note, scribbled a reply on it, and handed it back to the guy. I felt smoke blasting from my ears as my anger started to brew.

I stood up quickly, unable to tolerate the scene any longer. "If your group has finalized its agenda and duties have been assigned to each member, you're free to leave. I expect detailed outlines on my desk by our next session on Wednesday evening. Class is dismissed."

All of the groups dispersed. I kept my eye on Radiance and *lover boy* as the other members of their group walked away. He touched her arm and whispered in her ear before he pulled out his cell phone. My high level of restraint surprised me. It was the only reason why I didn't storm up the steps, grab Radiance, and drag her out of the room before she accepted the young man's phone. I saw red when she stored her number on his contact list.

"Ms. Alexander, I'd like a word with you before you leave."

I could tell that she'd been totally caught off guard, hearing my request. She was nervous and even jittery as she gathered her purse and backpack. And she had every reason to be. Her naïve behavior in response to being hit on by some young punk was beyond unacceptable. How could she even look at another man when we'd just fucked like a pair of wild rabbits in the shower a few hours ago? My body was still trying to recover from the over exertion, and memories were continuously replaying in my mind. A mountainous erection crept up on me when I recalled the hazy look in her eyes as I squeezed her breasts together so I could suck both of her nipples at the same time while she bounced and rotated her hips on my lap, taking my cock in fully.

"You asked to speak to me, Professor?" she asked as her *friend* walked past my desk.

I waited until after he'd exited the room before I spoke. "Go and lock the door."

She walked slowly to the door, locked it, and turned around with uncertainty clouding her features. She was a smart girl, so I imagined she sensed that something wasn't quite right.

"Come here."

She stood in place for a few seconds before she made short and timid steps in my direction. "Yes?" she asked in a child-like voice.

"What's that young man's name, Radiance?"

"Jordan Henderson. Why?"

"You're no longer in his group. I'll assign you to another one."

"But we've already delegated responsibilities. And our ideas are damn good."

"You will not work with a man who looks at you like he could eat you alive! You can work with another group or work alone. I don't give a fuck if you don't even do the assignment at all! But you will *not* work with Mr. Henderson! And why did you entertain his flirting?"

"I didn't. I just thought he was being nice."

"You gave him your phone number."

"He needs it so we can discuss our project. We selected him as our group leader. We all gave him our numbers, Eli."

"He doesn't need yours anymore because you're no longer in his group. It's final."

I gathered her in my arms and kissed whatever words she may have had in response right out of her mouth. She tried to push me away and break the embrace, but her strength was no match for mine. Plus the suction that my lips had on her tongue was too strong. She couldn't disengage our mouths without causing herself pain. I picked her up without breaking the kiss. I placed her on the edge of my desk and wedged my body between her legs. Her denim mini skirt crawled high above her thighs, and I couldn't have been happier.

My hand trembled as I reached down and eased the crotch of her panties to the side. I found the sweet hairy spot that I had grown to love, juicy with desire. I entered her wetness with two fingers and slid them out. I strummed her clit in slow motion to the sound of her soft coos and heavy breathing. I was teasing her into a fit with my fingers when I would've gladly sold my soul to Satan, himself, for a nickel if I could fuck her into submission right there on top of my desk. My dick was stiff and hot with raw need to be inside of her, but I didn't have protection.

I released her mouth. "When Mr. Henderson calls, you will tell him that you're no longer in his group. Do you understand?"

"Aaahhh . . . yesss . . . ."

"Good girl," I said, continuing my assault on her clit with my fingers.

"Aaahhh . . . Eli . . . mmm . . . baby . . . ."

I leaned in and blew in her left ear and pinched her right nipple at the same time.

"Ah, shit! Damn it, Eliiii!"

The earthquake inside of her body registered off of the Richter scale. She nearly jerked off of my desk. I covered her lips with mine to swallow her loud groans and curses. It pleased me to give her pleasure, but she was going to have to return the favor tonight—*all night.*

~♥~

I looked out the window for the hundredth time, hoping to see Radiance pulling into the driveway. It was almost nine o'clock, and she and Croix had not returned home yet. On campus before we parted ways, she'd told me that she was going to her ex's sister's house to collect the remainder of her belongings. Against my better judgment, I had allowed her to go without Sergio as I'd initially planned. She had convinced me that it would be better if she and Croix went alone to prevent potential questions and any speculation about her present living situation. Her ex's sister had been calling, questioning her whereabouts and demanding to see Croix over the past week, but Radiance had refused to speak with her until this morning after she had taken the child to school. That's when she agreed to go to the house to allow Croix to visit his aunt while she packed the rest of their things.

The visit started over three hours ago. She should've been home by now or at the very least, she could've called me to say she was running late. Mama Sadie had prepared dinner for us, but I was pretty sure it had turned cold by now. And I had purchased new Xbox One games, a bunch of action figures, and other toys and books as a surprise for Croix. I hurried to the window when I heard a car and saw headlights. I snatched the curtain back and released air from my cheeks.

"What took you guys so long?" I asked as calmly as I could the moment they entered the house.

"We'll discuss it later, Eli. Now isn't a good time."

I shifted my eyes from Radiance's troubled face to stare at Croix. "Hey there, little buddy. How're you?"

"I'm fine. Mommy's sad, though."

"Who made her sad, Croix?"

"The man on Auntie J's phone. I heard him screaming at her. He's *mean*."

I watched Radiance turn her back to me before she wiped tears from her eyes. "Let me fix you a plate of food, little man. Do you like chicken and dumplings?"

He nodded and smiled. "It's yummy!"

"Good. Go and wash up for dinner while your mother and I talk and heat up the food."

"Okay." He took off running down the hall.

I reached for Radiance and spun her around to face me. "Who was Croix talking about? Who did you speak to that made you so upset?"

"Satchel. He's pissed off and raising hell because I moved out. As long as I was living with Janelda, he could keep tabs on me, but now he can't. His boys on the outside got word to him that I no longer work at the Pleasure Palace. He's going crazy because he doesn't know where Croix and I live or how I'm paying our bills."

"That's none of his damn business!"

"I told him that," she said on a deep sob. "We're not together anymore. Yes, I will always be grateful that he spared me from going to prison by telling the truth about me being totally in the dark about his drug dealings. And he's Croix's father, so we'll always have a connection. But I don't love him anymore. He knows that, Eli."

I embraced her and let her cry on my shoulder. "It's okay, babe. It's okay. Hush now."

"There's more," she said, pulling back.

"Tell me."

"Satchel is due out on an early release for good behavior, and according to him, it'll be soon. In a few weeks, he's supposed to enter a local halfway house to help him transition back into society. He said if I don't come back to him, he's going to fight for custody of Croix, and I'll never see him again! Eli, I can't lose my son! He doesn't even know Satchel. He was only two years old when he went to prison."

"That bastard can't take Croix away from you. I won't let him. You're a wonderful mother, sweetheart. There's no way he can prove you unfit. He's a fucking criminal, damn it!"

"Yes, I know, but he has pictures of me giving a man a lap dance at my homeboy's CD release party. He said he'll tell the judge that I was a stripper and that I only pretended to be a hostess at the club."

"Your former boss can refute that. All of the people you used to work with can."

"I know."

"What did your ex's sister have to say about all of this?"

"Janelda was so mean to me. She said I owe her my half of a six hundred-dollar past-due electric bill. I swear I paid my bills in that house in full every month according to whatever she told me I owed."

"I'll give you a cashier's check to give to her just to shut her up. What else? Whatever is broken, Eli will fix it."

"I'm hungry and tired. What can you do about that?" she asked with a smile on her face that made my heart flutter.

"I can warm up the food that Mama Sadie prepared for us, and afterwards, I'll run a warm bubble bath for you, so you can soak away your worries and exhaustion. Then later on, after Croix goes to sleep, I'm going to lick and stroke all the tension from your body. How does that sound?"

"It sounds like a plan." She kissed my lips softly and smiled. "Speaking of Croix, where is he?"

"I think he may have found some surprises in his bedroom."

"Eli, you didn't," she said, frowning.

"I'm sorry, but I did."

"Croix, it's dinnertime sweetie! Where are you?"

He bounced into the room holding a brand new Spider-Man action figure. "Mommy, look what I found in my room!"

"Eli bought new toys for you."

He jumped in my arms, and I lifted him up high in the air and spun him around in circles.

He giggled like crazy. "Thank you, Eli," he said after I placed him on his feet. "I like my games and my super heroes and my books. Will you read a story for me tonight?"

"Of course I will."

Chapter Ten

Radiance

I stood quietly outside of the bedroom door peeping and listening to Eli read a story about a lost brown teddy bear to Croix. It warmed my heart to see my baby so happy. He had no memories—good, bad, or in between—of Satchel. Only pictures and phone calls had kept them loosely connected over the past three years. I used to take Croix to visit his father in prison down in Wrightsville, Georgia right after he was shipped off, but I stopped when I learned about his other *women*. His main side piece was a chick named Felicity, and she'd claimed the baby she was carrying at the time of Satchel's arrest was his. He swore to me that they'd never been romantically or sexually involved and that she was just one of the females he used to have slinging for him over in Ridgewood. I didn't know what to believe. Basically, it was her word against his. But she was big and pregnant with *someone's* child. So I figured if the man I'd once slept with every night and shared a son with could hide an entire drug operation from me in my own apartment, he could hide anything. Therefore, I decided to end our relationship. And I never took Croix to see his father again.

Janelda and I had had many arguments on the subject, but I'd stood my ground. If Satchel had loved his son and wanted to be the primary male influence in his life, he would've kept his ass on the right side of the law to avoid prison. But he'd chosen to live life in the dirty and fast lane, placing Croix and me at risk. Then on top of that, he'd had the nerve to cheat on me with a bunch of women, and had possibly had another son with one of them. I hadn't deserved his treatment, and neither had our son. And there was nothing that he could do or say to make me come back to him when he got out of prison. I was done with him. Of course, once he was out, I would allow him a chance to get to know Croix. It would be the right thing to do, but I wasn't going to be a part of the package. So Satchel needed to accept that before he stepped one foot out of the pen.

I didn't know what God had in store for me in the future, but I sure wouldn't mind if Eli could be included. Although crazy circumstances had brought us together, I was falling for him after such a short period of time. He was arrogant, stubborn, and controlling as hell, but there was something sweet and appealing about him that made me want to be wherever he was. He was a very kind and generous man. And the sex was slap-ya-mama good! I couldn't get enough of him, and he seemed equally hungry for me every night when we made love. And each morning that I woke up in his arms, I felt no regrets. I couldn't wait for him to finish reading to Croix so he could open up his bag of tricks in my bedroom tonight.

As if he'd read my mind, Eli looked up and caught me staring at him with lustful eyes that I couldn't even conceal. He read the last few words in the book and closed it. Croix's eyes were half closed, which meant it wouldn't be long before he would drift off to sleep. Eli ran his fingers through Croix's curls and kissed him softly on the forehead.

"Good night, Eli," he said sweetly right before he yawned.

"Sleep well, my little buddy. I'll see you in the morning." He turned to me. "How was your bath?"

"It worked like a charm. I was lonely, though."

He nodded, obviously catching my drift. "I'm going to shower. Don't take too long tucking him in."

"I'll be there shortly." I crossed the room, brushing past Eli as I did. I sat on the side of the bed. "Did you enjoy Eli reading to you?"

"Yes, ma'am. He reads good just like you. I want him to read the airplane book for me tomorrow."

"How do you know he'll be here tomorrow?"

"He said so. Mommy, you're *silly*."

"I know, baby." I pecked his cheek. "Go to sleep and dream about something special."

"Okay. I'll dream that Eli is my daddy and you and I can move into the castle with him and never, ever leave."

Where the hell had that come from? I was stunned without a comeback. Croix's words were pretty heavy for a little kid. What did he know about having a daddy or a woman and man living together? He didn't even know what a traditional family looked like outside of the children's shows and movies he watched on TV. I could count on one hand how many times my baby had asked about his father. And on each of those rare occasions, it hadn't taken very much effort to satisfy his curiosity because it was impossible for him to miss a person he had no memories of.

I couldn't deny that Eli had been more than kind to Croix since the night they'd met. And because of it, my baby was crazy about him. They clearly had a strong connection. There was genuine affection in Eli's eyes whenever he looked at my son, and it made my heart sing. But I was smart enough to know that he had no intention of becoming a permanent part of Croix's life. Hell, he damn sure wasn't trying to make me his wife or even a longtime partner. We were on the temporary plan, and I was okay with that for now. I was a big girl, and I understood that our season at Diamond Estate would soon come to an end. My fear was that Croix would become so emotionally attached to Eli and his guest house that he would be crushed when it was time for us to leave. The thought of that tore my heart to pieces. To spare my son from the heartache, I would have to limit his interaction with Eli. But who was going to protect *my* heart when my time with him came to an end?

I forced my thoughts away from the future and focused on the present. Right now I had an irresistible man in my bed waiting to make hot, passionate love to me. And he was taking excellent care of my son and me every day, providing us with everything we needed or could ever want. I wasn't about to let my concerns about the future rob me of the joy I deserved tonight. Only God knew how my life would unfold in the days, months, and years to come. Therefore, it would be useless for me to dwell on my future. So in the paraphrased words of the late, great Whitney 'Nippy' Houston: Tonight was the night, and Ray was feeling all right. I was about to make love to Eli the whole night through. And yes, I'd been saving all my love for him.

I kissed Croix one more time on his cheek seconds after his eyes closed. He was my precious angel, and I loved him more than I loved myself. Closing the door behind me, I made quick steps toward the master bedroom where Eli was waiting for me. Our timing was perfect. He emerged from the bathroom at the same time I entered our love nook. I closed the door and took in the perfect male specimen before me in all of his natural glory. Wrapped in a white towel from the torso down with his long, damp hair flowing freely, Eli reminded me of Eros, the Greek god of love, passion, procreation, and sexual desire. I considered myself one lucky sistah to have him all to myself night after night.

"I'll be leaving town for San Francisco on business tomorrow afternoon. I would love to take you and Croix with me."

"We would love to go with you, but we can't."

"Why not?"

"I have to work."

"You work from home, and you work for *me*, Radiance. You can take off whenever you want to. That's a perk for sleeping with the boss." He winked at me and smiled.

"I don't want perks. I want to do my job well and earn my salary just like your other employees. So this weekend while you're in San Francisco, I'll be here on the computer working on a sales campaign for your Tampa resort."

"I want you and Croix to go to San Francisco with me, so consider yourself on leave this weekend."

"No. I'll be working."

"I don't think so, sweetheart."

Eli sat down on the bed and picked up his cell phone from the nightstand. I watched him push a number on his speed dial list and wait for someone to answer his call.

"Kelly, this is Mr. Jamieson. Radiance Alexander, the new girl I hired to work in the sales department from home, has been terminated." He ended the call.

~♥~

"Do you like this big car, Mommy? Do you, huh? I do. It's *cool!*" Croix said excitedly, bouncing on the butter-soft leather seat.

"It's a *limousine*, sweetie, and I like it."

"Wow! Mommy, look at that giant bridge!"

"That's the Golden Gate Bridge, little buddy. I'll make sure we take a ride across it while we're in town."

"You promise?"

"Sure," Eli said, smiling and running his fingers through Croix's hair.

I wanted to smile too, but I refused to curl my lips because I was still pouting over being fired. I had only known Eli on a personal level for a few weeks, yet he had caused me to lose *two* jobs. And if he had one ounce of remorse about it, I couldn't tell. He was the picture of contentment, smiling and pointing out buildings and other Bay Area landmarks to Croix. He was a bully as far as I was concerned, but sometimes he could be a teddy bear. There were moments when he could be so gentle, affectionate, and sweet. That was the Eli I could ride with.

I released the toxic resentment I'd been holding on to toward him when I thought about the much softer and milder side of him that he'd shown me just last night after I threw a temper tantrum over being fired. He actually apologized and offered me my job back, but my stubbornness wouldn't let me bend. I told him that I didn't want to work for him and that I would find another job that would allow me to work from home. Although he was against my decision, he didn't say another word. We got in bed, and he held me until just before sunrise. And that's when we made slow, lazy love with the sound of a scattered morning rain in the background. An hour or so later, I woke up to breakfast in bed and a dozen of yellow long stem roses. Then before we boarded Eli's private plane for San Francisco, he treated me to a surprise shopping spree at Phipps Plaza. I was a lucky girl.

Chapter Eleven

Eli

"Yes, Mama, we're fine. San Francisco is beautiful. Croix is so excited. He's bouncing off the walls. We'll bring you lots of souvenirs," Radiance assured her mother, smiling.

The smile on her face was priceless. I lived to make her and Croix happy. After our little spat last night, I made a promise to myself that I would never upset her again. A happy Radiance was much more pleasant than an angry one. Her smile and sparkling eyes drew me in every time I looked at her. And the way she gave herself to me so freely and passionately each time we made love had brought out my greed. My appetite for Radiance had no end. I couldn't imagine her leaving Diamond Estate any time soon or *ever*.

I tossed my leather binder on the table and bolted from my chair. The thought of us parting ways caused my chest muscles to tighten. I needed air. I hurried toward the sliding glass doors and opened them. As soon as I stepped out on the terrace, I inhaled a long stream of fresh air. I closed the doors behind me and exhaled slowly. Placing my hands on the rail, I lowered my head to take in the sight of nearby Union Square. I needed a distraction to buy me a few minutes before I'd be forced to face an inevitable shocking reality. I was in *deep shit*! For the first time in my life I had acted without a plan, and now I had no clue what my next move was supposed to be. It had been totally out of character for me to carry Radiance out of the Pleasure Palace that night like a sack of potatoes. And then, as if I hadn't behaved foolishly enough, I moved her and her son onto my property without a second thought. I had acted spontaneously on emotion before thinking things through.

My current dilemma was now that Radiance and Croix had become a part of my personal world, I wanted them to stay beyond our original agreement. Once she finished graduate school, she expected to leave me and venture out on her own. *No fucking way!* My heart screamed, and my emotions caused my entire body to shudder even in the balmy springtime weather in the Bay. I wouldn't allow Radiance and Croix to leave as we'd agreed. No, I couldn't hold them hostage, demanding that they stay, but I could make life so comfortable and wonderful for them that they would never want to leave. I was going to win Radiance's heart just like she had won mine. My young student and house guest had cast a spell on me over the short time we'd been involved. I wasn't sure how she had pulled it off, but her hooks were deep inside of me. And I was going to hook her too. I was on a quest, and I had the perfect plan. Radiance was about to be properly courted and pampered like a princess.

"Eli, you only have a little over an hour to prepare for your lunch meeting."

I turned around and faced Radiance just as she joined me on the terrace. She was an eyeful of loveliness with her hair pulled back in a simple ponytail and her face free of makeup. We had lounged around our presidential suite at the Four Seasons in our pajamas all morning after an early breakfast and watching television with Croix. He was now taking a nap, which gave me some time to hang out with his mom.

"I'm prepared. It's a pretty simple deal. The land is available, and I have the money to purchase it." I opened my arms to her, and she didn't disappoint me when she walked into my embrace. "I want to take you and Croix out to dinner this evening before I meet with a group of investors over cocktails. Do you guys like seafood?"

"We do."

"Great. We have a six o'clock reservation at Sutro's at the Cliff House. Croix will get a kick out of the bird's eye ocean view. And maybe we'll have time to explore the beach."

"He'll love that."

"What are your plans for the afternoon? You have a car, a driver, and a pile of my money at your disposal."

"I think I'll take Croix sightseeing. He was flipping through some pamphlets and tourists maps last night. He wants to see the entire city and take pictures to show his friends at school."

"I wish that I could tag along, but—"

"You're here on business. I understand."

"Do you?"

"I do. My daddy was a hardworking man, and he tried to give my mama and me the world. Grinding is what made you wealthy and successful, Eli. I admire your vigorous work ethic. Someday, when I'm the CEO of my own empire, I'll work just as hard as you do to leave Croix a legacy he can be proud of."

I searched her eyes for honesty and found it. Pandora used to tell me that she understood too, but she didn't mean it. While I worked my heart out day in and day out to expand my company and its brand, the only thing she did was complain. She enjoyed the money, expensive gifts, and exotic trips around the globe, but those luxuries were never enough. She was a spoiled brat. And she was selfish too. I never asked her for much, but the one thing I wanted more than anything else in the world was the single thing she had refused to give me—a child. I guess that's why I was so fascinated with Croix. He was a constant reminder of the son that I had begged Pandora for but had never received. However, she had shared McKenzie with me, and we'd built a solid bond. But the precious little girl wasn't mine, and her mother used to constantly throw it up in my face.

I pulled my thoughts back to the present and checked my watch. "I need to get dressed, babe. I should be back around four. I trust that you and Croix will meet me here."

"We will."

I kissed Radiance like I would never see her again before I left her on the terrace so I could get dressed for my business lunch.

"Eli, the food was awesome, and the atmosphere was so romantic. It put me in the mood. I started to invite you to the ladies' room so I could take you in a stall and molest you."

I looked a few yards ahead to make sure that Croix was still busy collecting shells along the beach before I grabbed a handful of Radiance's soft, round ass. She squealed and scrambled away from my roaming hands. The sound of her laughter was infectious.

I chuckled lightly in response. "You can do any damn thing you want to do to me when I return to the hotel later. You won't get a fight from me. I like the nasty side of you, babe."

"Who? *Me?*" she asked jokingly, her eyes filled with mischief. "I'm not nasty. I'm a *lady*."

"You're a lady in my class and in the presence of your son. I'm sure you behave like an innocent little girl around your mother too. Mama Sadie and Sergio think you're a perfect angel. But *I* know the wild and raw Radiance Alexander, and I like her just fine. She's anything but a lady in the bedroom."

"There's a time and place for everything, Professor Jamieson. I'm like a chameleon. I know when and where to switch it up."

She approached me slowly in a catlike saunter. When her lips connected with mine, I swear I heard the heavens rejoice in song. I wrapped my arms around her and lifted her feet from the white sand. Like a joyous child, she giggled and shrieked against the evening ocean breeze.

"Trapper!" I heard a deep, familiar voice shout. "Hey, man, I'm up here. Trapper!"

I looked over my shoulder and searched the cliff above. My eyes zoomed in on Marlon, my attorney slash lifelong best friend who was more like a brother to me. *Why the hell is he here so fucking early?* I wondered silently as he made his way down the winding stairwell toward the beach. I knew without a second guess that the drink in his hand was a dirty martini. I placed Radiance on her feet and glanced down the shore at Croix. He was sitting in the sand playing with his bucket, his shovel, and a pile of seashells. I looked away from him and braced myself for a thousand questions from Marlon.

He and I embraced and clapped each other's back. It was the same way we had greeted each other consistently since we were four and five years old. Born to different parents on opposite sides of the track in Atlanta, Marlon and I were closer than any other two friends on the planet. I was happy to see him, but I was also nervous in light of the situation. I had purposely scheduled the cocktail meeting between the investors, Marlon, and me two hours after my dinner date with Radiance and Croix. But his early arrival was about to shake things up. I could feel it in my gut.

Before Marlon could speak, I rushed into introductions. "Radiance, this is my brother from another mother and my attorney, Marlon Lawson. Bruh, this is the lovely lady I've been telling you about. Her name is Radiance Alexander."

Their right hands joined in a friendly shake before Marlon leaned in and brushed his lips across Radiance's knuckles. If it had been any other man, that smooth move would've earned him a punch in the nose, but it was *Marlon*, my brother and best friend.

"It's a pleasure to meet you, sweetheart. My mama told me how beautiful you were. *Damn!* She wasn't lying either."

Radiance's face wrinkled in confusion. "I don't understand. Who is your mother?"

"Marlon is Mama Sadie's one and only *biological* child, babe. But *I'm* her favorite out of the four children she raised because I'm the baby."

"Yes, my mama raised Eunice, Homer Junior, this narcissistic fool, and me at Diamond Estate. She was the housekeeper and nanny for the senior Mr. Jamieson and his wife, Ms. Abigail, for as far back as I can remember. We were one big happy mixed family."

I nodded. "We were. Every weekend when it was time for Mama Sadie to go home, I would hide her pocketbook so she couldn't leave. After a while, she got smart and started taking me home with her to avoid the madness. When my mother passed away shortly after my tenth birthday, Mama Sadie moved in and raised me. Marlon never missed her because he came over every day after school, and he'd stay until his uncle picked him up in the evening. During the summertime, my dad used to ship us two off to camp up in the mountains. Those were the good ole days."

"It sounds like the two of you had a wonderful childhood together."

"Hell yeah, we did!" I assured her.

"Well, I'll leave you guys alone to talk. I'm going to go and dig in the sand with Croix." She pecked my lips before she turned and headed down the beach. Marlon and I stood in place, watching Radiance cross the sand to join her son.

As young boys, we were known as the terrible twosome on Diamond Estate. We got into trouble constantly, and Mama Sadie used to whip our butts with a wooden spoon every damn time we did. I was usually the mastermind behind our evil deeds, but Marlon was always my willing sidekick.

I guess I was so troublesome back then because my father was never around. I knew that he loved us, but I used to miss him terribly. He was just too busy, driven by his desire to become rich and successful that sometimes he forgot about his family. My mother turned to alcohol and prescription drugs to fill the void of his absence. The combination eventually killed her. Eunice ended up marrying early to get out of the house, and Homer Junior hauled ass for the navy as soon as he turned eighteen. He's been there ever since.

Marlon and I remained in Georgia for college. One could say we were mama's boys. He entered Morehouse College a year before I headed off to Athens to study business at the University of Georgia. We never lost contact. In fact, the brief separation only strengthened the bond between us. After Marlon finished law school at Mercer University in Macon, Georgia, he and I moved into a condo together in Buckhead while I finished up my master's degree in business at Georgia Tech. Even then, I had a part-time position in my father's company. I was the only one of his children who wanted to follow in his footsteps.

Sadly, a few months after my graduation, Homer Jamieson Senior died of a massive heart attack. He left half of his millions to me. The other half was divided to his specifications between Eunice, Homer Junior, Marlon, and of course Mama Sadie. However, the entire company fell into my hands because my siblings wanted no parts of it. Marlon handled all of the legal work, but he didn't have any interest in working for Diamond International on the business side. So I was the lone Jamieson in the family empire, but I had a jewel of a woman in my personal life. I was falling hard for Radiance, and she definitely was feeling me too.

Chapter Twelve

Eli

"Wooo weee!" Marlon drawled when Radiance was out of earshot. "You are one lucky dude, Trapper. You're hitting *that* every night?"

"A gentleman never kisses and tells."

"I know. That's why I'm asking *you*, bruh. Is she the one who has you walking around barefoot outside all times of the morning, singing to the sun and shit?"

"Go to hell, Marlon."

"I live there. I'm married to *Golden*. Remember? And since we're on the subject of *marriage—*"

"Let's not go there tonight," I said, walking away with my hands stuffed inside my pants pockets. I did a quick about face. "And why the hell did you come here an hour before the meeting anyway? You weren't supposed to meet Radiance."

"You're obviously not trying to keep her a secret. She's whipping around Atlanta in your cars, and the two of you are practically shacking up on the estate. And then you had the nerve to bring her and her son out to San Francisco. It doesn't seem like you're keeping things on the low to me."

"I know! I know! Damn it! My life is complicated as fuck!"

"Yeah, it is. You need to fix it."

"How can I? I don't know any more information than I did two years ago. *You're* my damn lawyer. What the hell have you and the other legal experts at your firm come up with? Have your investigators found her?"

"Nah, man. There ain't nothing new, bruh. I'm sorry."

"That's exactly what I thought."

"Hey, man, as your brother and best friend, I understand. Believe me. I do. Radiance is a whole lot of chocolate in one scoop. Hell, I would've kidnapped her fine ass too. But as your attorney and advisor, I must warn you that you're walking way too close to the edge."

"I can't keep putting my damn life on hold."

"I know, and I don't expect you to. I've got a colleague in Augusta looking over the case for me. He thinks he's found a new angle that hasn't been explored yet. Give him a week or so to research it and get back with me."

I nodded and looked down the shoreline. Radiance was on the damp ground in her expensive black dress, helping Croix build a sand castle. The sight of them having fun together at my expense made life worth living. "I care about her, Marlon," I whispered. "It's not just some meaningless fling going on between us."

"Does she feel the same way?"

"I'm not sure right now. But she definitely will after I'm done putting the moves on her."

"And then what? After you make her fall in love with you, what will you do? I hope you don't expect a hottie like her to settle for being your *mistress* for the rest of her life. She's probably cool with your complicated situation right now because she's young, and it's fascinating to have a sugar daddy. But what're you going to do when she starts demanding that you put a ring on it?"

"Leave it alone, Marlon."

"Have you even discussed it with her?" he pushed against my wishes.

"No," I growled, rubbing my hands over my face.

"Wait a minute." He walked closer to me and stopped when we stood eye to eye. "She doesn't even know, does she? You didn't tell her. Damn you, Trapper!"

Radiance snuggled closer to me as she slept peacefully in my arms. I kissed her forehead and wrapped my arms tighter around her perfect body. My feelings for her were growing stronger with each passing day. And because of it, I knew that it was time for me to come clean with her. As usual, Marlon's advice had been on point. Radiance deserved to know the truth. And I'd had every intention of making a full confession the moment I returned to the suite from my business meeting. But the sound of smooth jazz and the scent of jasmine greeted me at the door. Instantly, I got caught up in the rapture of romance. I experienced a testosterone rush when I entered the master bedroom and saw Radiance relaxing on the bed, wearing one of my crisp white dress shirts.

My well-rehearsed speech I had committed to memory on the limo ride back to the Four Seasons completely vanished from my brain. The only thing I could think about was getting Radiance out of that shirt. And after I got rid of it, we pounced on each other like a pair of wild dogs in heat. I think it was our most intense lovemaking session ever. I only hoped that it wasn't our *last* one. But unfortunately for me, it wouldn't be my call. The future of our fate would be in Radiance's hands tomorrow morning after I revealed the whole truth about my situation. She was so innocent and unassuming. She trusted me. It had never been my intention to hurt her or Croix, but my failure to plan could possibly do just that. The very thought of it caused my heart to crumble into billions of small pieces.

After all, I had chosen her. And she had been none the wiser. But no matter what, I was going to tell Radiance everything I should've told her before we got involved. Now I would have to accept whatever decision or reactions she was going to throw my way.

~♥~

"Look at him. He's out like a light. All of the excitement at the Golden Gate Park wore him out." Radiance spread a blanket over her sleeping son. "He'll probably sleep through lunch."

"I'll order him something from room service the moment he wakes up."

Radiance stared at me with questioning eyes. "Don't you have a meeting or some other business to tend to?"

"No. My business in San Francisco is officially over. That's why I was able to take you guys to breakfast and to the park."

"So now that you have some spare time, what would you like to do?" She wrapped her arms around my waist and laid her head on my chest.

My body responded as it always did whenever I was close to her, inhaling her alluring scent. She was more addictive than any drug. But it wasn't time for us to mate. We needed to have a conversation. I had prolonged the inevitable with breakfast and a trip to Golden Gate Park, but now it was time to face the music. "Let's go in the sitting area."

"I'd rather go to the *bedroom*," she whispered seductively and ran her fingers through my hair.

Hell, I want to take you to bed too! I ignored the mounting temptation and gently guided Radiance out of Croix's bedroom. I closed the door and led her to the sitting area. My nerves were all over the place. I felt like

---

my stomach had knotted into a tight ball of tension, and I couldn't take in enough air.

"Sit down with me. We need to talk, babe."

"What is it, Eli? You're acting strange."

"Radiance, there's something that I should've told you the night I moved you and Croix into my guest house. At the time it didn't seem important, but after that first night you and I spent together, I knew that you had a right to know. I just couldn't figure out how to tell you."

"Tell me now, Eli. I'm listening. Just spit it out."

I released a breath and looked her directly in her eyes. "Radiance, I'm married."

"What?"

I placed my hand on her thigh, but she swiped it away. "I'm *legally* married, but I've been separated for two years now. Pandora, my estranged wife, left me. Shit, I don't even know where the hell she is! I've been trying to serve her with divorce papers ever since she left, but no one can find her."

Radiance stood up quickly with tears flowing down her cheeks. "You should've told me! Why did you allow me to fall for you when you knew you had a fucking wife, Eli? Why? I feel so *used*." She ran from the sitting area.

"Radiance, come back here this instant!"

"Go to hell, Eli! Take your lying, two-timing, married ass straight to hell!"

I ran to the master bedroom and found her throwing clothes, shoes, and toiletries into her suitcase. A heavy stream of tears continued pouring down her face. Her sadness and disappointment punched me hard in the gut. She was visibly hurt.

"Radiance, stop packing and listen to me."

She ignored me and disappeared into the bathroom. I followed her.

"Pandora and I would've been divorced by now if it wasn't for the stupid prenuptial agreement we signed. She *must* be served notice of the divorce in person, Radiance. I only agreed to that ridiculous clause in the agreement to protect my money and my company. I worked hard for everything I have. I wasn't about to let her take one thin dime from me, so I agreed to certain outlandish terms against Marlon's advice. It was a stupid compromise."

She pushed past me with her hands filled with lotions, perfumes, and makeup. The only sounds she made were light sniffles as she continued to cry pitifully. She wouldn't even look at me.

"A team of investigators have been searching for her all over the world. She doesn't want to be found. McKenzie, her thirteen-year-old daughter, doesn't even have a clue where she is. She dropped that poor girl off at a boarding school in Switzerland and went along her merry way. Pandora has been spotted in Dubai as the guest of a wealthy oil tycoon. A few months ago, some friends of Homer Junior ran into her in Monte Carlo, and last year she sent me a post card from Bangkok. She could be anywhere right now. I don't know where the hell she is, Radiance! Damn it! Listen to me!"

She sat down at the desk and logged on to the laptop that we shared. I looked over her shoulder and noticed that she was searching for airline tickets on the Delta website. She had enough money in the bank to get home without me. I had made sure of that with a whopping deposit before we left Atlanta. I could've begged her like hell not to leave me, but I couldn't stop her.

"You don't need to travel with Croix alone in your emotional state, Radiance. You're too upset. He's a smart boy. He'll sense that something is wrong. Please stay until it's time for us to leave tomorrow morning."

"I was fine taking care of my son and me before you came along. Croix and I will be okay without you. If it kills me, I will pay you back every penny for all you've done for us. I'm not a beggar or a prostitute or one of your charity projects. You will get your money back."

"Where will you and Croix live?"

"Don't worry about it. There're shelters for homeless women and children all over Atlanta. And my MARTA pass is still good. We'll make due until I find a cheap apartment and get my car out of the shop."

"You are *not* going to a homeless shelter with Croix! I won't allow it! This is absurd, Radiance! Stop acting like a child!" I grabbed the laptop from the desk and hurled it across the room. It crashed into pieces when it slammed against the wall. "You and Croix will leave San Francisco with me tomorrow on my private plane as planned. When we return to Atlanta, I will make arrangements for the two of you to move into a place of your own if you wish to leave Diamond Estate. I'll pay for your car repairs as well, although I'd prefer to buy you a new one. That's not important right now, though. Just know that you and Croix will leave San Francisco with me tomorrow and not a second sooner.

Chapter Thirteen

Radiance

"Who is it?"

"It's me, Mama. Open the door."

The sound of the chain and locks disengaging rattled before the door opened slowly. I was greeted by a bright smile. "What a pleasant surprise. Come on in here, you two."

"Grandma!"

"Lord Jesus, look at my grandbaby," she said, bending down to meet Croix at eye level. She kissed his cheek. "What brings y'all here this time of the evening? And don't lie to me, Ray. Eli called me. I know you moved out of his guest house over a terrible misunderstanding."

"He had no right to call you!"

"How come? He calls me every week. This one wasn't any different."

"He's married, Mama."

"I know. He told me." She turned around and walked toward her small living room. "He told me *everything*, in fact."

I followed my mama and sat down next to her with Croix close behind me.

"Croix, go and get a few cookies out of the cookie jar in the kitchen. Then go to my bedroom, sit in the big chair, and watch TV, sugar."

"Yes, ma'am." He took off running.

"Let Mama ask you something, Ray. Were you and Eli fooling around a little bit?"

"*Mama!*" I felt my face burning with embarrassment.

She laughed and shook her head. "I figured so."

"I didn't answer your question, Mama."

"You didn't have to. I brought you into the world. I know you better than anybody else. You wouldn't have gotten upset and moved away from that comfortable house if Eli was just your landlord and professor. It wouldn't have made a bit of difference to you if he were married or not if there was nothing going on between the two of you. Y'all crossed the line, didn't you?"

I nodded as a fresh stream of tears escaped my eyes.

"What're you crying for? Do you regret it?"

"No, ma'am, I don't regret it. I just wish he wasn't married. He should've told me."

"Yes, baby, he should have. But in his heart, he's been divorced for a long time. That woman left him because he asked her to give him a child. She was a spoiled little rich girl, living off of her daddy's fortune. She married one rich man before Eli and had a daughter that she never wanted for security. Eli refused to pay her to give him a baby, so she took off."

"How do you know all of this?"

"Eli told me. You see, I listened when he talked to me. I asked questions too. That man has spent over a million dollars trying to find that manipulative tramp so he can dissolve their marriage. Now that you and Croix are in his life, he's more determined than ever to find her. And he will. The only mistake he made was he didn't tell you about it."

"What would you do if you were me, Mama?"

"I would take my behind back to that guest house. Then Eli and I would have a little talk. And I would help him locate that fool he married so he can hurry up and divorce her."

~♥~

I was too tired to make the cab ride back to Diamond Estate, so Croix and I spent the night with my mama. I was still upset with Eli although I understood his situation much better after my conversation with Mama. She was a wise woman, and I loved her to pieces. I only hoped that her wisdom would follow me someday. I was the spitting image of my mama with my daddy's dark complexion. It was a blessing to have her good looks, but I wanted to be smart like her too. She had been right about Satchel from day one, and I trusted her on the advice she'd given me about Eli. She wasn't a fan of my relationship with my college sweetheart. She used to tell me all the time that he talked too fast and too much. She swore it had nothing to do with his thick Caribbean accent he'd inherited at birth from his native homeland of St. Croix, United States Virgin Island. Mama just believed that Satchel was a slick hustler who had never meant me any good.

Right before she tucked Croix and me in on the sofa bed in her living room, she encouraged me to follow my heart. And that's exactly what I intended to do. I was going back to Diamond Estate to Eli. He had assured me that Croix and I were welcome to return anytime. So as soon as I picked up my son from school tomorrow, we would catch a cab back home.

~♥~

"I'll get your bag for you, Ms. Alexander."

"Thank you, Sergio." I smiled at the gentle giant as he approached the cab. I paid the driver and helped Croix from the back seat. "Come on, baby. Let's go inside."

"Mr. Jamieson will arrive home late this evening, ma'am. Is he expecting you to be here?"

"No, Sergio, he's not. I wanted to surprise him. Do you think that's a good idea?"

He grinned and nodded. "Yes, ma'am. Boss will be happy to see you." He removed the keys from my hand and hurried to the door to unlock it. He placed the suitcase on the floor in the front hall. "Have a good evening," he told me before he dropped the keys in my open hand.

My eyes nearly popped from their sockets when I stepped inside the house. There were dozens of red roses in exquisite crystal vases everywhere. The fragrance in the air was heavenly. Every table, shelf, and sturdy flat service was occupied by roses.

"Mommy, Eli turned our house into a garden! Look at all of the flowers!"

"I see, honey."

"I'm going to check out my room."

"Yeah, you go and do that," I mumbled, looking around in awe.

I walked to the master bedroom and discovered more flowers and a dresser covered with gift boxes wrapped to perfection in shiny silver paper. I ripped into the first one and was shocked out of my mind by a pair of diamond teardrop earrings. They were *huge*. Another box contained a gorgeous diamond tennis bracelet set in brilliant platinum. The lone gift bag was filled with several bars of Miha's organic soap that smelled amazing. I nearly fainted when I opened a box of CoCo Mademoiselle perfume. I'd only dreamed of wearing such an expensive fragrance, but Eli had found me worthy enough to own a bottle.

As I continued opening presents like a kid on Christmas morning, Croix came running into the room with a fancy red sports car in one hand and a remote control in the other. "I've got balloons *everywhere* in my room! Look at my new car! Come see my spaceship, Mommy."

"Mommy's coming, sweetie," I said seconds before I noticed an envelope with my name scribbled on it lying on the edge of the dresser. I stared at it for a moment while hundreds of tiny butterflies danced in my stomach. Too anxious to wait another second, I picked it up and tore into it with shaking hands.

My dearest Radiance,
If you're reading this letter, it means my prayers have been answered. Thank you for coming back to me. One night apart caused my soul to sink into painful darkness. It felt like I had died and been cast to hell. I'm sorry that I didn't tell you about Pandora. I made a terrible mistake by withholding something so important from you. Please know that from this day forward, I'll always be true to you. And I promise that I will locate Pandora as soon as possible. so that I can move forward with my life with you and Croix. I'll see you later tonight.
Eli

I pressed the single sheet of paper to my chest, trying to control the runaway beat of my heart. Eli had missed me. The thought of him alone and sad because I wasn't with him last night caused hot tears to pool in my eyes. The man was under my skin, deep into my pores, and flowing through the warm blood in my veins. Mama believed I had fallen in love with him. Maybe she was right. She was seldom wrong about anything.

"Mommy!" Croix yelled from his bedroom "Are you coming?"

"Yeah, sweetie, I'm on my way!"

~♥~

"It's almost dry, baby. Just hold on." I pulled the brush through Eli's hair repeatedly as I moved the blow dryer's nozzle over the long, thick, wet tresses. "You need to sip more tea. I don't want you to catch a cold."

"The pilot thought we would miss the storm, but he was wrong. Marlon tried to tell him. He wouldn't listen."

"You guys should've spent the night."

"Hell no! My sister-in-law, Golden, would've had a conniption. Plus Sergio had called to let me know that you were here," he said in a gravelly voice as he ran his finger up and down my inner thigh. "I had to get back home to you."

"Flying on a private plane from Toronto Ontario, Canada to Atlanta in bad weather wasn't a smart move, Eli. It was *dangerous*."

"I know, but we had to follow the lead that one of the new investigators I hired had on Pandora. She was at a casino in Toronto supposedly with a wealthy Canadian investment banker two days ago according to sources. She had left the country by the time we got there. I was so upset that I insisted that we return home."

"You'll find her. I know you will."

"Will you be okay until I do? I mean, does it bother you that I'm still *legally* married to Pandora?"

I tapped the brush against my chin while I seriously considered Eli's question. "Do you still love her?"

"Of course not."

"Well, I'm fine then."

Chapter Fourteen

Eli and Radiance

"It's been over a month since I hired the new team, and we're no closer to finding Pandora than we were two years ago! Those guys have swept the upper Mediterranean coast from Spain to Turkey, but she's managed to stay two steps ahead of them. The entire situation is driving me nuts!"

"I told you not to marry her," Marlon reminded me with a smirk on his face.

I glared a hole straight through him.

"Shut your mouth, Marlon! He doesn't need you poking fun at him right now." Mama Sadie rubbed my back soothingly in a circular motion. "Stop fussing and eat, Eli. Your food is getting cold." She sat in the vacant chair next to me. "When was the last time you spoke with McKenzie?"

"I called her two days ago. She hasn't spoken to her mother in over a month. Supposedly, she was calling the child from the Dominican Republic during their last conversation. That poor sweet kid . . ."

"You've got to bait her, Eli. You need to come up with something to lure Pandora back to Atlanta."

Marlon smiled and nodded his head. "Mama's right, bruh. Think long and hard. What would cause Pandora to rush back to your side?"

"Money."

"Nah, man, she has plenty of that. It would take her a lifetime to spend all of the millions her daddy and granddaddy left her."

I stared into my wineglass in deep thought. Mama Sadie was on to something. Everyone, including Pandora, had triggers and weaknesses. There had to be something or someone who could bring her back to Atlanta. I didn't know who or what it was, but I sure as hell was going to find out and *soon*.

"Should I pack food for Radiance and Croix, Eli?"

I abandoned my pondering to give Mama Sadie my full attention. "Yes, ma'am. They'll probably be hungry when they return."

"Where are they this evening anyway?"

"Radiance was nice enough to meet Croix's aunt in the park for a brief visit. I wasn't exactly in favor of it, but it's been a while since the little fellow has seen his aunt."

"Family is important to a young child," Marlon pointed out.

"I suppose so, but Croix's family is a little unsavory."

"But they're still his family."

I studied Marlon's face. He was right. One could not choose his or her family. We all had to accept the one God had chosen to give us. "You're right."

"Pump your legs, baby, so you can swing high. Auntie is gonna take a walk so she can smoke a cigarette."

"How am I pumping, Auntie J?"

"You're doing a good job, Croix." She turned toward the bench where Bambi and I sat catching up. "Come walk with me, baby."

"I'll be right back," Bambi told me, rubbing her hands together nervously.

"Cool."

Croix was having so much fun playing in the park. And he did seem happy at first when he saw his aunt, but she couldn't compete with the swings, sliding board, and merry-go-round. After a brief hug and a peck on the cheek, he ran off to play with a group of children. Now he was giggling as he soared high in the air in a swing.

I thought about Eli as I sat watching my baby. I wondered what he was doing. Would he eat dinner without me or would he hold off until I arrived? Either way, I couldn't wait to get home because I missed him terribly. Our relationship was blossoming into something beautiful. We spent lots of time together talking and laughing. I enjoyed our evening walks across the estate with his dogs running free all around us. Croix loved to chase after his four-legged friends.

Eli and I also had quiet times when we'd sit out by the pool and look at the stars after Croix went to sleep. Just being with him caused my entire body to tingle. The chemistry we shared was *flammable*, which was the reason why our lovemaking had yet to slow down. We were still hungry for each other every night. And tonight would be no different. The moment Croix closed his eyes I was going to give Eli all of me. The thought of him working his magic on my body caused me to squirm in my juices on the park bench.

"Damn, girl, you must be thinking about *me*. I knew you missed a nigga."

My head snapped to my left, and my stomach instantly churned. I was literally nauseous. Somehow I managed to swallow the rising bile bubbling in my throat. "Satchel, what the hell are *you* doing here?"

I'm sure the smile he flashed my way was meant to be sexy, but it fell way short. He licked his lips and sat down next to me. I scooted to the other end of the bench. My eyes locked on Croix. I didn't want him to see his father. I hadn't prepared him for introductions because I had no idea we would see him so soon. *Damn you, Janelda!* I felt like screaming.

"I see my boy over there looking just like me. He's got your hair and your complexion, but that li'l nigga looks like his pops."

"Do not use that derogatory racist term to describe *my son!*" I hissed through gritted teeth.

"Oh, my bad. I forgot. You're on that *swirl shit* now."

I rolled my eyes and sucked my teeth at his ignorant ass.

"Yeah, I heard you're dating some white cat. My boy, Theo, said he saw you and my son at the movies with a white dude, looking like a swirly family and shit." He laughed at his humorless joke.

I grabbed my purse and stood up only to be yanked by my arm forcefully to sit again. I pulled away from Satchel's grasp. "If you ever put your hands on me again I will call the police. I swear to God I will! Do you understand me?"

"Forget you, Ray. I didn't come to see your ass anyway. I came to see my son." He stood from the bench and headed for the swings.

I hopped up and ran a foot ahead of him to block his path. "Please don't do this, Satchel," I begged, pulling his arm. "Croix doesn't know you. If you go over there now and tell him you're his father, it'll confuse him. He'll be scarred for life. It'll be too much too soon. Don't you understand? Give me some time to talk to him. A child his age needs to be prepared for major changes like this. Please give me some time."

Even through the heavy flow of tears blurring my vision, I saw a wicked grin spread across Satchel's face. He seemed amused by my emotional plea. At that moment,

I hated him. Hell, I hated myself for ever loving him and having his child. I cursed the day we met. But even in the midst of my loathing, I thought about my son. I loved Croix, and I would do anything to protect him from whomever threatened to harm him—even his *father*. I would kill Satchel in cold blood before I'd allow him to disturb Croix's happiness and peace of mind.

"Okay," he finally said, still grinning like the evil bastard that he was. "I'll give you some time, but make it quick because I only have six weeks in the halfway house. As soon as I get out, I'm gonna get my own spot, start stacking some paper, and then I'm coming for you and my li'l man."

"You can have a relationship with your son. I have no problem with that at all, Satchel. But leave *me* out of it. It's over between us."

"It ain't over until *I* say it's over! We're gonna be a family like we planned back in college, Ray. Croix is *our* son, and we're gonna raise him together. Ain't no other man, especially not some *cracker*, is gonna raise my son. You can cancel that shit."

"You can't force me to be with you. I don't love you anymore, Satchel. I've moved on."

"Well, if I can't have *you*, you can't have *Croix*. I guess I'll have to file for sole custody."

"No judge is going to remove custody from me and give it to you, you *convicted felon*!"

"You're probably right. But I'm gonna file anyway just so I can enjoy watching you go through hell." He laughed like his words were actually funny. Then he got serious all of sudden and penetrated me with a menacing glare. "Have my son here the same time next week. Tell him he's coming to meet his *daddy*." He walked away as quickly as he had appeared out of the blue.

I looked around and caught a glimpse of Janelda and Bambi out of the corner of my eye. They were walking toward the sliding board where Croix was now playing with the other children. I wanted to run over to Janelda and slap that smirk off of her face. She had set me up. Bambi's darting eyes and jittery body language told me that she hadn't been a willing participant in my ambush. I could see her sympathy for me in her eyes. I mentally dismissed both women and ran to the sliding board. I took Croix by the hand and led him out of the park.

~♥~

"I really wish you would eat something, sweetheart. You haven't eaten anything since lunch. Please eat."

Radiance wiped her tears away with my handkerchief. "How can I eat, Eli? My stomach is bubbling like hot boiling grits."

"Damn it! I should've followed my instincts. It was foolish of me to allow you to meet that wicked woman alone. From now on, Sergio will drive you and Croix to any meetings you schedule with your ex or his sister."

"I don't think that's a good idea, Eli. It'll only give Satchel another reason to make good on his threat. I can handle him and Janelda. I just need you to hold my hand when I talk to Croix. I'm so worried about my baby."

"Of course I'll be with you whenever you decide to tell Croix about his father. He means a lot to me, Radiance. His well being is very important. You've done a great job raising him on your own. I don't want his father to enter the scene and destroy the foundation you've built for him. That's why Sergio will accompany the two of you to all visits with Satchel and Janelda in the future. The matter is not up for discussion."

"Is Sergio violent by any chance?"

"Extremely."

Chapter Fifteen

Satchel

"What's good, man?"

I shook it up with Big Mo, my roommate at the halfway house. I sat down on my bed. "I'm grinding and trying to keep myself motivated for these next six weeks. I had a visit with my son yesterday, but his mom was trippin'. She wouldn't even let me talk to him, man. I had to sit on a fuckin' park bench and watch him play like I'm some kinda stranger and shit. My li'l shorty don't even know I'm his pops."

"How come he don't know you, man? Didn't you write to him and call him while you were locked up? Didn't his mom take him to visit you?"

"I tried to keep in touch, but my girl was on some crazy bullshit 'bout a bitch I knocked up. But I don't even fuck with that chick or her baby. Hell, I ain't ever seen the lil' nigga 'cause I don't want him. Me and his mom created a mistake that I refuse to deal with. But *Croix* . . . that's my heart, man. I got my girl, Ray, pregnant with him on purpose. I wanted a baby with her 'cause I loved her. I still do, but her ass is trippin'."

"So what're you gonna do about the situation?"

"There ain't much I can do while I'm in here. I need to make some fast cash and pile it up. And I've gotta get my hands on some heat too."

Big Mo frowned and shook his head. "Man, you need to forget about quick money and guns. That shit is gonna land you back in the pen. You're one of the lucky ones. You got out early, landed one of the better jobs, and you got visitation with your son. Don't fuck it up, dude. Work hard at that dry cleaner and save every dime you can. Above everything else, get to know your *son*."

"Yeah, you're right," I said with my mouth, but my heart was saying the total opposite. I needed some real money in my pocket *now*, and I had major plans that required me to carry heat. My boys, Pete and Nuevo, would help a nigga out. I was gonna call them from work tomorrow and ask them to hook me up. Janelda would do anything I asked too. Ray was damn stupid if she thought she was gonna run the show. I wasn't gonna let her keep me away from my son. And she wasn't about to reject me. I was her *first*. Classy chicks like Ray never forgot their first loves no matter how many men ran through them later on. I didn't have any information on her white sugar daddy, but I would have my boys check the cracker out. Then I would have his ass murked if I had to. Ray, our son, and I were gonna skip Atlanta and head down to Saint Croix to live a good life amongst my family just like we had planned back in college. That's just how it was gonna be.

"I'm about to go and call my sister, man," I told Big Mo. "She's been holding me down. I owe her a lot."

"All right. I'ma go and work out."

I left the room and went to the community area. Luckily, there was a phone available. I picked it up and dialed Janelda's number.

"Hello?"

"Yo, Bambi, let me holla at my sister."

"Hold on."

I pulled out a chair from one of the tables in the room and sat down. I figured that Janelda was relaxing after getting off work an hour or so ago. She had put in a lot of over time when I was on lockdown in order to keep money on my books. I used to get a care package loaded with all of my favorite snacks and shit on the regular too. Plus my big sis had visited a nigga once a month without a miss. Janelda was loyal as fuck to a nigga, so I knew she would help me fix my situation with Ray and our son.

"What's up, li'l bruh?"

I smiled at the sound of her voice. "I'm good. What's going on with you?"

"I'm working like a Hebrew slave, trying to cover these bills. Ray's foul ass left me in a mess. She hauled ass without notice, and a bitch had debts hanging. She owes me at least a grand, but I know I won't see a single penny of it. I only let her stay here because of my nephew. You know I love that kid."

"Yeah, you do love Croix," I mumbled while I processed my sister's words. I didn't wanna call her a liar, but I couldn't believe that Ray had moved out of Janelda's house without settling her bills. That was so unlike my baby. Usually, she was all about business.

"I talked to Mama and Daddy last night. How come you haven't called them, Satch?"

"I'll call them soon. I just hate to hear the disappointment in Pop's voice whenever we talk. He had big dreams for me, and I failed him. Ma understands that I got caught up in some bullshit, but Pops ain't got no mercy for me. I'm gonna make him proud, though, as soon as I get my shit together. Hell, I may even go back to school. But what I know for sure is that I'm gonna get Ray back in my life so we can raise Croix together."

"Forget about Ray. She's moved on, Satch. Concentrate on building a relationship with Croix. And you need to find Felicity so you can meet your other son. Every little boy needs a daddy. Focus on your *children*."

Janelda was right, but I refused to admit it. My mind was made up. I wanted my family back. Yeah, I had screwed up big time by selling drugs and getting caught. But I had risked my freedom to take care of them. The way I saw it, Ray owed me another chance for keeping a roof over our heads and food on the table. Plus she knew that no other female alive could ever take her place in my heart. No matter how many chicks I had been with, Ray was the only one I had ever loved. And somehow I was gonna make her fall in love with me again.

~♥~

"Thanks for the loan, the phone, and the gun, bruh," I said, clapping Nuevo on the shoulder. "You came through for a nigga. "You did too, Pete. I'll move these ounces in two days and break you off your cut. This shit is *strong*."

Pete grinned, flashing his diamond encrusted platinum grill. "That's that *loud*, boy. It don't get more potent than that. Weed heads be feenin' for that shit. Be careful and don't get caught. I ain't trying to see you go back to the tank, man."

"I heard you. Anyway, I gotta get back to work."

I opened the back door of my man, Nuevo's midnight Lincoln Navigator and placed my feet on the sidewalk. I was thinking about Ray and Croix. I couldn't wait to see them again in a few days. I hoped she'd had a little talk with my son so he would know what to expect. I was his *daddy*, and it was time for us to be properly introduced as father and son. Too much time had passed without us having contact. I was ready for my boy to know me.

I entered the building and headed to the back. Janelda had eased me Ray's number, so I was about to hit her up. I removed my new cell phone from my pocket and dialed the number I had committed to memory. Ray was gonna be surprised to hear from me, but she needed to get used to hearing my voice 'cause I was gonna keep in contact with her and our son. I had every right to check on Croix to make sure he was okay.

"Hello?"

I snatched the phone from my ear and stared at the screen. I had dialed the correct number all right, so I wanted to know why the hell a man was on the other end of my phone. I just knew that Ray didn't have that cracker screening her calls and shit. "Who the fuck are you and where is Ray?"

"Who the fuck are *you*?"

"Look, man, I'm Satchel Young, Croix's father. I need to holla at Ray about *our* son."

"Radiance is taking a nap right now. I'll tell her you called as soon as she wakes up."

That arrogant cracker hit me with the click like I was some insignificant nigga without any ties to Ray and Croix. He didn't know who he was dealing with, so I was gonna have to school him.

I was pissed the hell off by the time I got off work. Ray had not returned my call or even sent me a simple text message. I had my pride, so I wasn't about to hit her up again. If she wanted to play games, she had the right nigga 'cause I would move heaven and earth to see my son after three and a half years. If Ray thought that I was gonna disappear, she was a damn fool. Right now it felt like she had me by the nuts 'cause I was on partial lockdown and had limited funds, but that was all about to change. I knew my rights. In the cage, you had a lot of time to research the law and other things. Even as a convicted felon, I still had paternal rights. I had signed

Croix's birth certificate the day he was born, *and* Janelda had hired me an attorney after my sentencing so I could legitimate my li'l homie from prison, and there wasn't a damn thing that Ray or her white man could do to change it.

A clap of thunder boomed, and bright lightning flashed across the sky. I hoped the bus would come before the rain began to fall. I hated my life, but I knew that my current situation was only temporary. *Patience*, I mentally reminded myself. I needed a healthy dose of it.

Chapter Sixteen

Radiance

I woke up to a warm, soft kiss on the back of my neck. I wiggled when it turned from a kiss into a full wet pull of my sensitive flesh between lips and teeth. I tried to turn over onto my back, but I was in a body lock so tight that I couldn't move. A long muscular leg was resting over my entire body, and arms, strong and protective, encircled me. I looked on the nightstand to check the time on my cell phone, but it was missing. I pressed my ass into a certain erect masculine member vibrating against me, and Eli released a deep breath and cupped my breasts, teasing my nipples with his thumbs and middle fingers. We'd spent the day in bed, closing out the rest of the world.

"What time is it? I don't want to be late picking up Croix from school."

"We still have time. It's only one o'clock. Mama Sadie took the day off. Maybe we can go out to dinner."

"Croix and I would love that."

"Good. I think I would like an early dessert," Eli growled in my ear before sliding his hand down my stomach until he reached my wetness. He inserted one long finger between my hairy lips.

My clit got stiff, and liquid love gushed out of my pussy in abundance. I was slightly tender down there from all of our earlier sexual activities, but I could handle a slow and easy lovemaking session if Eli wanted me. "It looks like it's about to rain," I whispered, panting.

"Maybe."

"Where is my phone, Eli? I need to check my messages before we get this party started."

"No one important called . . . just your *ex* demanding to know who I was and where you were."

I sat straight up in bed. "*Satchel* called me? I never game him my—"

"Of course his sister gave him your number. You had to know that she would, babe."

"What did he say?"

"He wants you to return his call so you two can discuss Croix."

I looked down into Eli's face and found his eyes staring back at me. "It's time to tell Croix about his father. The visit is in a few says, so we might as well get the conversation over with."

"I agree. We'll talk to Croix over dinner this evening."

"Fine."

"Are you enjoying the ice cream and fruit, sweetie?"

"Yes, ma'am. It's *good*!"

I looked into Eli's eyes, and he smiled and nodded, encouraging me to start the conversation. He squeezed my hand underneath the table, lending me the strength I needed.

"Croix, remember the picture of the man in the blue jumpsuit sitting on the mantle over Auntie Janelda's fireplace?"

He nodded. "He's my daddy. He's in prison."

"That's right, sweetie. He went to prison, but he's out now, and he wants to visit you."

"Is he coming to our house, Mommy?"

"No," I said, laughing nervously. "We're going to meet him in the park just like we did last week with Janelda and Bambi. Only this time, *Satchel*, your father, will be there too."

"Is my daddy nice?"

I didn't know how to answer that question. Once upon a time, Satchel was a sweet and very caring young man. But he had changed. I didn't know the new Satchel at all. He seemed distant, selfish, and cold when he surprised me in the park. Yet he wanted a relationship with his son, and I couldn't deny him that even if I wanted to.

I exhaled. "Your daddy has missed you, sweetie. He loves you very much, and he's looking forward to getting to know you. But Mommy will be with you at all times."

"And so will your buddy, Sergio," Eli added with a smile that didn't quite reach his eyes.

"I like Sergio. He's big and strong." Croix's smile faded as he eyed Eli. "What about *you*, Eli? Aren't you coming to the park with us? I want you to see me swing high in the sky."

"Um . . . I won't be there. I . . . um . . . um . . . have to work, little buddy. Maybe I'll join you at the park some other time."

"Okay."

Thank God the conversation had gone better than expected.

~♥~

"Ms. Alexander, you seem nervous. There's no need for you to be. I'll never be more than two or three feet away from you and the kid. That's the boss' order. You and Croix are safe with me."

"I know, Sergio."

We had arrived at the park early to give me a little time to get my nerves and emotions in check. I hadn't spoken to Satchel or Janelda, but I'd received a text message from him at midnight, reminding me about the visit. I'd found it very disrespectful of him to contact me so late. Anything he needed to say to me regarding our son should've been done before nightfall. I had to talk Eli off the ledge because he attempted to grab my phone so he could call Satchel back to give him a tongue lashing. I couldn't allow him to do that. There was nothing good about stoking the flames in our very complicated situation. I wanted peace for the sake of Croix by any means.

The fine hairs on my nape bristled suddenly, and a cool stream of air crept up my spine. Satchel had arrived. I could feel his icy presence down in my bones. I turned around quickly and saw him trekking in our direction. I guess he was still handsome and in great shape. His flawless caramel skin and bulging muscles used to light my fire on sight. And his smooth hairless baby face with a crater-deep dimple in each cheek had once been my weakness. Today, I felt nothing but anxiety. I squeezed Croix's tiny hand and raised my chin in Satchel's direction. "Here comes your daddy, sweetie. He's the man in the jeans and purple t-shirt."

Sergio moved his massive frame closer to us in full protective, bodyguard mode. He kept his eyes on Satchel even as they were hidden behind the dark round lenses of his sunglasses. He was a big man, standing at least four inches over six feet with a muscular body built like a trained assassin. Eli had said he was one of the most dangerous men he knew. I hoped he wouldn't ever have to prove it in front of me or Croix.

Satchel looked Sergio up and down a few times as he narrowed the gap between us. I swallowed the marble size lump in my throat when Croix tugged on my hand gently to get my attention. He smiled at me, and it made my heart pause. His innocence was pure, and he was so unassuming.

"What's up, Ray?" Satchel spoke to me, but his eyes were fixated on his son.

"Croix, this is your daddy, Satchel Young. Satchel, this is your son, Croix Bryson Young."

"Hi," my baby whispered bashfully and dropped his head.

"What's up, li'l man? Come and give your daddy a hug."

Before I could say anything, Satchel scooped Croix up into his arms and squeezed his tiny body in a bear hug. His eyes closed when Croix squeezed him back. When he opened his eyes, he frowned when he saw Sergio standing to my left, staring straight through him.

"Who is *he*, Ray?"

"His name is Sergio, and he's a friend of ours."

Satchel laughed. "Damn, so it's like *that*? You couldn't bring our son here today to visit his daddy without your boo thang taggin' along? I thought we were better than that, baby. We got solid history, girl."

"Sergio is not my man. Like I said, he's a friend."

"*Eli* is Mommy's man."

Satchel looked at our son. "Is that so? Do you like this Eli cat?"

Croix smiled and nodded his head energetically.

"Well, Daddy is gonna have to meet Eli so I can make sure he's treating you and your mama all right. Let's go and swing now. Show your pops what kinda speed you've got."

Satchel headed toward the swing with Croix in tow. I was like his shadow, glued to his heels. And Sergio was in step just a foot or two behind us.

"That ape is too damn big to catch me if I take off running with Croix, Ray. You could've left his big ass at the zoo."

"I'm faster than I look, you little big-mouth punk. But if you run and I can't catch you, I'll just shoot you. I'm an expert marksman. I never miss my target."

~♥~

"So how did the visit go?" Eli sat on the bed and leaned over to peck my cheek.

I closed my book and notebook and placed them on the nightstand. "It went well. Croix didn't have much to say to his father, but they played a lot."

"And what did Mr. Young have to say to *you*?"

"We made a verbal agreement. He'll visit Croix at the same time and place every week. We discussed ideas for his birthday party next month, and then he gave me a wad of cash, which he promised to do every other week."

"You don't need his money, Radiance. I provide generously for you and Croix."

"You do, Eli, but Satchel has a financial obligation to his son. I have taken care of Croix alone for most of his short life. It's time for his father to step up now."

"I don't like it, but I suppose you have a point."

"He gave me five hundred dollars. I can't imagine where he got that kind of money from since he works at a dry cleaner. I wouldn't be surprised if he's doing something illegal again."

"He may be, but that's not your concern." Eli removed his dress shirt and wife beater and tossed them on the loveseat. "On another note, Pandora has been spotted in Greece. One of the investigators flew out this afternoon to hunt for her. If he finds her, he'll serve her the divorce papers right away. Regardless if she signs them or not or fails to appear in court, according to the prenup, I will be declared free from the marriage within sixty days."

"And then what?" I couldn't help but ask. My heart needed to know if there was a permanent place in his life for me.

"I'll let you decide. I'd like for you and Croix to stay here forever, but your plan is to leave me after you finish school."

Forever was a long time. I did want a life with Eli, but not as his permanent house guest. My heart yearned for more. I loved him. I could no longer deny it. I wanted him to find Pandora and divorce her so that we could have a future together, but I was afraid to reveal my feelings to him out of fear that he didn't feel the same way.

"I'll stay here with you for as long as you want me to."

"Good. Then it's settled." He removed the remainder of his clothes, giving me a delectable eye treat. "I'm going to shower. Don't fall asleep. I have plans for you, babe."

Chapter Seventeen

Eli and Radiance

"How is the party going?"

"It's going all right, I reckon, boss. Croix is all over the place. He's having a blast. You really outdid yourself with the animals, the train, and the Ferris wheel. His friends are enjoying the cotton candy and pop corn stand too. Croix is like a rockstar to them."

"He's a great kid. He deserves the best. Keep a close eye on him because I don't trust his father or his aunt."

"I've got it all under control, boss. Everything is as smooth as butter. Mama Sadie and Ms. Alexander's mother are getting along like old friends. And the kids from Croix's class are really into the clown and the music. Satchel and his sister are on their best behavior too."

"And how is *Radiance* doing?"

"She's fine. Marlon and Golden are helping her serve the kids. She looks happy, but I think she misses you, boss."

I sat down behind my desk at my office in my casino in Atlantic City. I missed Radiance like crazy. It had been three days since I'd left for my business trip, and I was close to losing my damn mind. I was actually having withdrawal symptoms from sleeping alone and the lack of good loving. And I hated the fact that I was missing Croix's sixth birthday celebration. I had spared no expenses whatsoever in making sure he had everything he wanted and then some. Now if only I could have exactly what *I* wanted: *Radiance*. She had promised me that she would stick around Diamond Estate beyond her graduation. I was happy about her decision, but it wasn't enough. My feelings for Radiance had evolved. I loved the woman, and I wanted her in my life *permanently*. But I didn't want to tell her that just yet. I needed my marriage to Pandora dissolved first.

I had grown frustrated with the situation. My men were zigzagging around the globe trying to find her, following every lead they stumbled upon. But Pandora was a ghost, fading in and out like the wind. It angered me just thinking about the hide-and-go-seek game she was playing with my life. I prayed every day that Radiance would continue to be patient with me. My greatest fear was that she would wake up one morning and tell me that she couldn't wait for me any longer. I needed to do something to assure her that I was doing everything within my power and resources to find Pandora. I wanted her to know that she and Croix would be in my life forever.

I smiled when the light bulb turned on inside my head. I knew exactly what I should do.

~♥~

"Um, Sergio, what's going on here? What're you and these men doing with my things?" I asked, walking into my bedroom. Boxes filled with my clothes and shoes were everywhere.

"I'm just following boss' orders, ma'am."

"What did Eli tell you to do? Am I being evicted?"

"No, ma'am. You're *moving*."

"*Moving*? Where the hell am I moving to?"

"You and Croix are moving into the main house."

I didn't know what to say. I would've been excited if I wasn't so damn pissed off. Eli had given Sergio and a crew orders to move Croix and me while he was out of town without telling me. He had big nerve. We'd spoken this morning, but he never mentioned his plans to me. I removed my cell phone from my purse, prepared to call him on his private line and give him the business.

"Ms. Alexander, here you go, ma'am."

I stared at the phone in Sergio's hand a few seconds before I took it. "Hello?"

"I take it that you like my surprise, babe."

"Actually, I don't," I snapped.

"What's wrong?"

"You should've told me about your plans, Eli. Don't I have a say in this?"

"I thought you'd be happy to move in with me. Croix will have more space to roam about and a much bigger room and bed. And I won't have to wander back and forth between the two houses. It'll be easier for us to spend time together now that we'll be under one roof."

"I understand that it'll be much more convenient for us, but I wish you had talked to me about it first, Eli. That's all."

"I'm talking to you *now*, sweetheart. We couldn't live in separate houses forever. Now stop pouting. I'm on my way to the airstrip right now to board the jet. I'll be home tonight, and I expect Croix to be in his new bedroom and you in my bed. Have I made myself clear?"

"Yes, you have. I'll see you tonight."

~♥~

The flowery scent of her skin greeted me the moment I entered the master suit. I was excited as I approached

the king plus four-post bed. The outline of her volup-
tuous body was distinct underneath the covers. My cock
jumped to full mass. I wanted her, and the few days I'd
been deprived of her gave me the right to take her even if
I had to wake her from a peaceful sleep.

I stripped quickly, losing a few buttons on my dress
shirt in my rush. Radiance stirred in her sleep when I
lifted the covers and joined her in bed. I pulled her body
on top of mine and palmed her ass with both hands,
squeezing it until she moaned.

"Eli, you're home."

"Yeah, babe, I'm home. I like the sound of that. I rushed
to *our home* because I missed you so damn much." I
captured her lips in a long, slow kiss filled with more
passion than I'd ever felt. "Did you miss me?"

"I did."

"Show me," I whispered against her parted lips before I
eased my tongue inside her mouth.

I rotated and grinded my dick against her crotch, dying
to have my way with her, but I wanted to pace myself
and relish every second of our reunion. Within seconds,
I flipped her over onto her back. I wanted to eat her into
surrender and bury my cock so deep inside of her that
our bodies would conjoin like Siamese twins from the
inside out. I removed Radiance's silk blue chemise and
matching boy shorts. Her unique feminine scent intoxicated me with a single whiff. I loved the way she smelled.

I sucked one hardened chocolate nipple and then the
other one alternately. Each twirl of my tongue around
the erect peaks caused Radiance to moan and squirm. I
snaked down her body and spread her legs as far apart as
I could before I dived inside her pussy with my tongue. It
was hot, wet, and welcoming. My face was saturated with

her honey as I licked, sucked, and hummed my appreciation for the sweet treat I had craved over the past few days. And as if we had developed a secret sex language of our own, Radiance purred and sang my name in a soulful melody as I slurped down her juices with unashamed greed. When I stroked the tip of her clit slowly and grazed it with the edges of my teeth, her back arched several inches off the bed, and she began to convulse fiercely through an orgasmic tidal wave that ripped through her body. It was so strong that I could feel it. Precum seeped from the head of my hard penis as I enjoyed the way I had pleased Radiance. Making her feel good gave me more pleasure than I could measure.

As her jerks and squirms subsided and her breathing returned to normal, I positioned my body between her thighs and entered her with one smooth motion. Our bodies fit just right together; like we had been designed solely for one another. When I hit her G-spot and rolled my hips to tap it again, another flood of her love juice flowed. The feel of her warm wetness saturating my cock caused my heart to skip a few beats. She squeezed her inner muscles tightly around my dick, and I swear I saw shooting stars.

"I'm about to annihilate this sweet pussy! It's *mine*, damn it! It's the best pussy in the world."

"Oooh, Eli," Radiance shrieked, pressing the sharp edges of fingernails into the flesh on my back, piercing it. "Uh . . . uh . . . I'm about to cum, baby!"

"Cum on this dick, babe! It's *yours*! Cum on it, damn it!"

"*Eli, I love yooou!*"

My release took me by surprise because I'd been trying to hold it back. But the moment I heard those four words and felt Radiance buck and jerk underneath me at the same time, the dam broke. Semen, heavy and fast-flowing like a fire hydrant, rushed from my body, depleting me of millions of babies. I was drained and limp, but I was satisfied beyond my wildest fantasy.

~♥~

Eli was already seated at the breakfast table when I entered the kitchen. I had just returned from taking Croix to school.

"Good morning," I whispered shyly. Oddly, bashfulness had overtaken me.

Eli shot me the sexiest smile ever after lowering the newspaper from his face to sneak a peek at me. "Good morning, babe. How did you sleep?"

"Like a dead woman."

Out of all of the many times that Eli and I had made love, the night before had been our most passionate episode to date. The mutual hunger we'd had for each other after being separated for a few days had been our undoing. It got wild and almost dangerous up in the master suite. We christened it totally on my first night as its new occupant. At one point during the night, I thought Eli was going to break me in half. Fortunately, I had survived the pleasurable pain and could write a book about it.

"Would you like me to serve you breakfast? I don't mind."

"No, thank you. Although the food smells good, I'm going to grab some fruit, a slice of toast, and some juice before I leave. I'm not all that hungry for anything heavy."

"I see. Let's talk about it."

I looked away because I was somewhat embarrassed for allowing my feelings get the best of me last night. I had told Eli that I loved him. I was kind of humiliated and

hurt that he didn't voice his feelings for me. I was glad
that we were now sharing his bed. I sincerely appreciated
the gesture, but I wanted to know how he felt about me.
His actions said he loved me, but I needed him to look
me in my eyes and tell me. "Let's talk about *what*, Eli?" I
asked after some time of dealing with my emotions.

"Did I do something wrong last night, Radiance?"

*If you don't realize that I opened my heart to you
while we were making love, but got nothing in return
from you, I refuse to point it out,* I so desperately wanted
to say, but my words wouldn't flow. So instead I told him,
"You were amazing last night."

Chapter Eighteen

Radiance and Satchel

I hurried inside the down home soul food restaurant and spotted Satchel in a booth near the back right away. He had sent me a text message while I was in the library earlier, asking if we could meet somewhere and talk. Against my better judgment, I had agreed to have lunch with him at the Busy Bee. I was still in my feelings about Eli and what had happened between us last night, so I needed something to take my mind off of the situation. I slid onto the bench inside the booth across from Satchel.

"What's so important that we couldn't discuss it over the phone?"

"I'll be moving into my own place next week, Ray. I think it's time for us to step up the visitation with my son."

"What are you talking about, Satchel? You see Croix for two hours every week. He said you took McDonald's to his school Monday and ate lunch with him. That was nice of you, by the way. I think you two are bonding well."

"Yeah, we are, but I have a lot of time to make up with him. I was hoping that you'd let me scoop him up from school next Friday so we can hang out at my spot for a few hours. Soon, I'll want overnight visits, and then eventually, weekends."

I held up both hands. "Pump your breaks, player. I think you're moving too fast. It's only been eight weeks, Satchel. What's the rush?"

"I ain't rushing, girl. I just wanna get to know my son. I can't build a solid relationship with him by only spending two hours a week with him in the park with you and that ape watching me."

"Okay. When are you moving out of Janelda's house and where will you be living?"

"I told you I'm moving out next week." He smiled and rubbed his hands together. "I locked down a townhouse in the Camp Creek area. It's *fat*, baby."

"How can you afford a townhouse, a brand new Navigator, and a thousand dollars a month in child support working at the dry cleaner, Satchel? Are you slinging again? Because if you are, I won't allow our son to visit you unsupervised in your home. I'd be a fool if I did."

"Ain't nobody slangin' shit! Janelda kept a stash for me while I was in the pen. She invested about twenty-five grand for me, and it turned over a few times. Life is good, baby girl, and we could be sharing it together. You, Croix, and I could be a family again if you would stop being so damn mean. I love you, Ray. I always have and I always will." He reached across the table and stroked my cheek with the back of his hand.

I flinched, and every muscle in my body contracted with tension. I quickly swatted his hand away. "That ball has bounced."

"So you mean to tell me that *Eli*, your white mystery man, is putting it down like that? I know he's sponsoring you 'cause Croix said y'all live in a castle and have a bunch of whips and shit. And you come to the park with your beefy-ass bodyguard every week. That white dude may be rollin' you in dough, but does he *love* you? I don't see no bling on your finger," he taunted me, smirking.

"My relationship is none of your business. By the way, how is *Felicity*? And how many times have you visited *her* son? He should be around three now, right?"

"There you go throwin' up old mistakes again. I ain't tryin' to hear shit about that girl and her baby. She knew the deal from the rip. That situation has nothing to do with this one. I just want regular and longer visits with Croix at my spot. I'm asking nicely, Ray, but I ain't afraid to fight you."

"Don't threaten me because you can't win. I'll think about the visits. I knew this was coming. I just wish that you wouldn't rush it."

"Yeah, you think about it long and hard 'cause I want to be a major part of my son's life.

My dick bricked up on me when I watched Ray's fine ass sashay out of the restaurant. That white dude must've been blowing her back out and spreading those hips on the regular. The thought of another man touching her intimately caused jealousy to bubble up inside my gut. In my heart, Ray still belonged to me. I remember all those nights we used to do that hard-core, ghetto-style fucking until the sun came up. We were young, energetic, and crazy in love back then. I missed that body. My girl had a nigga feenin' for her like a junkie itchin' for a rock.

I was gonna give Ray some time to consider my visitation request. But if she decided to deny me more time with my son, I would have to take matters into my own hands. Fuck the court! I didn't trust attorneys and judges too much. In their eyes, I was just another black convicted felon out on parole. They wouldn't see my heart filled with love for my son and his mother. I had mad love for my family, and I wanted us to hook back up again.

I threw a couple of bills on the table to cover my meal and Ray's glass of sweet tea. I thought about how nice it would be to take her and Croix for a surprise trip to the

Virgin Islands to visit my parents and other relatives. My mom and pops had only seen my son twice in his life. The first time was when he was a small baby. They saw him again as a toddler when they came for my trial. My folks were long overdue to see their only grandchild again. But a nigga had to put in the work to make it happen. I needed to win Ray's trust first. Without that, everything else was just an impossible dream.

~♥~

Three weeks had passed, and I had yet to give Satchel an answer about extended visitation with Croix. I had to admit that he had been on his A game. He had shown up on time each week with gifts and clothes for my baby. And he paid child support consistently. He and Sergio were even cordial to each other during visits, discussing sports and cars from time to time. I wanted to allow Croix to spend two or three hours with his father unsupervised, but Eli was against it. He didn't trust Satchel even a little bit, and he'd forbidden me to take Croix anywhere near his father without Sergio being there. I was so confused, so I called my mama for advice.

"I agree with Eli, baby. Satchel cannot be trusted, I tell you."

"But he's Croix's father, and he's been great. You should see the two of them together. They love each other to death, and they enjoy their visits. And Satchel is on parole, Ma. It's not like he's stupid enough to run with Croix and hop on a plane somewhere."

"I don't trust him any further than I can throw him. Give it a little more time, and get legal advice if you have to. Just wait until the Lord gives you a sign, baby."

"Okay, I'll wait, but Satchel is getting impatient. He calls every other day to ask me the same question. I can't keep putting him off. What if he hires an attorney and drags me into court?"

"Then you'll get a chance to tell the judge your suspicions about him selling dope again."

"I'll wait until I have no other choice."

"Good for you, darling."

~♥~

"Okay, Ray, what's really going on, girl? Why are you clockin' the time I spend with my son. It's summertime. Croix's out of school now. He should be spending the night with his daddy and going to the movies and the arcades with me. We're working on almost two months now. What's the *real* deal, though?"

"I've increased your visits to twice a week."

"Yeah, but I'm tired of going to the park. It's hot as hell outside. And whenever it rains, we have to reschedule. I want my son to visit me at my crib so we can lie around, watching TV, and playing video games like normal fathers and sons. I know he does that with Eli and that big ape 'cause he told me. I want Croix at my spot tomorrow evening from six to eight."

I ran my fingers through my hair nervously. Time was up. Satchel had turned up the heat on me. I couldn't put off the visit any longer. If he got an attorney involved, he could be awarded joint custody because he was Croix's legal and biological father by every measure of the law. I couldn't risk that.

"All right. Give me your address, and I'll bring him over, but I'm not going to leave him, Satchel. I'm staying. I have to."

"Cool. I don't mind entertaining you. It'll be just like old times when we were a family."

"Don't do that," I said, shaking my head. "It's all about *Croix*. I'm just going to tag along so he'll be comfortable. Don't get it twisted, okay?"

"I hear you, but a nigga can hope."

~♥~

"Now remember that no one can know that we're visiting your daddy at his house, especially not *Eli*. Do you understand, sweetie?"

"Yes, Mommy. It's our secret."

"That's right, baby."

I pulled Croix along by his hand until we reached the front door. I rang the doorbell and bit down on my bottom lip while I waited for Satchel to answer. I didn't feel comfortable at all, but a girl had to do what she had to do. The door opened slowly.

"Hey, li'l man! Welcome to your daddy's house. Come on in." He picked up Croix and stared at me with lust in his eyes. "What's up, Ray? You're looking good, girl."

"Thank you," I said, following him inside. I took a seat on a brown leather sofa and watched Satchel lead Croix from room to room, showing him his townhouse.

It was much larger on the inside than it'd appeared from the exterior. Satchel had done a boss job decorating with a masculine color scheme of brown, rust, and beige. If I didn't know any better, I would've sworn that some chick had helped him select the African artwork and the huge decorative mirrors.

"Let's go upstairs," I heard Satchel say to Croix. "I want you to see the room you'll be sleeping in one day. Do you like the Avengers?"

"Yeah! Iron Man is my favorite."

"Well, you're going to love your room then."

I followed them upstairs and was pleasantly surprised by the furniture and décor in both bedrooms. True to his father's word, Croix's room was decked out in all things Avengers from the comforters on the bunk beds to the rug on the hardwood floor. The master bedroom was black and gray as was the adjoining bathroom. I didn't want to linger in Satchel's sleeping quarters, but a framed picture of me on the dresser caught my eye. I shivered involuntarily at the eerie feeling the picture gave me. *I'm not his woman anymore, so why is that picture there?*

"You're welcome here anytime, baby," Satchel whispered in my ear.

I zapped from my thoughts when his warm breath fanned over my skin. "No, thank you. I'm far from homeless."

The rest of the evening went by smoothly. Satchel had ordered a bunch of Chinese food, and he and Croix pigged out. I wasn't hungry at the time. And I preferred to eat dinner with Eli anyway. Father and son played video games and wrestled in the middle of the floor while I responded to Eli's text messages. He wanted to know where we were and when we were coming home. I lied and told him we were out window shopping. I felt horrible about lying to him, but there was no way he could ever find out that we were visiting Satchel in his home. He would pitch ten fits. I couldn't handle that.

"Thanks for bringing him, Ray," Satchel said when he walked us to the car after the visit. "It meant a lot to me."

"You're welcome, but I'm not comfortable sneaking around like this. Eli wouldn't approve of us being here."

"You didn't have to come, Ray. I'm Croix's father. I would never do anything to hurt him. It's okay to leave him here with me for two hours."

"I'm not ready for that just yet."

"You're gonna have to trust me one day."

"I will, but not right now. Good night."

Chapter Nineteen

Eli

"I won't be home for dinner, Mama Sadie. I have a late meeting this evening. It'll be catered by an Italian restaurant for our convenience. Radiance and Croix will be dining alone. I'm sure Sergio will eat more than his share before he leaves for the evening."

She let out a throaty laugh. "You *know* he will." She squeezed my shoulder with the soft hand that used to bathe me, spank my butt, and wipe away my tears when I was a child. "I'll make sure that Radiance and Croix have a delicious supper. You know she's in love with you, don't you?"

"Of course I do."

"I suspect you feel the same way about her."

I nodded my affirmation and crossed my arms over my chest. I felt a lecture coming on, so I mentally prepared myself. "Go ahead, Mama Sadie. Tell me what's on your mind. The words are on the tip of your tongue."

"Those investigators better find that wife of yours *quick*. Do you hear me?"

"Yes, ma'am, I hear you. But they've been trying their best. It just seems that Pandora out slicks them every damn time they get close to her."

"Then I suggest you give them a helping hand."

"What more can I do, Mama Sadie? I have done—"

"Bait her."

"*What*?" I asked with furrowed brows, totally confused.

"Bait that heifer, Eli! If Pandora knew you had moved on and given your heart to another woman, she would catch the first thing smoking back to Atlanta just to try to win you back. She's got folks watching you, son. That woman knows she's still your wife, and that's why you haven't gone public in *Atlanta's high society* with a new female companion. Pandora is satisfied with that, but you're stuck in her trap. And if you don't free yourself soon, Radiance and Croix are going to leave you."

Mama Sadie had a point. Radiance and I were together on one hand, but we really weren't together on the other. As much as I enjoyed my privacy, it was destroying my life. I loved Radiance, so why had I kept her a secret all these months? She was no longer one of my students, and we were two consenting adults who were living together at my request. I had been a damn fool without even realizing it. Somehow, I'd slipped and allowed Pandora to manipulate me by the balls from afar for two years. But her little game was about to end now.

"Tell me what to do, oh wise queen."

"Call McKenzie and put a bug in her ear about Radiance. Tell her that you're in love and couldn't be happier. The next time McKenzie speaks with her mother, she'll tell her that you've put her in the wind."

"Then what?"

"Pandora will rush back here and try to be a wife to you again. She still wants you, and she always will, baby. She just wants you on *her terms*, which means she'll do anything except have your child. You two were fine until you started fussing about having a baby. She left you soon after that, but she took your name with her. Call McKenzie so she can help get Pandora back here."

"I don't know if that'll work," I mumbled, scratching my chin in deep thought. "Pandora is smart. She knows that once she returns, I'll have her served with the divorce papers immediately. There's nothing she can do after that. The divorce will be finalized in sixty days with or without her consent."

"That may be true, son, but it won't stop her from trying to rekindle the old flames between the two of you before the judge bangs the gavel. Of course, that'll never happen, but Pandora doesn't know that. For sixty days, she will hunt you like a hound dog sniffing behind a rabbit. She's going to try every trick in the book to get you under the sheets. But what you and Radiance have is strong, and Pandora can't destroy it."

"So I'll use McKenzie to get Pandora here by telling her about Radiance?"

"Unh-huh. Then slap those papers on her the moment she arrives. But don't allow her to get close to you after that, Eli. In fact, keep her far, far away from you."

~♥~

"This is Eli Jamieson."

"Good afternoon, my dear stepfather. How are you?"

I froze in midstride in the center of the corridor. It was *McKenzie* on the line. Thank God that she'd finally returned my call after three days. "I'm well, sweetheart. How are you? Are you making good grades in school?"

"School is great, and I'm getting along fine. I was surprised that you called the other day so soon after our last conversation. It's not my birthday."

Her last remark landed like a sucker punch to my belly. "I'm sorry that I don't call you more often, McKenzie, but your mother has insisted that I limit my contact with you since we separated. And legally, I don't have the right to push against her where you're concerned."

"I understand."

"Speaking of Pandora, how is she these days?"

McKenzie chuckled. "It's funny that you should ask. Mother called me two weeks ago and promised to come for a visit this coming weekend. I don't believe her, though. Do you know how many times she's promised to come and spend time with me but failed to show up?"

"Unfortunately, I imagine you've heard that empty promise more times than you can count. I'm sorry, darling. Maybe Pandora will surprise you this time."

"I doubt it, but I'll be right here waiting just in case she does."

"Please say hello to her for me. I hope she's well."

"I will." McKenzie fell silent for several seconds before she added, "I'll also ask her to return to the States to give you a divorce. It's so unfair of her to make you put your life on hold."

Bingo! That's the opening I needed! I screamed inside my head as I hurried to my office and closed the door. "My life isn't on hold at all, McKenzie. I've met someone, and we're very happy. As a matter of fact, we've been living together for a few months now."

"Really? That's wonderful, Eli. I'm so excited for you. But . . . but . . . does this woman know that you're still legally married to my mother?"

"Yes, she does, but she's not concerned about that. Radiance loves me, and she's willing to wait patiently for me until Pandora returns to Atlanta, so we can dissolve our disastrous marriage once and for all."

"I'm sure she's a sweet lady, but it may be a long time before you'll be able to marry her. My mother is as stubborn as a bull at times. She can be very cunning too. She still thinks of herself as Mrs. T. Eli Jamieson all while jet setting around the world care free."

"Radiance and I are in love, so we don't care about Pandora's schemes or our bogus marriage. As long as we're together, we'll be happy." I looked at my watch. "I have to go now, McKenzie. I'm expecting my broker any minute. I promise to call you again soon."

"Okay. It was nice talking to you, Eli. Take care."

"You do the same, sweetheart."

~♥~

I was tempted to call McKenzie to find out if Pandora had arrived for her weekend visit or not. But I figured that if I were to do that, the real reason for calling my stepdaughter earlier that week would be exposed. So I pushed that thought out of my head and concentrated on the beautiful woman who had captured my heart as she stood cooking at the stove.

I had decided not to tell anyone except Mama Sadie that I had spoken to McKenzie. I didn't want to get Radiance's hopes up only to have them crushed if Pandora failed to visit her daughter. Mama Sadie was used to the disappointment my ex-wife often caused. But she always prayed and relied on her faith whenever we got a lead on Pandora's whereabouts. I had considered sending one of my investigators to Switzerland just in case my ex did make an appearance, but it didn't seem like a smart move. More than likely, she wouldn't show up, but Mama Sadie believed if Pandora did visit McKenzie that she would learn about Radiance just like we had planned. We just needed to wait because only time would tell.

"Dinner will be ready in a few minutes. Can you get Croix from the great room for me please?"

I smiled at Radiance, realizing just how lucky I was to have her in my life. I couldn't wait to make her my wife. "Sure, I'll get him."

I walked down the hall and entered the great room. Croix was deeply engrossed in a race car game on his

Xbox One. He didn't even notice me walk in. I watched him for a few moments, grateful that I'd been blessed with such a precious gift. No, I wasn't his biological father, but I couldn't have been fonder of him. I would be honored to call him my stepson someday. And I would give him a sibling or two when the time was right.

~♥~

"Where are you, babe?"

"I'm on my way to pick up Croix from summer camp."

"Isn't it kind of early?"

"Um . . . well . . . I'm going to take him to visit my mama for a little while if that's okay with you."

"Of course it is. What time will you two be home?"

"Expect us around six o'clock. We'll be there just in time for dinner."

"Good. I'll see you then. Don't be late."

"We won't, Eli."

I hung up the phone and stared at the calendar on my desk. It had been exactly one week since I'd spoken to McKenzie, and I hadn't heard a peep from Pandora. Maybe she'd been a no show in Switzerland as usual. It was a shame that she lacked the decency to keep a promise to her only child. She was a cold piece of work, and the sooner I got her out of my life, the better. I reached for my phone to call Jake, my lead investigator.

Chapter Twenty

Satchel and Radiance

"Did you hear me, Satch?"

"Yeah, I heard you! Pops got prostate cancer! Fuck!" I threw the video game remote control across the room and watched it break apart when it crashed against the wall.

"There's a five o'clock flight to Miami this evening. I'm going to hop on it and spend the night with Auntie Lois. She and I'll catch a direct flight at eleven-fifteen in the morning to Saint Croix. Daddy wants his baby sister by his side for the surgery."

"What about *me*, Janelda? Hell, I wanna be there too! He's my damn daddy!"

"You can't leave town, fool! You're on parole. I'll call you every day with an update. I swear I will. Just pray for Daddy. That's all you can do."

"I'll do that, but it won't be the same as me being there. I should be in St. Croix taking care of Pops and comforting Ma."

"But you *can't*, so get over it. Anyway, don't you have a visit with Croix in a little while?"

"Yeah. Ray just sent me a text message 'cause she's running a few minutes late. She *claims* she's not feeling well, so she had to stop by the store to get some medicine for her stomach. She better not stand me up. I ain't got time for her bullshit today of all days."

"Has she canceled a visit since y'all started this new arrangement?"

"Nope."

"Her vanilla king must be on board now."

"Nah. His punk ass thinks I visit Croix at summer camp twice a week. That's the lie Ray came up with, and he believes her. If only he knew . . ."

Janelda laughed. "Yo, I've got to run, li'l bruh. Kiss my nephew for me and tell him Auntie J loves him to the stars and back."

"Will do. Be safe, sis."

~♥~

"Are you okay, Mommy?"

"I'm fine, baby. I just have an upset stomach. That's why we stopped at the drug store to buy the icky pink stuff I just drank. I should feel fine in a minute."

"Maybe you should call Eli and tell him you're sick."

"I can't, sweetie. I have to take you to visit your daddy. Remember we can't tell Eli about that."

"We can't because it's our secret."

My stomach rumbled and rolled as I pulled into the visitor's parking space in front of Satchel's townhouse. I took a few deep breaths and exhaled them slowly before I exited the car with my purse on my shoulder. A wave of nausea hit me the moment my feet touched the ground. I felt dizzy, so I leaned against the driver's side door and willed the earth to be still. I gave Croix a weak smile when I felt his little hand take hold of mine.

"Come on, Mommy. Daddy and I will take care of you."

We walked hand in hand to the door. Croix rang the bell. My tummy growled and tumbled violently again. I couldn't hold the contents down any longer. As soon as Satchel opened the door, I pushed past him and sprinted as fast as I could to his bathroom. My purse fell to the floor on the way.

"Ray, what's wrong with you, girl? Did you eat some bad food or something?"

I couldn't answer Satchel. I was too busy emptying my belly into his commode and trying to balance myself on wobbly legs. Croix came in, wrapped his arms around my right leg, and rested his face on my hip.

"Mommy's okay, baby. I just have a sour stomach. Run and tell your daddy I need a glass of water."

"Yes, ma'am." He took off running.

I turned on the cold water on the tap and cupped my hands underneath the stream. When my palms were filled to capacity, I lowered my face into the water. I looked into the mirror afterwards and grew concerned about my frail appearance. My face was fully flushed, and a gloss had filled my eyes. *What the hell is wrong with me?* I wondered.

I grabbed a handful of tissue to dry my face before I left the bathroom. I was light-headed, and my stomach was still rolling like ocean waves.

"Damn, girl, you scared me," Satchel said, handing me the red plastic cup filled with ice cubes and water. "Are you all right?"

"I've had an upset stomach since yesterday. I don't know what it could be because I haven't been eating much lately."

"Sit down and relax while Croix and I play video games."

I nodded because I couldn't speak over the bile bubbling in my throat. I took a sip of water, and it went back down seconds before the room started spinning. The cup of water slipped from my hand, and the cold liquid splattered all over my feet. I felt myself going down, but Satchel caught me right as the room turned as hot as fire and was swallowed by blackness.

I knew exactly what was going on with Ray's health the moment she collapsed in my arms. I had been through this with her before, and we'd both survived. I placed her on the sofa and covered her with a light blanket. I knew from experience that all she needed was a long nap and lots of TLC. My heart ached knowing that she would now have the same kind of lifelong connection with Eli that she shared with me. I figured that our chances of ever reuniting were now slim to none. Actually, I knew it the first day we met in the park, but I was hoping I could win her back from Eli somehow. It definitely wasn't gonna happen now. As it stood, my ultimate goal was to build a strong and lasting bond with our son. I wasn't about to cry over losing Ray 'cause it was my fault that she'd called it quits between us in the first place.

It took a while for me to convince Croix that his mommy was gonna be all right after she fainted. My son had heart, though. He didn't even cry when he saw Ray pass out although I could tell that he wanted to. But he manned up and trusted his daddy. I assured him that when she woke up, she would feel much better and that I would make sure they got home safely. His smile let me know that he believed me, but it kinda got under my skin that he kept asking me to call Eli, though. However, he was just a kid, so I sucked it up.

Thankfully, he forgot all about his mommy's white lover once the delivery guy brought the subs and salads. We dug into the food and watched half of a Disney movie

before an idea suddenly popped inside my head. I tried
to fight the temptation, but I couldn't. I knew what I was
about to do was dead wrong, but I couldn't stop myself. I
found a pen and a piece of paper and scribbled a note to
Ray on it. I placed it near her purse on the coffee table so
she couldn't miss it. I ran upstairs and grabbed my wallet
and two thick stacks of bills from the mini safe hidden
inside a secret compartment in the wall of my walk-in
closet.

"Let's roll out, li'l man," I told my son when I returned
to the living room.

"We can't go anywhere. Mommy's sleeping."

"We'll be back before she wakes up. I promise," I flat
out lied. "I'm gonna take you to get an ice cream cone."

"Cool!"

We left my spot and drove straight to the Dairy Queen.
As promised, I bought Croix a scoop of vanilla ice cream
on a waffle cone. Then we headed to Janelda's house so
I could holla at Bambi. We arrived twenty minutes later,
and fortunately, Croix had fallen asleep on the drive. So
I left him in my SUV while I went to talk to Bambi on the
front porch. She answered the door after a few knocks

"Yo, I need to swap vehicles with you."

"How come?"

"You don't need to know why." I reached inside my
pocket and pulled out a few bills. "Take this as a rental
fee. I need your car."

"You won't be driving my car anywhere until you tell
me what's going on."

"I'm about to run down to Miami to catch up with
Janelda so I can fly to Saint Croix with her and our auntie
in the morning. I gotta check up on my pops. I need your
whip 'cause my Navigator is considered a drug dealer's
ride in certain parts of Florida. A parolee ain't tryin' to
get stopped by the badges. You understand, girl."

Bambi nodded her head. "Let me get my key." She returned in less than thirty seconds with a single key in her hand. "You're gonna have to put some gas in it."

"I will. Don't worry." I reached out and hugged her chubby ass after we exchanged keys. "I'll see you in a week. Thank you, Bambi."

"It ain't no problem."

I turned to leave but quickly did an about face. "Do me one more favor?"

"What's that?"

"Don't call and tell Janelda that I'm driving down. I want to surprise her and Auntie Lois."

"All right."

I walked away hoping Bambi wouldn't get pulled over by the police in my truck. I wasn't too worried about it, though 'cause she hardly ever went anywhere. But at the moment, I couldn't sweat it anyway 'cause I needed to get the hell out of town. I looked over my shoulder to see if Bambi was standing on the porch watching me. She wasn't. I ran and unlocked her car first. Then I ran to my whip and gently picked up Croix from the back seat. I carried him to Bambi's car, placed him in the back, and strapped him in. He looked so peaceful without a care in the world.

I hopped in the driver's seat and sped toward the interstate.

I woke up to the sound of my stomach growling from hunger and a painfully stiff neck. The nausea was gone, and I was grateful for that. It wasn't until I sat up and looked around that I realized where I was. Then the memory of me vomiting my guts out in Satchel's bathroom came to me. Everything after that was sort of blurry. But

I did remember my body feeling weak and limp before the temperature spiked off of the thermometer. Then the darkness came.

"Croix!" I yelled, jumping to my feet. "Croix, where are you, baby?"

The silence caused me to panic. I could actually hear my pulse thumping in my ears. I ran to the front window and looked out. I nearly fainted again when I didn't see Satchel's SUV in its designated spot. It was nighttime, so I had no idea where he could've taken Croix or why. I reached for my purse so I could get my cell phone, but the piece of paper lying next to it snatched my full focus.

>*Ray,*
>
>*I decided to take Croix on a surprise mini vacation. Forgive me for not asking for your permission, but I knew you wouldn't approve. Please understand that I need this time to bond with my son. I'll bring him back in a few days, so please don't report this as a kidnapping. You had to learn to trust me with my son at some point, so I decided to force your hand. He's safe, so there's no need to worry. We'll see you soon.*
>
>*Satchel*
>
>*P.S. Congratulations.*

"Oh my God! He took Croix!"

Chapter Twenty-one

Eli

"Sit down and take it easy, bruh. Sergio and his friends will find them."

I stopped pacing to glare at Marlon. "How can I take it easy when Radiance and Croix should've been home *four* hours ago? They never made it to her mother's house. Ms. Gloria hasn't even heard from them! Something has gone wrong. I can feel it deep down in the pit of my stomach. Damn it!"

"We've checked all of the hospitals, and no one fitting either of their descriptions has been admitted to any of them."

"They could be in a ditch on the side of the fucking road! Something bad has happened. Radiance would've called me by now if she could."

My phone rang before Marlon could respond to my rant, and I answered it right away. "Radiance, where the hell are you?"

"It's Gloria, Eli. It sounds like you haven't heard from my baby and grandbaby yet."

"No, ma'am, I'm sorry I haven't. This is so unlike Radiance. I can't help but worry that something terrible has happened to her and Croix. I hope I'm wrong."

"You've got to think positively and have faith. That's what I'm doing. I've been praying ever since you first called. I'm about to have another little talk with Jesus as soon as we hang up."

"You do that while my assistant and his crew continue searching for them. I'll call you as soon as I learn something. Goodbye for now." My phone rang again immediately after I ended the call. I checked the caller ID this time and was relieved to see Radiance's name along with a picture of her, Croix, and me. "Radiance?"

"He took my baby, Eli! Croix is gone! I trusted that bastard, and he kidnapped my baby!"

"Calm down, sweetheart. *Who* took Croix?"

"*Satchel* did! I took Croix to visit him. I was trying to be nice and fair," she explained on a pitiful sob. "But when I got sick and passed out, he ran off with my baby! I don't know where they are! Oh God, please help me, Eli! I want my son!"

Her tearful plea shattered my heart, but I couldn't make sense of anything she'd said. I needed more information. "Babe, where are you?" I asked as calmly as I could.

"I'm at Satchel's townhouse in Camp Creek. I'm so sorry I lied to you about where we were going, but I felt like I had no other choice. It was a mistake . . . a *big, big* mistake. My baby is gone because I didn't listen to you or Mama."

"Radiance, darling, it's not the time to play the guilt game. We need to find Croix right now. Give me your ex's address so I can come for you. Calm down and relax. I'll be on my way as soon as you tell me where you are."

~♥~

It was a hard task to hold my emotions in when Radiance opened the door to let Sergio, his goons, Marlon, and me inside of her ex's townhouse. Rage overtook me each time I read the note he'd written to her. Graphic, deadly thoughts crossed my mind. I wanted the motherfucker dead! But before I decided Satchel's punishment for tricking Radiance into a secret visitation agreement and kidnapping Croix, I needed to come up with a plan to get the child back to his mother. I was willing to do anything—legally, illegally, or otherwise—at this point. I simply wanted to make Radiance's tears go away forever.

"Janelda knows exactly where my baby is. Satchel confides in her about *everything*. Take me to her house, Eli. I want to confront that evil bitch! If she won't tell me where her brother took my child, I'm going to kick her ratchet ass!"

"I think we should call the police," I suggested, rubbing Radiance's back. "We need to file a kidnapping report against the worthless bastard."

"*Technically*, it's not a kidnapping, bruh," Marlon advised. "The dude *is* Croix's legal father. He has a right to travel with his kid although he should've informed Radiance, the custodial parent, of his plans first. Unfortunately, her actions placed Croix in his father's physical custody. The only crimes the punk-ass loser has committed at most are parole violations. He may catch an abduction charge too."

Crashing noises from upstairs drew my attention away from the conversation. Sergio and a trio of his outlaw buddies were trashing Satchel's place. The way I saw it, vandalism was a petty crime when compared to an ex-con fleeing town with his son without permission from the child's mother. He was one sick son a bitch.

"Let's go, Eli! Please take me to Janelda's house. If you won't take me, I'll go by myself. Either way, I'm going to get my son."

"All right. Marlon, you drive Radiance's car and follow us in my truck. We're going on a little adventure."

~♥~

Marlon and I stood behind the bushes on the left side of the unkempt lawn waiting for Janelda or her mate to answer their front door. Radiance had knocked twice and rang the doorbell, but no one had answered yet. I could tell by her body language that she was growing more impatient by the second. I envisioned her kicking the door in like Black Widow from the Avengers if one of the ladies didn't answer the door soon. That would not be a pretty scene.

I didn't condone any sort of violence, especially when it came to a man putting his hands on a woman. But as angry as Radiance and Sergio were over Croix's disappearance, I was expecting World War III the moment the door opened. My man, Sergio, was standing on one side of the door, and two of his three buddies were on the opposite side. The other guy was behind the wheel of my Range Rover, ready to get us away from the scene as quickly as possible if need be. I had given Sergio and company specific instructions to only search the house for Croix, bring him out unharmed, and protect Radiance. They were not to lay a finger on Janelda or her lover.

When the door finally opened, my heart started beating a million times per second. Through cracks in the overgrown shrubbery, I saw Radiance push past a heavyset woman with braids and force her way into the house. Sergio and his boys stormed in right behind her.

"They're in," Marlon announced as if I hadn't seen the same thing he had. He took off running toward the front porch.

I rushed to follow him, hoping like hell that Croix was safe inside. I heard Radiance calling his name, and the young lady was screaming bloody murder. I decided to enter the house.

"Where is he, Bambi? Don't fuck with me, girl! I will kill you about my child!"

I did my best to restrain Radiance, but her adrenaline-induced strength and anger made it impossible. She broke away from my hold and rushed the woman. She slammed her against the wall hard and got directly in her face. Sergio and his buddies were running through the house, kicking in doors, shouting for Croix.

"Where is Janelda and Satchel? Wherever they are, Croix is with them. You know it, Bambi, so quit playing games!"

She threw both hands up in the air as tears fell from her eyes. "Okay! Okay! Janelda is in Miami with her aunt. Her daddy's got cancer, so they're flying to Saint Croix at eleven-fifteen in the morning. Satchel is on his way down south to catch up with them, but Janelda don't know it because he made me promise not to tell her. I don't know where Croix is. I swear I haven't seen him since his birthday party."

"You're lying!" Radiance grabbed Bambi by the neck and squeezed. She banged the back of the frightened woman's head against the wall repeatedly as she strangled her with her bare hands. "Where is my son, heifer? Where is he?"

I had to step in to prevent a first degree murder by strangulation. "Radiance!" I yelled, trying to pry her hands away from Bambi's neck. "Let go or you'll kill her. Then we'll never get the answers we need."

Radiance released Bambi's neck and allowed me to lead her away to the other side of the room. I turned around at the sound of a loud thud. It was Bambi falling to her knees, coughing and gasping for air. Seconds later, Sergio and his friends returned to the front room, but Croix wasn't with them.

"Croix ain't here, boss. We looked everywhere . . . even outside. I'm sorry, Ms. Alexander."

"Nah, don't be sorry, Sergio. I'm about to torture Bambi for helping Satchel and Janelda hide Croix, and then *she'll* be the one sorry." She lunged toward Bambi, but I held her in place.

"Look, ma'am, you need to tell us any information you know about this situation," Marlon said. "My brother won't be able to keep his woman off of your ass much longer."

"I-I . . . I've told y-you all I . . . I know. Janelda is in Miami," she whispered through ragged breaths. "And Satchel is on his way there. I haven't seen Croix. I swear to you on my life I haven't laid eyes on him since his party."

"Why the hell is Satchel's truck here, Bambi? I know his Navigator when I see it. He was here, and Croix was with him."

"Yeah, Satchel did come by, but Croix wasn't with him. He asked me to swap rides with him because he didn't want to make the trip to Miami in his truck. Lots of drug dealers down there drive Navigators, so he didn't want to risk getting pulled over by the police since he's on parole and all."

"So he took your Honda Civic and left his truck with you?"

Bambi nodded instead of speaking her answer to Radiance because she was coughing and massaging her neck.

"And you never saw Croix?"

"I didn't see him."

"Well, we know for a fact that he's with his father because the cocky punk left a note for Radiance telling her he was. Maybe he had locked Croix in the truck and told him to keep quiet, still, and out of sight until he came back outside with your key."

"Satchel didn't come inside the house. He stood on the porch the entire time he was here. I went and got my key and exchanged it for his."

"Croix was either too scared to let you see him, or he was asleep," Radiance said, starting to cry again. "My poor baby . . ."

"Did you watch Satchel pull off in your car?" Marlon asked.

"No, sir, I didn't because I was watching a movie, so I was in a hurry to get back inside to catch the ending."

"That's why you never saw my little buddy. He was in that truck. His father removed him and placed him in your car as soon as you re-entered the house. That twisted bastard!"

"*Now* I think we should call the police," Marlon suggested.

"Hell no! *We're* going to handle this situation ourselves. The authorities will only arrest that thug and throw him back in prison. I want to make him suffer first for the way he devastated Radiance." I turned to Bambi. "I need the address of Satchel and Janelda's aunt in Miami. Do you have it?"

"No, sir. I've never met her before. I don't even know her last name."

"It's Lois *Blyden*," Radiance told them. "She lives in Coconut Grove, but I don't know the—"

"Wait! The box she shipped Croix's birthday presents in is still in the laundry room. There's a return address on it!"

Everyone ran to the back of the house behind Bambi. Sure enough, Mrs. Lois Blyden's address in Miami was on the box.

"How long ago did Satchel leave here, Bambi?" Radiance asked.

She looked at the clock on the wall. "My movie came on at eight, and it was almost over when he got here. It's a little bit after two now, so I'll say he pulled off around ten o'clock."

"He's been on the road for about four hours now, bruh. What's your plan?"

"Sergio, make arrangements to have Ivan fly us to Miami pronto. Have an SUV waiting at the airstrip for us when we arrive. And I need you and your men to be armed."

"I'm sorry for attacking you, Bambi," Radiance apologized, approaching the young woman. "But I'll *kill* you the next time I see you if you give Janelda or Satchel a head's up on what's about to go down. And don't even think about calling the police. That'll cost you your life too."

"I won't say a word to anybody, Ray. I promise. I love Croix like he's my own son. I want your man to find him. And then I want these men to kick Satchel's ass."

Chapter Twenty-two

Radiance

"I'm going with you, Eli! Croix is my son! I *need* to be there."

"It's too risky, Radiance. I won't allow it. Plus you're not well. Look at you," he said, waving his hand before me. "You're flushed, weak, and probably dehydrated. You passed out for several hours. You aren't flying to Miami with us! The discussion is closed!"

I flopped down on the bed and covered my face with my hands as I cried my eyes out. I wanted to fly to Miami with Eli and the rest of the men, but he was determined that I wouldn't. I needed him to understand that every minute I was away from Croix I lost a little piece of my soul. Why couldn't he get it?

He sat down on the bed next to me. "Look at me, babe."

I turned the other way defiantly.

"Radiance, I don't have the patience nor am I in the mood for one of your temper tantrums. Now look at me!"

I turned around slowly to face him, but I made sure that the look in my eyes was lethal enough to stab him in his heart.

"You have to trust that I'm making the best decision for your safety. I can't have you in harm's way, sweetheart. I love you, and it's my duty to always protect you." He wrapped his arms around me and pulled me close.

My heart did a tap dance, and my spirit took flight at the sound of those three special words. Eli had finally professed his love for me, and I was overwhelmed with emotion. I allowed my tears of joy to fall freely and relaxed in his arms.

"Your mother will be here soon to watch after you while I'm gone. I love you, but I don't trust you to stay here alone and behave." He laughed deeply. "You'll probably book a flight to Miami as soon as I leave if there's no one here to stop you."

I raised my head from his shoulder and pulled back to look at him head-on. "You know me too well."

He smiled and nodded. "Of course I do. You're my *heart*, Radiance. Every man knows his heart."

"When will you guys be leaving?"

"Ivan, my regular pilot, wasn't available, so Sergio had to find a substitute. The young man won't be able to get here before five-thirty for a six o'clock takeoff. We have another two hours."

"What's the plan when you get to Ms. Lois' house?"

"You don't need to know that, sweetheart. The less you know, the better. Just trust me that we'll find Croix and bring him back home to you."

"What's going to happen to Satchel?"

"That's not your concern either."

"Please don't let Sergio and his posse kill him. No matter how terrible of a person Satchel is, he's still Croix's father. How will you be able to look that precious child in the eyes every day, knowing that you ordered his dad's death?"

Eli released me and stood up. As he began to pace back and forth in front of me, I saw conflict in his handsome features. My words were resonating with him, but there was a death wish for Satchel tugging at him as well. I knew that he was livid that Croix was missing and I was on the brink of a mental meltdown because of it. But in his heart, he knew that it wouldn't be right for him to have Satchel killed.

"I won't let Sergio and his boys kill the lowlife hoodlum. They *will* rough him up, though, but he'll survive. Then we'll notify the authorities."

"Thank you."

After a long hot shower, I put on a bright green caftan and wandered downstairs to the great room. Mama looked so out of place sitting among a group of men sipping coffee and strategizing.

She placed her coffee mug on the end table and stood up. I walked into her arms when she reached out to me. There was nothing more comforting than a hug from the woman who'd birthed me.

"How are you feeling, baby?"

"I'm much better now, but I won't be one hundred percent until Croix is in my arms."

"Are you hungry?"

"Yes, ma'am, I'm starving."

"Let's go to the kitchen so Mama can fix you something to eat. Eli and these other men don't need us hanging around."

I followed Mama to the kitchen and took a seat at the table. "Eli insisted that you come here to be my body-guard and babysitter. He doesn't trust me to stay put."

"He's a smart man," she said, searching the refrigerator.

I didn't respond. There wasn't much I could say. Eli and Mama knew that I wouldn't have stayed here like some spineless female without a brain. I most definitely would've hopped on a plane to Miami and caught a cab to the Coconut Grove address I'd memorized from the box in Janelda's laundry room.

I smiled when I saw Mama pull the ingredients for her famous omelets from the fridge and place them on the counter. She reached for a skillet from the rack above her head. The sound of her humming a hymn as she prepared to cook took me back to my childhood. Fond memories of her, my daddy, and me talking and laughing at the breakfast table flooded my mind.

"We're about to leave, babe," Eli announced from the kitchen's entrance.

I abandoned my memories and turned my head in his direction. He extended his right hand to me, and I left the table immediately.

He snaked his arms around my waist and drew my body snuggly against his. "Don't give Ms. Gloria any trouble. I would hate for her to have to spank you."

"She won't have to. I'll be good."

"That's my girl." He kissed my lips. "I'll call you as soon as we land."

"I'll be waiting. Be safe."

"No doubt. I love, you Radiance Alexander."

"I love you too."

~♥~

"Ugh!" I growled as my stomach tumbled again. I heaved, and another portion of my delicious ham, cheese, and spinach omelet spilled from my mouth and into the commode.

Mama patted my back like she used to do every time I threw up yucky Brussels sprouts or liver when I was a little girl. "How long has this been going on, baby?"

"It's been a few days." I flushed the commode and stood up straight.

"You should make an appointment to see your doctor. Something ain't right. You can't hold down food, and then you fainted yesterday. You need a checkup, baby. Call your doctor."

"I don't have time to see Dr. Wexler today. I need to be right here waiting to hear from Eli about my son. I'm just stressed out, Mama. All of the lies and sneaking behind Eli's back so Croix and Satchel could visit got the best of me. Now I'm even more stressed out because that fool took my baby. It's a wonder that I can drink water."

"It may be stress, but I still want you to see your doctor soon. Now make an appointment before I go and find one of Eli's belts and whip your behind!"

Of course, I did as I was told as soon as the clock struck nine. I made an appointment to see Dr. Wexler in two days at ten o'clock in the morning.

Chapter Twenty-three

Satchel and Janelda

"I want my mommy!"

Ice cold milk and a whole McDonald's hot cake, dripping with syrup, hit the back of my head and neck.

"Stop it, Croix! You're acting like a spoiled little punk, and Daddy don't like it!"

"I want my mommy! Take me to my mommy!" He started kicking the back of the seat in front of him and crying at the top of his lungs.

"We're going to the beach. Don't you wanna swim in the ocean and hunt for seashells?"

"No! I don't want to go anywhere without Mommy! You better take me home *now*! I don't like you anymore! You're mean! I don't want you to be my daddy! I want Mommy and Eli!"

My son was pissing me the hell off with his baby bullshit. Plus I was tired as a mothafucka after driving all damn night without rest. I wasn't feeling Croix's little temper tantrum, and he had one more time to mention that cracker, Eli. I had a mind to pull over to the side of the road and whoop his little rotten ass, but I didn't have time to deal with him. I needed to get to Auntie Lois' house. It was seven-forty-five in the morning. No doubt she and Janelda were up preparing for the trip. We would have to get to the airport earlier than usual so I could purchase tickets for Croix and me.

I was a few blocks away from my aunt's house, so I was relieved. I looked over my shoulder at my son and saw tears pouring down his little sad face. I couldn't deny it. He did look pitiful, and it made me feel some type of way. I knew snatching him from Ray the way I did was foul, but I was gonna deliver him safely back to her in a few days. He needed to get used to being around me, though. At the time I came up with idea, it seemed like it was the only way I could make that happen. So I went for it.

I pulled up to Auntie Lois' house and exited Bambi's whip quickly. I walked around and opened the back door. As soon as I did, Croix started screaming and throwing his breakfast at me. I released his seatbelt and picked him up. The little dude was strong. He was punching and kicking me like a grown-ass man. I had to cover his mouth with my hand so the neighbors wouldn't hear him screaming. That's when he bit me.

I held him upright so he could see the anger in my face. "If you bite me one more time, I will *never* take you back to your mommy. Do you understand me?"

His little eyes bucked wide in shock, but he nodded his head. He knew I wasn't bullshitting. I ran to the door and banged on it a few times.

"Oh hell nah!" I yelled and stumbled backwards. My eyes had to be playing tricks on me. Ain't no way in hell my stupid-ass brother was standing on Auntie Lois' porch holding my nephew. I slapped my chest hard with my palm, struggling for air and asked, "What the fuck are you doing here, Satch? You ain't supposed to be here, dude! What the hell did you do?"

"Man, move! I'm tired and I gotta pee. Here, take him." He handed me Croix before he headed down the hall to the bathroom.

I sat down on the sofa with my nephew in my arms. I wiped the tears and snot from his face with the back of my hand. "Are you, okay, sugar?"

"I want my mommy!"

Auntie Lois came, flying into the living room from the back of the house. "What's going . . ." her voice faded when she saw Croix on my lap.

"Apparently, your dumb nephew kidnapped his son from his mother and fled down here! Ray would never have let Satch travel more than three feet away from her with this boy, Auntie!" I rocked Croix in my arms as I tried to figure out what to do. I wasn't about to go to prison because of my brother's stupid bullshit. "Come and hold him, Auntie Lois, while I try to talk some sense into that ignorant-ass nigga's head."

I handed Croix over to my aunt, rushed down the hall, and knocked on the bathroom door.

"What the hell do you want, Janelda? A nigga can't relieve himself without you fuckin' with him?"

"Why did you do it, Satch? Why did you kidnap your own son? I know damn well Ray didn't just let you take him. Either she's dead or in a coma. That's the only way you could've traveled all the way down here with him." I felt nauseous all of a sudden as fear gripped me. "Did you hurt Ray? Please tell me you weren't crazy enough to hurt that girl!" I banged on the bathroom door again.

"Man, I would *never* lay hands on my baby mama. How're you gonna ask me some foul bullshit like that?"

"You know what? I don't even want to know what happened. This is *your* mess and not mine! I ain't going down with you, nigga! I swear I ain't. You can get on the plane if you want to with that boy, but you're on your own! Auntie Lois and I don't have shit to do with it!"

"Fuck you, Janelda! I don't need your ass anyway! I'm going to visit my daddy, and my son is going with me no matter what you, Ray, or that cracker she's in love with says!"

It was useless. Satch had lost his fucking mind. I walked down the hall confused and scared out of my skin. Just as I reached the living room, the front door popped off its hinges, and two mean-looking men stormed inside the house with high-power handguns drawn. Auntie Lois screamed and immediately dropped to the floor with Croix in her arms when we heard another loud boom at the back door. Two more men burst into the house with weapons aimed in our direction. I spun around in a circle, not knowing what the hell to do.

I held my hands up in the air. "Don't shoot! Please don't shoot!"

A gorgeous white man with long, dark hair walked coolly into the living room with an equally handsome brother a beat behind him. Both men looked directly at Croix. My nephew smiled and wiggled out of Auntie Lois' arms. He ran to the smooth white dude and jumped up and landed in his arms.

"No one came here to harm you, ma'am, so you can relax. We only came for Croix," Mr. Vanilla told me in a deep rich voice just above a whisper. "But if you're wise women, you'll tell me which room Satchel Young is hiding out in right now."

"He's in the bathroom. It's the first door down the hall on your left," my aunt whispered nervously.

I was so fucking scared and upset that the only thing I could do was point in the direction of my brother's location.

All four armed men ran toward the bathroom. One kicked the door in. I heard things crashing to the floor in the bathroom and lots of cursing. It sounded like a war zone. Then the chaos spilled out into the hallway and to other rooms throughout the house.

The biggest guy, who was rocking a long ponytail, ran back into the living room. He walked over to the man holding my nephew and rubbing his head affectionately. "He got away, boss. It looks like he jumped out the bathroom window. Should we go after him?"

"No. As the only lawman among us, I've got to tell y'all to fall back. We'll notify the Georgia and Florida authorities about everything. They can handle it from this point on."

"Damn it!" The man who was obviously in charge shouted.

"Chill out, Trapper," the black dude said, patting his friend's shoulder. "Let's not upset Croix anymore than he already is."

Just then, I recognized the black guy from Croix's birthday party. That's where I had seen the Hulk look alike too. The man I wasn't familiar with was the boss holding my nephew. I figured he was Eli, Radiance's man. But his friend had called him *Trapper*.

"Ladies, I'm Eli Jamieson," he announced as if he'd peeped inside my head. "I'm deeply involved with Radiance Alexander, which means Croix is like my son. I apologize for invading the house and destroying property. But I couldn't go back home to Atlanta without Croix." He turned to the black guy and nodded.

"For your troubles, Mr. Jamieson would like for you to have this," he said, reaching inside his breast pocket. He removed a check. "You should be able to make all necessary repairs and replacements with it. If it isn't enough, please don't hesitate to call the number in the upper left corner to let us know."

"Thank you." I grabbed the check and looked at it. The amount was five figures deep. It was probably more than the entire house was worth and then some. My bottom lip dropped to my chest. "*Damn!*"

Auntie Lois let out a fake, exaggerated cough and eyed me like I was a stranger. I sucked my teeth and passed her the check.

"Our business here is done. I have who I came here for," Eli told my auntie and me. "Have a safe flight to Saint Croix, ladies."

"Thank you."

"We will."

The Hulk stepped to me boldly. "When you see your brother, tell him Sergio is looking for him. He can run, but he can't hide forever."

With that said, the six men filed out of the house and headed for a midnight blue Mercedes SUV. I wanted to kiss Croix goodbye and tell him I loved him, but the possessive hold Eli had on him was a clear sign that I wouldn't be allowed to. I stood on the porch, relieved that my nephew was on his way home to his mother, but I was still furious with Satch. His stupidity and selfishness had caused all of the madness. I would probably never see Croix again because I was sure Radiance had lost all trust in me. I hoped the police would catch Satch's dumb ass and throw him back in the pen.

Chapter Twenty-four

Radiance

"I never want to see my daddy again. Don't make me, Mommy."

I stroked Croix's cheek and kissed his forehead. "Don't worry, baby. Your daddy is out of our lives for good. The police are looking for him right now so they can take him back to prison for a long time."

"Can Eli be my daddy now?"

I was at a loss for words by my baby's question. Kids truly did say the darnedest things.

"If you want me to," Eli rushed to say from the other side of Croix.

"I want you to be my *new* daddy."

"Sure, little buddy."

I snuggled closer to my son in the bed with so much gratitude in my heart. The three of us had been lying in the dark for an hour talking. A thunderstorm had delayed the return flight from Miami to Atlanta until that evening. I had sat patiently by the window waiting for Eli's truck to pull in the driveway. Although I knew that Croix was safe with him, I wanted him home with *me*.

When the SUV full of men finally arrived, I ran outside and grabbed my son and released all of my pent-up emotions through tears. I hadn't allowed Croix out of my sight since then. After he'd eaten his favorite meal

of spaghetti and meatballs prepared with love by his
grandmother, I gave him a hot bubble bath. I was about
to tuck him in bed when he asked if he could sleep with
me. There was fear in his eyes because of the trauma he'd
been through, so I couldn't tell him no. And of course
my sweet Eli didn't mind, so we were cuddled up like a
family in bed. It felt so right. I never wanted the feeling
to end. My life was better than any fairytale, and I hoped
with all my heart that it would always be this way.

~♥~

"It was sweet of you to say what you said to Croix last
night."
"I said a lot of things to him. What exactly are you
talking about?"
"You know, when you agreed to become his father. It
made him happy, but hopefully, he'll soon forget about
it."
Eli took a sip from his coffee mug. "Why would you
hope such a thing? My little buddy asked me to be his
father, and I accepted."
"I thought you only agreed to keep from hurting his
feelings."
"I said it because I *meant* it. As soon as the investigators
find Pandora, you and I will have some serious decisions
to make about our future. Croix gave us a jumpstart last
night."
Wow! He wants to be a father to another man's son.
The thought of it was heart-warming, but there was a
question that I needed him to answer for me. "Why didn't
you and your wife have a baby?"
"I wanted a son or daughter very much, but Pandora
isn't a big fan of children."
"But she has a daughter."

He sighed in what I believed was frustration. "Yes, she has a daughter that she shipped off to boarding school and rarely ever calls or visits."

"That's a damn shame. I would *never* abandon Croix."

"I know you wouldn't, sweetheart, because you're a wonderful mother."

"And I think you're going to be a great father figure to my son."

"I hope so." He checked his watch. "I have to run soon, babe. I've got a ten o'clock walkthrough at a potential property. What's on your agenda today?"

"Nothing. I'm still not feeling my best, so I'm going to hang around here and read and watch a few movies. I'll probably nap a lot too."

"Why don't you and Ms. Gloria go to the spa? You both deserve a little pampering after the day from hell we all had yesterday. Sergio can make the arrangements and drive you there."

"I think Mama would like that, Eli."

"Sure she will. What woman doesn't like manicures, pedicures, massages, facials, mud baths, and full cosmetic makeovers? I'll have Sergio call you with your appointment time."

"Thank you, baby. You're too good to me." I got up from the kitchen table and kissed his lips. "I love you."

"I love you too," my man said, grabbing a handful of my ass and squeezing it.

~♥~

"Congratulations, Radiance. You're pregnant. I'll get you started on prenatal vitamins right away. As for the queasiness . . ."

I didn't hear much of what Dr. Wexler said after he dropped that bombshell. His words started to sound like Chinese Ebonics in my ears. Nothing made sense anymore. I marched like a zombie behind him from the examination room to his office. I left twenty minutes later with two prescriptions and a few pamphlets, but I didn't even remember the doctor handing them to me. I had an appointment in six weeks. I sure as hell couldn't recall scheduling it.

Even as I drove Eli's silver Infiniti out of the parking lot, my mind was pretty much a blank. My body felt numb too. I couldn't determine if I was crying because I was happy to be carrying Eli's child or if I was afraid that my pregnancy was a terrible mistake. I was so confused.

I knew that he'd wanted a baby with Pandora, and he had made a commitment to help me raise Croix. But I wasn't sure if Eli wanted to become the father of a newborn at the age of forty. I wished I could read his mind or look into his heart. I needed a sign from heaven. I wanted to give Eli a baby for reasons that I couldn't explain. I couldn't think of a more precious gift for a woman to give the man she loved. I only hoped that the man I loved would gladly accept my gift.

"You've been quiet since I told you I had to make an unexpected trip to Dallas tonight. Are you upset with me, babe?"

I placed a stack of t-shirts in Eli's suitcase and shook my head. "No, I'm not upset. You're a businessman. I understand that you have to travel without notice from time to time. I'm just tired."

"Why don't you rest then? Sergio can come upstairs and finish helping me pack."

"I'd rather do it. It'll give us a little bit of time together before you leave."

Eli walked up behind me and wrapped his arms around me. He kissed the back of my neck. "That's why I love you the way I do. You know how to take care of your man."

I experienced instant euphoria in the midst of the three-day inner turmoil I'd been living through. I was much better physically, but emotionally, I was still one hot mess. My pregnancy to date remained a secret. I hadn't even told my mama about the baby yet because I felt that Eli deserved the honor of being the first to know. He *was* the baby's father, and I loved him deeper than any ocean.

"I like to take care of you because you take damn good care of Croix and me."

"Give me a few days to close out the Dallas deal, and I'll be back to spoil you more than ever." He placed another soft kiss on my neck. "I may even have a surprise for you when I get back here."

I bet my surprise is bigger than yours, I could've told him, but the time wasn't right. While he was in Dallas, I was going to build up my confidence and put my big girl panties on to prepare myself to tell him that I was pregnant when he returned. Perhaps if I had kept my *real* big girl panties on, I wouldn't have been in the predicament I was in. But it was too late for that now. Eli and I were expecting a baby, and he had every right to know.

I was surprised to see my mama sitting at the kitchen table with Croix the next morning. She must've come to the estate while I was asleep. Sergio, no doubt, had driven her out for a visit.

"Good morning, you two." I kissed Croix on the cheek.

"Hi, Mommy!"

Mama offered me a warm smile, but she didn't say a word. She continued eating her breakfast.

"Did I oversleep?" I asked, hugging my mama.

"You were snoring, Mommy. I couldn't wake you up."

"I'm so sorry, baby. I guess I was really tired."

"How come you're so tired, Ray? Did you *work* last night?"

"No, ma'am. You know I don't have a job."

"Exactly. So tell me why you couldn't wake up before ten o'clock. Croix should be at summer camp, but he wasn't able to wake you up so you could get him dressed and feed him breakfast."

"I didn't sleep much last night, Mama. I sat up and waited for Eli's call. I couldn't rest until I knew he had landed safely in Dallas. We talked for a while, and by the time we hung up, I was wide awake. I watched TV until I finally fell asleep some time after three."

"Is that right?"

"Yes, ma'am."

"Baby," Mama said to Croix. "Take your juice box into the great room and turn on the TV. You can watch anything you want. I need to talk grownup talk with your mommy."

"Okay." He jumped down from his chair and dashed down the hall.

"Ray, is there something you want to tell me?"

"No, ma'am."

"Are you sure?"

"I'm sure."

I wrapped my arms around my waist nervously. Mama's question had made me feel uncomfortable. And I didn't appreciate the way she was looking at me. She was fishing for something, and I didn't like it.

"Well, you may not have anything you want to tell me, but I know for a fact that there's something you *need* to tell Eli."

"I don't have time to play games, Mama," I snapped. "If there's something on your mind, go ahead and say it already."

"Watch your tone, li'l girl. You may be an adult, but I'm still your mother. And I'm not the one playing games. *You* are! When are you going to tell Eli about the baby?"

Chapter Twenty-five

Radiance

After I got over the shock, I asked, "How did you know I was pregnant?"

"I'm your mother. I knew you before you knew yourself, baby. I've known you were pregnant since the day you got sick in front of me. I was just waiting for you to say something."

"I just found out a few days ago, and my brain has been scrambled ever since." I took the napkin Mama had offered me to wipe away my tears. "I want to be excited, but how can I be? I don't know if Eli wants a baby at his age or not. We've never discussed it before."

"If that man loves Croix enough to track him down and rescue him from his father, he will love his own child. Eli loves you, Ray, and I know that you love him back a million times over. You've got to trust in the love you share. Ain't nothing greater than love. Tell Eli. As soon as he comes home, tell him that he's going to be a father. I promise you that he'll be the happiest man alive."

"Do you think so?" I asked, wiping away more tears with the crumpled napkin.

"I know so, baby."

~♥~

"Lock the door behind me and set the alarm, Ms. Alexander."

"I always do, Sergio. Now go home. Croix and I will be all right until Eli gets here."

"Fine. Call me if you need me."

"I will."

I closed the door and secured the locks. Then I stopped at the bottom of the double marble staircase and activated the security system. With Croix already tucked in for the night, I had exactly one hour to prepare for Eli's arrival. The word, excitement, didn't begin to describe what was stirring inside of me. I was more than ready to tell the man I loved that I was carrying his baby. And because he adored me and was committed to our relationship, he would be happy.

It was bubble bath time, and it called for Eli's most favorite fragrance. I was always as helpless as a sheep before a fox whenever I bathed and moisturized in my passion fruit and maple scented body care products. Eli often told me that the scent caused him to drool at first whiff and gave him a never-ending woody. I laughed, recalling his silliness and sank deeper underneath the blanket of bubbles.

After twenty minutes of soaking and scrubbing my body thoroughly, I moisturized from head to toe. Then I sprayed my signature perfume in all of the important places. There wasn't a need to spend lots of time on my hair because by the end of the night, it would be all over the place. So I pulled my mane back into a simple loose ponytail at my nape. My sexy bedroom attire selection was a no brainer. Eli was obsessed with my cheetah print bra and boy short set and the matching four-inch stiletto slippers. I slid into the ensemble and then reached for my long-arm lighter. I wanted the fragrance of the mocha scented candle to welcome my man into our love nook. I lit the wick, and like magic, the security system chirped, signaling that *Daddy* was home.

My heart went into overdrive with anticipation. I couldn't keep still. On sheer feminine instinct, I left the master suite and floated sexily down the staircase with love on my mind. I wanted to greet Eli like the king that he was.

"Welcome—"

"Oh dear, God! You're practically naked, darling. And you . . . you . . . you're *black*."

"Yeah, I'm a sistah. Who the hell are you?"

The mystery woman who had somehow managed to get past the security system threw her head back and laughed. Her long blonde curls cascaded down her back. Skinny as a malnourished child, she planted her bony fists on her imaginary hips. Her baby blue eyes flashed with arrogance. "You must be *Radiance*."

"I am," I confirmed, rolling my neck like any girl from the hood would have.

"I'm Pandora, but you may call me *Mrs. Jamieson*, my dear."

"Nah, boo boo, I will call you *trifling*! You're only Eli's wife on paper, but *I* own his heart."

She threw her head back and laughed again. "You are so *cute*! And you're a spicy little thing too. But good looks and attitude won't keep a man like Trapper, darling. Little skimpy cheetah outfits won't either. I should know because out of all of the many women who vied to become Mrs. T. Eli Jamieson, only *I* was able to get him down the aisle. He chose *me*."

"That was *then*," I said, strolling slowly toward her, sizing her up. "I'm with Eli *now*, and he loves me. So you need to turn your little anorexic ass around and get the hell out of this house."

"I'm the queen of this castle, dear, so if anyone should be packing their bags, it's *you*. I'm Trapper's *wife*. You were his playmate while I was away, but Mama's home now. It's time for Trapper's concubine to leave."

That did it. I snapped and lunged toward Pandora, determined to choke her ass to sleep.

"What the hell is going on here?" Eli shouted, jumping between Pandora and me with his arms extended. He looked back and forth between us with wide eyes. "What are you doing here, Pandora? You have no right to be in this house! You don't live here anymore!"

"My goodness, Trapper. Is that any way to greet your *wife*?"

"Our marriage is over, Pandora. It ended when you left here two years ago."

"Excuse me, sir," a male voice interrupted. "Where should I put these?"

Eli, Pandora, and I turned toward the front door. There was a man dressed in a dark suit and tie standing there holding two designer pieces of luggage. Eli turned away from the man without giving him an answer. He stared at me briefly before removing his suit coat.

"Put this on," he whispered to me as he placed the coat around my shoulders. Then he escorted me to the bottom of the staircase. "Stay here, please. Don't go near Pandora. I don't want to see you in an orange jumpsuit and handcuffs. You're much too pretty for that." He winked before he kissed my lips and walked away.

I cast my eyes on a visibly shaken Pandora while Eli gave the chauffer instructions about his luggage and tipped him. Her baby blues weren't shining as brightly as they were when she'd first arrived. Eli's defense and open affection toward me had robbed her of her thunder. I could tell that she was crushed. Her countenance was now flat, and I clearly saw nervousness in her body language. I offered her a dazzling smile just to taunt her ass when she looked at me. Nobody would ever come for Radiance Alexander and get away with it. Pandora had started this mess when she interrupted the special night I had planned for Eli. And I was pissed to hell and determined to finish it.

I jumped when I heard the front door slam shut. I watched as my man stomped toward Pandora like he was ready to pounce on her. She stood under the chandelier like a stick figure with her arms folded across her flat chest. I sat down on the first step to watch the showdown.

"Why are you here, Pandora?"

"I missed you."

Eli laughed, but the anger in his eyes told me that he was anything but happy. "Bullshit!"

"It's true, Trapper. I've had lots of time to think about our marriage and to work on some personal issues. I know exactly what I want now."

"I'm dying to hear this. Please do tell."

"I want to be the perfect wife to you and give you the one thing you want more than anything else in the world. I'm ready to give you a baby, Trapper.

~♥~

"Why is this happening, Eli? Why did that bitch decide to come back to Atlanta all of a sudden? Uggghhh! And why the hell did you invite her to spend the night in this house?"

Eli reached out and grabbed me around the waist when I attempted to walk past him as he sat at the foot of the bed. With force, he pulled me onto his lap and held me in place. "I'll answer the last question first. Marlon convinced me to be nice to Pandora. He thinks it'll improve my chances of persuading her to sign the divorce papers. So as a goodwill gesture, I offered her the downstairs guest suite for the night. But she's going to get a rude awakening in the morning when she'll be served with the divorce documents.

I nodded my understanding although I didn't like the fact that Pandora was sleeping downstairs. "What made her come back here out of the blue after all this time?"

"I baited her, sweetheart."

"How?"

"I called her daughter, McKenzie, and told her that I had fallen in love with a young, sexy, irresistible woman named Radiance." He squeezed my ass and bit my earlobe like he was ready to make me climb the wall.

"Did you really do that?"

"I sure did."

"Why Eli? What made you call McKenzie to tell her that?"

"Mama Sadie thought it was a good idea, and she was on the money as usual. You see, she figured if Pandora knew that I had moved on with another woman, she would rush back here and attempt to break us up so that she and I could reconcile."

"Mama Sadie is one smart old woman. She was right about Pandora. That heifer twirled in town like a tornado just like Mama Sadie said she would, and she wants you back, Eli. Will you reconcile with Pandora now that she's willing to have your baby?"

"Don't insult me, Radiance," Eli snapped. "A house full of babies wouldn't make me remain in a marriage with Pandora. I don't love her anymore. Sometimes I wonder if I ever did."

"What's going to happen now that she's back? I don't want any surprises, Eli. My heart can't take any unexpected drama, so give it to me straight. No chaser. No bull."

"Pandora will be served with divorce papers early tomorrow morning by a processor. The transaction will be documented by Marlon for verification. Then in sixty days, regardless if she signs the papers or not, I'll be a free man."

"No you, won't," I corrected and swatted him teasingly on the shoulder. "You belong to *me*."

Eli chuckled lightly. "I stand corrected, Ms. Alexander. In sixty days, no matter what, I will no longer be married to Pandora."

Chapter Twenty-six

Pandora

"*Fuck!*" Trapper sent the thin stack of papers flying into the air. They dropped to the carpet like leaves blown in the wind. "How the hell did we miss this, Marlon and Thomas? How did we miss it, damn it? How?"

I stifled a laugh as I watched my handsome husband have a conniption right before my very eyes. Marlon and his other attorney, Thomas DeFore, sat speechless and still across the table from Whitley Warren, my attorney, and me. The three gentlemen had expected our first meeting since I'd been served with the divorce papers to go a whole lot smoother. They had underestimated the great Pandora, and now I had them all by their sweaty balls. It served Trapper right. How dare he dishonor me by bringing some hood rat and her son to live in our home?

He's a man, so I didn't expect him to remain pure and celibate for the two years I was traveling the world, trying to find myself. Every man has needs, and Trapper is not the exception. I knew there would be lovers here and there, but I never would've imagined that he would fall in love. And with a *black woman*? That was a slap in the face. Sure, Radiance's extraordinary beauty couldn't be denied. She was drop-dead gorgeous with an amazing body. I was anything but a lesbian, but I wanted to fondle her perfectly round breasts and grip her plump ass just to see what they felt like. I could clearly understand why Trapper was so smitten by her, but he'd had no right to enter into an exclusive relationship while he was still married to me. Hit it and quit it was the game I had played with my string of suitors over the past two years. Trapper should've been smart enough to do the same. But since he had committed the ultimate no-no against me, I was about to make him pay.

"We didn't miss anything, Mr. Jamieson," Thomas finally said. "The clause Attorney Warren referenced is not applicable in this matter."

"Of course it is," Whitley shot back. "It's quite clear in fact. Mr. Jamieson committed adultery. He and his mistress, Radiance Alexander, are cohabitating. My client, Mrs. Jamieson, his *legal wife*, witnessed this upon her return to the home she and her husband shared for three years."

"Mr. Jamieson hasn't denied that he's involved with Ms. Alexander or the fact that they live together on his estate," Marlon stated eloquently. "Our argument is that Mrs. Jamieson abandoned the marriage for two years and had multiple affairs with various men during that time."

"Do you have pictures or eyewitness' statements or even sworn affidavits to prove your accusations against my client, Mr. Lawson?"

"No, I don't at this time. But there have been countless reports of Mrs. Jamieson's philandering all around the world since she separated from Mr. Jamieson."

I couldn't help but laugh at Marlon. He was grasping for straws. He hated me, and he'd do anything to rid Trapper of me. "Oh, dear brother-in-law, you can't believe every piece of vicious gossip you hear. I have *never* cheated on my husband. That's why it . . . it b-broke my h-heart when I . . . I . . . I came home and found a scantily-dressed woman in my house!" I turned on the water works like

Meryl Streep. I accepted the tissue Whitley had offered me and blew my nose for effect. "I was devastated and humiliated," I continued pitifully, fake sobbing like crazy.

"Stop it, Pandora!" Trapper shouted, banging his fist on the table. "Those crocodile tears don't move me! You took off two years ago and left me. I had no idea where you were. You've been spotted all around the globe with one rich and foolish victim after another. I don't give a damn about all of the losers you've been with! They can have you! Sign the fucking papers and let me out of this bogus marriage! Do you hear me?"

"Mrs. Jamieson has no problem with signing the divorce papers, sir. Her issue is the compensation clause in your prenuptial agreement. Will you honor it, Mr. Jamieson?"

"Hell no!" Marlon shouted, pushing back in his chair.

Thomas shook his head in the negative. "Absolutely not."

"I will give you twenty-five million dollars of my hard-earned money over my dead body!" Trapper roared at me. "I don't owe you a fucking dime!"

"According to the compensation clause you do, sir," Whitley pointed out. "It's a clear line item. It specifically states that if the dissolution of marriage is the direct result of proven infidelity, the unfaithful party must pay his or her spouse a one-time financial compensatory award in the amount of twenty-five million dollars. It's here in black and white, gentlemen."

"It ain't going to happen," Trapper said with a devious smile on his face. "I'd rather die and go to hell."

I sighed. "Well, I guess we should seek marriage counseling, my dear, because we will remain Mr. and Mrs. Jamieson until death do us part. And I'm afraid you're going to have to ask your little chocolate Barbie doll to get out. I refuse to share my home with my husband's whore."

"Fuck you, Pandora! Radiance and Croix aren't going anywhere."

"Chill out, Trapper. I got this. Mrs. Warren, please advise your client that Mr. Jamieson is the *sole owner* of Diamond Estate and all properties under Diamond International. Therefore, as of today, Mrs. Jamieson's presence at any of these businesses or my client's private residence will be considered trespassing."

"Duly noted, Mr. Lawson."

"She needs to take her ass to the nearest Motel 6," Thomas mumbled under his breath.

"I think this matter should go to mediation, gentlemen," Whitley suggested.

"We disagree. Your client left her husband to wander the world. She was involved in numerous extramarital affairs while she was away, and because of that, she owes my client twenty-five million dollars and a divorce."

I smiled at Marlon and looked him dead in his eyes. "Prove it."

~❤~

"Ah, shit! You got that magic mouth, baby. I'm 'bout to rain down your throat!"

I hollowed my jaws and allowed that big black dick to hit the back of my throat. I sucked harder and slurped before I pulled back to circle my tongue slowly around the gigantic head. The doctor had circumcised him perfectly. His dick was beautiful and delicious.

"Fuck! Damn it! Here comes my nut!" he announced and yanked my hair hard with both hands, causing my scalp to burn.

I flattened my tongue as warm creamy cum slid over my tonsils. I swallowed deeply, taking all of that sweetness in. I stood from my knees and looked at the face of one satisfied man. I was sure I had earned my keep for at least another week. My money transfers hadn't come through from my offshore accounts yet, so I wanted to hold on to every dime I had until then. My money was a little funny at the moment because I was spending like a maniac while I criss-crossed God's green earth. Plus I had made some unsuccessful investments over the past two years. And it didn't help that Dale, McKenzie's father, had stopped paying his half of the tuition and housing at the boarding school. Now that he was married and had a newborn son, he wanted McKenzie to move to Texas to live with him and his family. I refused to even entertain the notion, so he stopped his financial assistance with her schooling. He continued his measly child support payments, which barely covered my weekly spa treatments and psychic readings.

"Let me hit that pussy now," Jihad ordered.

I dropped down on the bed, spread my legs wide, and smiled. Instantly, his dick got hard again. It was *huge*. Shit, he was a big and powerful man, standing well over six feet at a weight no less than two hundred and fifty pounds. A wealthy champion boxer by profession, Jihad was rough and violent by nature. There was nothing gentle about him. My insides were about to take a pounding. I prepared myself for the torture because I wanted to sink my claws deeper into his prize-winning bank account.

Like a wild beast, Jihad pounced on me. He rammed that fat, ten-inch dick inside of my pussy with no mercy whatsoever. He didn't even put on a condom, but it was fine because I'd had a tubal ligation a week after Trapper started begging me to give him a child over two years ago. I screamed out in pain when Jihad started pumping in and out of me like a mad man.

"Nah, girl, you gotta take this dick like a brave bitch," he growled, lifting my legs over his broad shoulders.

His thrusts were forceful and uneven. Each time he shoved himself inside of me, I wanted to die. It was so painful. He was buried deep inside my body to the hilt. It felt like his penis was in my chest. My inner walls had collapsed just to accommodate him. His body weight labored my breathing. I barely weighed a hundred and twenty-one pounds. He was crushing me.

"I'm slaying this pussy! Take this dick. Take it! Take it damn it!"

I was taking it all right because I wasn't ready to spend money on a house or apartment right now. So I had to do whatever was necessary for me to maintain my princess lifestyle until Trapper surrendered the fight and paid me the money I had asked him for. I couldn't wait for my offshore accounts to transfer to the States either. After that, I would be set.

I had never been so happy to feel a man ejaculating inside of me. Jihad had finally gotten his rocks off, and I was relieved. He rolled off of me and landed on his back. Almost immediately, he fell asleep, snoring like a grizzly bear. While he slept, my mind floated back to Trapper. He was probably at Diamond Estate making love to Radiance like *she* was his wife. And here I was in agony after being fucked savagely in exchange for money and a place to lay my head like I was some common whore from a truck stop.

I made a mental memo to call Whitley in the morning to tell her to put some pressure on Trapper and his legal duo. I was willing to settle for a smaller amount of money if I had to. I simply wasn't going to set Eli free to continue his life with Radiance without compensation. If he wanted out of the marriage, he would have to pay for it. Of course, he didn't really owe me the money because I was the first to commit adultery. But he nor Marlon or anyone else could prove it beyond a shadow of doubt because I had been extremely cautious. Since leaving Trapper, I'd slept with a Greek oil tycoon, Saudi royalty, a Spanish ambassador, a Brazilian soccer player, and a French movie maker, just to name a few. I had been no saint. I had simply been careful not to go public with any of my lovers. Sure, I had been spotted on all seven continents, but never in the company of a man to my knowledge. I was much too smart for recklessness.

Trapper's boldness with that Radiance tramp had come as a total shock to me, though. I still had a hard time accepting the fact that he had actually moved on. During my most recent visit to Switzerland, I was surprised when McKenzie told me that she had spoken to Trapper. She was happy to report that he was in love with another woman and was sharing Diamond Estate with her. That revelation got me back to Atlanta as fast as I could get here. I had rushed home to win my husband back, but all I got was a disappointing surprise. Trapper was truly in love. I could see it in his eyes. Even when I lied and told him that I was willing to give him a child, he still rejected me. His heart belonged to Radiance. She would be the one to bear Trapper's children, and nothing sickened me more.

In my own weird way, I still loved my husband, but I loathed him at the same time for turning his back on me and our marriage. I know it sounds selfish and audacious of me. I may even appear to be crazy, but he was supposed to have waited for me to clear my head and return home. Then we could've ended our marriage amicably if that was what he wanted. But he had brought Radiance into the equation, and now I wanted the payout.

Chapter Twenty-seven

Eli

"Is Mommy coming downstairs for breakfast?"

"No, she's not, little buddy. Sergio is going to take a tray of food upstairs to our room. She's going to eat there. Go ahead and finish your bacon and eggs. Sergio will drive you to summer camp as soon as you're done."

"Okay."

I poured myself another cup of black coffee and took a sip. I didn't have an appetite even though Mama Sadie had baked a pan of her famous buttermilk biscuits. They had been my favorite since I'd started talking and walking. My stomach was upset this morning because my relationship with Radiance was on a rocky road. I was pissed that Pandora had come back to town wreaking havoc on our lives instead of doing the right thing by giving me a divorce. Even after meeting with her one on one yesterday at Fogo de Chão Brazilian Steakhouse, nothing had been resolved. The woman was unbelievable.

I had the money to give her to dissolve the marriage. I could've easily paid Pandora to dismiss her from my life for good. But I refused to give her one red cent because she didn't deserve it. She had abandoned the marriage, and she was a good-for-nothing adulteress. No matter how many times she denied it, I knew it to be true, and I was determined to prove it. I had contracted the same team of investigators that had searched for her to find evidence on her many international affairs. I needed concrete proof. Four investigators were actively working on the case from every angle twenty-four hours a day. I was sparing no expense because I wanted my life to return to normal so that Radiance, Croix, and I could be happy again.

"Are you ready to go to summer camp, champ?" Sergio asked Croix from the entrance of the kitchen.

He nodded. "I'm ready. Let me go and kiss Mommy goodbye first."

"Okay. I'll be waiting right here."

"How is Radiance? Is she eating?" I asked Sergio when Croix left the kitchen.

"She promised me she would, but I'm not sure that she will. She seems so sad, boss. I think she's worried about the situation with your wife."

"That woman is no longer my wife," I spat.

"You know what I mean. Why don't you go ahead and drop that money on Pandora and send her ass far, far away."

"I will *not*. Radiance has made me promise not to pay Pandora a single penny. And Mama Sadie would kill me with her bare hands if I did. Besides, it's not about the money, Sergio. It's the *principle*. If I give in to Pandora about money that she's not legally entitled to, she'll make more demands. I can't allow her to get the upper hand. If I do, I'll never get rid of her. She'll drag the situation out for a long time until she has everything she wants. Then she'll more than likely still deny me a divorce just for spite."

"You're right, boss.

"I'm ready, big guy!"

Sergio and I turned and looked at Croix. He was dressed for the hot Georgia weather with his backpack in tow. He ran over to me and gave me a big hug before he took Sergio's hand and left the kitchen. I immediately ran upstairs to check on Radiance. I met Mama Sadie in the middle of the staircase on my way up. She had Radiance's tray of picked-over food in her hands.

"Eli, that's a mighty depressed woman upstairs in the master suite."

"I know." I sighed and raked my fingers through my hair. "She's worried that I'll be stuck married to Pandora for the rest of my life. I need Radiance to trust me on this. I'm getting a divorce."

"She may have some concerns about the marriage, but I think something else is bothering her too. Go up there and talk to her, Eli. Make her tell you what's on her mind."

"Yes, ma'am."

I hurried up the remainder of the stairs, taking them two at the time. When I entered the bedroom, I found Radiance in bed. She didn't move when I closed the door. I walked over and sat on the edge of the bed and rubbed her cheek. "What's wrong, sweetheart?"

"I thought when I found Pandora in this house that night that my prayers had been answered. I truly believed that once she'd been served with the papers, our lives would change sixty days later."

"The divorce will happen, Radiance. The little game that Pandora is playing right now is only a bump in the road. As soon as we get a picture of her with one of her flames or a sworn affidavit from an eyewitness, it'll all be over."

"Do you promise?"

"I swear to you on my parents' graves and everything sacred. Just be patient and trust your man, babe."

She sat up and wrapped her arms around my neck. "I love you so much, Eli."

"I love you too."

"When this is over, I'm going to give you the most precious gift that any man could ever ask for."

"Wow! I'm looking forward to that. Can you give me a hint about this surprise gift?"

"Nah. You'll just have to wait and see. But I promise you won't be disappointed."

I took Radiance's face between my palms and kissed her like my life depended on it. I pulled back. "You could never disappoint me."

~♥~

"Cheers," we said in unison and extended our glasses to meet in the center of the table.

The sound of crystal touching crystal chimed. With the exception of Radiance, we all sipped champagne from our flutes. She had asked for sparkling grape juice because of an upset stomach. Marlon, Golden, Radiance, and I had ventured out to a popular Buckhead supper club for a couples' night out to take our minds off of the Pandora situation. I thought an evening of fine dining, live music, and dancing was in order. Croix was at the estate under the watchful eye of his grandmother and Sergio.

Although Radiance was still a bit anxious about the delay of the divorce, she was much happier than I'd seen her in weeks. And she was eating again—*a lot too*. I figured food was her comforter while we awaited a breakthrough in the Pandora fiasco. Sex was too. She was going through a wild and horny stage that was taking its toll on an old man's body. Don't get me wrong. I could hang with her, and I *was* hanging, but we hadn't taken a break in almost three weeks. I was going to have to start taking vitamins or some type of energy booster soon if Radiance's ongoing sexual appetite continued.

"Dance with me, baby," she said, placing her hand on my thigh close to my crotch.

I kissed her cheek and stood up, pulling her to her feet as well. I led her out on the dance floor and twirled her around before we started moving our bodies to the music. Her laughter was contagious. I loved to see her happy. It was my life's goal to keep her content with a smile on her face. I also wanted to put a ring on her finger, and I was going to as soon as I got rid of Pandora's conniving ass. I was paying the investigation team time and a half to work longer hours and cover more ground. I needed evidence on just one of my ex's affairs like *yesterday*. If Marlon, Thomas, and I had to hop on my jet and track down every man that she'd come in contact with, we would. But I was trying to exercise patience, and leave the investigation to the professionals.

I wrapped my arms around Radiance's waist and pulled the back of her body against my front. She pressed her ass into my crotch and wiggled to the beat of the music. I got a stiff one on the spot like I'd done that night at the Pleasure Palace while she was giving me a lap dance. I'd been hooked on her ever since then. And judging by the way Radiance was backing into me, I still had the magic touch. I was sure we were going to tear each other apart the second we stepped inside our bedroom. Tonight was going to be just as passionate as all the other nights during my babe's horny season.

Marlon and Golden joined us on the dance floor when the band eased into Barry White's "Can't Get Enough of Your Love." We laughed and competed, showing off different dance moves. We even switched partners. We were having a blast. My problem with Pandora faded into the background as I watched Radiance rotate her hips and circle around a stiff and uncoordinated Marlon. Golden and I were in sync with a basic two-step and finger-snapping sequence. Tonight was a good night.

~♥~

"Mr. Jamieson, there's a Sheriff Eugene Talton from Dade County in Miami on the line."

I paused, wondering why a law enforcement officer from Miami would be contacting me. "Put the call through, Violet." I picked up the phone as soon as it rang. "This is Eli Jamieson."

"Good afternoon, sir. I'm Eugene Talton, sheriff of Dade County in Miami. I hope I didn't catch you at a bad time."

"You didn't. What can I do for you?"

"I called to update you on the investigation of the abduction of Croix Young by his father, Satchel Young, which took place a couple of months ago."

"I'm listening."

"The suspect hasn't been found, sir. It seems like Mr. Young dropped off of the face of the earth. We've been in constant contact with the authorities up there in Georgia. They don't have a lead on him either."

"He probably made it to St. Croix."

"No, he didn't. Mr. Young never made it to the island. The authorities over there were waiting to apprehend him, but he never showed up. He's a wanted man in St. Croix. The moment his foot hits the sand there, he'll be arrested."

"Maybe his aunt and sister are helping him stay under the radar."

"That's highly unlikely, sir. Mrs. Blyden has been very cooperative with the department. Her house is being watched around the clock too at her request. The poor woman is scared to death that her nephew will come back and try to start some trouble. She wants nothing to do with him. His sister feels the same way according to investigators in Atlanta. She even promised to turn Mr. Young in if he comes anywhere near her."

"So that hoodlum is just out there somewhere lurking around."

"Unfortunately, you're right. Mr. Young is at large, sir. But don't worry. If he's anywhere in the Sunshine State, we're going to catch him. And when we do, the judge is going to throw the book at him."

"I sure hope so. He deserves to rot in jail for what he did."

I ended the call with the sheriff and leaned back in my chair. I decided to beef up security at Diamond Estate just in case Satchel was bold enough to try to pay Radiance and Croix an unexpected visit. I was pretty sure that he didn't know much about me, especially not where I lived. Radiance had been careful to keep my identity and other pertinent details about me to a minimum when dealing with Satchel. Croix couldn't have revealed much because he was too young to provide very many details. And he had only been in his father's presence once without his mother. That was the night he was kidnapped. I seriously doubted that I had been the topic of discussion while father and son were on the run.

I buzzed Violet. "Get Sergio in here please."

"He's on his way, sir."

Seconds later, my longtime assistant entered my private office and closed the door. "What's up, boss?"

"I need a few extra men at the estate. The authorities haven't found Croix's father yet. I want Radiance and her son monitored closely until they catch that lunatic, but they aren't to know anything about this."

Germaine Solomon

"I'm on it, boss. Some extra men will be hired and assigned right away." He paused and walked closer to my desk. "I'll cover Ms. Alexander and Croix personally if you don't mind. I'm crazy about that kid."

I smiled because I felt Sergio's sincerity. He and Croix were very close. If it ever came down to it, the giant would slay Satchel in a heartbeat in order to protect the boy. "Of course you can be in charge of Radiance and Croix. They're comfortable around you. "

It was a rare and unexpected occurrence, but Sergio actually smiled.

Chapter Twenty-eight

Radiance

"You've picked up weight, baby. And look at your hips. They're spreading wider every day. It's time for you to tell Eli you're pregnant before he figures it out."

"One of the investigators is in Canada right now. A former resort manager is supposed to help him get his hands on some video footage of Pandora and a Toronto investment banker entering and leaving a suite together over a period of three days. That video will be the evidence Eli needs to prove that his ex cheated on him first."

"And what does any of that have to do with you telling Eli that you're pregnant with his child?"

"Mama, once Eli is on a sure path to divorcing Pandora, it'll be the perfect time to tell him I'm carrying his baby. Don't you understand? He doesn't need to worry about me and my pregnancy while he's trying to untangle himself from Pandora. His focus needs to be on running his company and finding evidence for his divorce."

"I don't like how you're handling this situation, baby, but I'll go along with it *for now*. I just think that it's unfair for Eli to miss out on doctor's appointments and sonograms all because you're waiting to tell him the most important news of his life."

"I'm doing what's best for Eli, Mama. I know I am. Plus he's going to get his hands on some evidence soon. And once he does, I'll tell him about the baby. Trust me."

"I *do* trust you, but I don't think you're doing the right thing."

"Anyway, I just arrived on campus for class. I'll call you later."

Mama worried too much about nothing. Eli was busy running his company and trying to end his marriage. He didn't have time to hold my hand through a pregnancy that was going smoothly. That's what *she* was there for. Mama had been to both of my doctor's appointments with me and seen my first two sonograms. The baby and I were healthy, so why was she making a fuss? I was going to tell Eli I was pregnant soon. I could feel it down in my bones that the investigators would find some hardcore evidence on Pandora's cheating ass any day now.

~♥~

"Hello?"

"Ray, it's me, Janelda. I got my number changed because Satch keeps calling me. Have you heard from him?"

"No, I haven't, and I don't want to hear from him. I was hoping that his crazy ass had died and gone to hell."

"Nah. He's alive. I just don't know where he is."

"He's not in *jail*?" I got up from the recliner quickly and walked out of the great room. I didn't want Croix to hear my conversation with Janelda about his father.

"Nah, Satch ain't in jail because the cops in Florida never found him, Ray. I assumed you and your man knew he was still on the run. I figured the sheriff down in Miami had reached out to y'all like he did to Auntie Lois and me. That's crazy."

"It is," I said, wondering why Janelda knew more about the status of Croix's abduction case than I did. Maybe she had been a part of it after all.

"Ray, are you still there?"

"Um . . . yeah . . . yeah . . . I'm still here. How was your trip to St. Croix?"

"It was fine, but we ended up leaving much later that evening because of my dumb-ass brother. Auntie and I had to go downtown to be questioned by detectives while her boyfriend came over to fix her doors and make other repairs to the house."

"How is your father?"

"Pops is recovering slowly, but his prognosis is good. He and Mama asked about you and Croix. I showed them pictures of him on my phone. I hope they'll get to see him again someday."

"Maybe. Anyway, thanks for calling, Janelda. Call again tomorrow, and I'll let you speak with Croix."

"That's a plan. Thanks, Ray."

"It's not a problem. We'll talk tomorrow. Goodbye."

"Yo, Ray, wait. I'm sorry about what Satch did to you and Croix. It was foul as hell. I just want you to know that although you and I've had our differences in the past, I had nothing to do with my brother's bullshit. Bambi didn't either. Neither one of us would ever do anything to hurt Croix."

"It's good to know that."

"Until tomorrow . . ."

"Yeah."

I ended the call with my mind racing. Satchel was still at large, and Eli and I had no clue until now. I wondered if he was stupid enough to come after Croix again. I had never given Satchel any hints about where we lived, but criminals were resourceful. They had a knack for uncovering any information necessary to help them commit crimes. Eli needed to know that Satchel hadn't been caught yet. I headed to his home office where he was in a meeting with Sergio and some other men.

As I rounded the corner, I heard his voice. I didn't want to interrupt the meeting, but I felt what I had to tell him was worth it. I tiptoed toward the partially ajar door and stood hidden right outside it.

"I spoke with Sheriff Talton again yesterday," Eli told Sergio and the other men. "We've spoken every day since his initial call."

"Is there anything new, boss?" Sergio asked.

"No. They still haven't found that thug. They did pick up a lead, though. A man fitting Satchel's description was spotted leaving a motel in the Fort Lauderdale area a few days ago. He was in a rental car that was later found on the side of the highway near Pompano Beach."

I felt like bursting into the office and giving Eli a piece of my mind. He already knew that Satchel was still on the run, and it seemed like he'd known for a while. Why in the world hadn't he told me? I was livid, but I calmed myself down so I could hear more of the conversation.

"What are the chances that he'll try to make his way back to Georgia, sir?" an unfamiliar voice asked.

Eli released a loud sigh. "I don't know, Morris. That's why I want continued around-the-clock security on the entire estate. Sergio, you and Ambrose have been doing a great job covering Radiance and Croix. Keep it up."

"Yes, sir."

"We will."

I couldn't listen to another word. I spun on my bare feet and made my way back to my son.

If I hadn't already agreed to attend the business dinner with Eli for one of his associates, I would've been at home sitting up in bed eating my favorite nighttime snack: a pint of Häagen-Dazs black cherry amaretto gelato. But I was a woman of my word, so I'd squeezed my expanding ass, tits, and thighs into a royal blue cocktail dress and left the house with an attitude. I was still very angry with Eli for not telling me that Satchel was still on the loose. I hadn't confronted him about it because I didn't want him to know that I'd been eavesdropping on him and his associates. *Technically,* I wasn't spying on him, but I'd never be able to convince him to believe that.

Anyway, it wasn't important how I had stumbled on the information. The main point was Eli should've told me that Satchel hadn't been caught by the authorities yet. I had every right to know something so significant that could possibly have an impact on Croix's well being and mine. I almost went into cardiac arrest when Janelda told me that fool was still on the run. Paranoia set in immediately. I was constantly looking over my shoulder at all times. That ain't no way for somebody to live. And now that Croix was back in school, I was even more on edge. Thank God for Sergio and my other shadow, Ambrose. I had to give it to the fellas. They were watching my baby boy and me like a pair of hawks. And they were real discreet about it too.

I was grateful that Eli cared enough about Croix and me to protect us, but I was disappointed that hadn't told me that Satchel was never arrested. I guess I couldn't be too upset with him because he wasn't the only one keeping secrets. I still hadn't told him that he was going to be a father, but I had a good reason for holding back. I wondered what his excuse was for keeping me in the dark about my fugitive ex.

"Champagne?" a passing waiter offered.

"No, thank you," I whispered, shaking my head.

Eli removed a flute from the tray. "Thanks," he said before he lifted the bubbly to his lips and took a long swig. "Are you enjoying yourself, babe?"

"No, but the food was delicious."

"I noticed how much you liked the veal shanks and seafood kabobs. How many of those raspberry tarts did you eat?"

"I only ate two."

Eli took another sip of champagne and laughed. "Did you count the half of mine that you gobbled down?"

"No. What's the big deal anyway? You weren't eating it. You know how I hate to waste food."

"Oh, I was eating it, sweetheart. You were just eating it faster."

I rolled my eyes to the ceiling. "I'm going to the little girls' room. I'll be ready to go home when I come back. There's a trick I want to turn on you tonight."

"Are you serious? I think you're trying to kill me, sweetheart. After last night and this morning, I don't know if I have the energy to do anything tonight, babe."

"Don't worry about it, old man. Radiance will do all the work." I winked and walked off toward the restrooms.

Chapter Twenty-nine

Radiance

I smiled and rolled over onto my left side while flashes of my early morning sexcapade with Eli drifted through my mind. I seriously needed to consider joining the rodeo, because I rode that man like a pro for twenty minutes before he asked me to let him hit it from the back. And then I backed that thang up on him so good that he promised to buy me a brand new car and a whole bunch of other expensive shit that I didn't even need. We fell asleep afterwards even though Eli had an eight o'clock business breakfast on his calendar. He almost missed it because he didn't wake up from his post-sex sleep until seven-twenty-five. I felt kind of bad for my man because I had been working him over. I just couldn't get enough of him now that I was pregnant with his little one.

My cell phone rang, interrupting my flashback of the good loving Eli had put on me before dawn. I reached over on the nightstand and removed it from the charger. "Hello?"

"How's my son, Ray?"

I sat straight up in bed, and a bolt of fury struck me like lightning. "Fuck you, Satchel! You don't give a damn about Croix, because if you did, you never would've taken him and run!"

"Look, Ray, I'm sorry. I don't know what the hell I was thinking, okay? I fucked up."

"Hell yeah, you did! My baby was traumatized by what you did. He never wants to see you again."

"Croix is my son, and I love him. I never meant to hurt him, Ray. You gotta believe that. I don't want him to hate me or be afraid of me."

"It's too late for your wishes now. Croix wants nothing else to do with you, Satchel. You won't ever see him again. I swear to God you won't. When the police catch your ass, you're going down for a while. By the time you see the light of day again, Eli would've adopted Croix, and you'll be long forgotten."

"Fuck that cracker! He ain't gonna adopt my boy! I'll block that shit no matter what I have to do! I'll kill that mothafucka before I let him take my son away from me! You're a cold-ass bitch, Ray! How're you just gonna erase me from Croix's life for some white dude?"

"*You* did it, Satchel, you evil piece of shit! Grow up and stop blaming other people for your mistakes. I went behind my man's back and ignored my mama so you could build a relationship with your son. And how did you repay me? You snatched him and ran when I was helpless."

"I don't consider being *pregnant* helpless."

I was stunned to silence for a few seconds, but I made a quick comeback. "How did you know I was pregnant?"

"I know everything about your body, girl. I was your *first*. And I've been through a pregnancy with you before. Your first child, my son, is the product of *my* seed. Eli ain't nothing but a bootleg second-hand redneck."

I laughed at Satchel's ignorance. "You may have been my first, but every day Eli gets plenty of this good stuff you wish you could have. And he takes care of your son like a real man is supposed to. So it doesn't matter who had me first because Eli is the one and only man who has me *now*. I can't wait until the police find your punk ass and lock you up."

"They gotta find me first, and so far, I've outsmarted them just like I did them fools who busted up my auntie's house."

"You can't hide forever. They'll catch you eventually, and I'll be the first person to ask the judge to stack the maximum time possible on you for what you did to my baby."

"I ain't worried about that shit. The only thing I care about is *Croix*. No matter what happens, he's my son, and ain't nobody gonna take him from me. I'll see him again one day. I guarantee it."

The call ended on that note. I felt like Satchel's last statement was meant to be a threat. I couldn't take any chances with my son. Eli had to be told about the phone call. There was no way around it. The situation was much too serious. In fact, it was so serious that Eli was going to have to come clean with me now. He had no other choice but to tell me that he'd known all along that Satchel was at large.

How could a day that had started off so magical have turned gloomy that fast?

~♥~

The detective offered me his card. "Call me immediately if Mr. Young contacts you again, Ms. Alexander."

"I will," I said, reaching for the card, but Eli intercepted it.

"If that punk contacts her again, she'll tell me, and *I'll* call you, Detective Washington."

The young detective looked at his female partner before he faced Eli and addressed him. "Of course, sir."

"Sergio, please walk the detectives to the door."

"Yes, sir, boss." He left Eli's home office with the two detectives following him.

Eli sat down next to me on the black leather loveseat. "I'm sorry. I should've told you Satchel was still on the run. I didn't want you to worry, though. You and Croix are safe at all times. I made sure of that the moment I found out Satchel hadn't been taken into custody yet. But again, I'm sorry. You had a right to know. Will you forgive me, babe?"

"You're forgiven, Eli."

"Good. How are you now? Are you okay?"

"I've had better days."

"I know, sweetheart. I know." He kissed my cheek. "How did Janelda react when you told her Satchel had contacted you?"

"She was pretty pissed. Her main concern is Croix. She's afraid that Satchel might try to snatch him again. I assured her that wasn't going to happen. Then she apologized to me a thousand times for Satchel's crap."

"There was no need for her to apologize. She's not her brother's keeper."

"Well, she *used* to be. That's probably why he's so screwed up. Once upon a time, she thought he could do no wrong. She would give him the shirt off her back. But today is a new day. Janelda is done with Satchel."

"Good for her. Hopefully, your mobile service provider will be able to help the police trace the call. By now Satchel could be halfway around the world."

"That's true."

"Don't worry, babe," Eli said, squeezing my thigh gently. "The police will find him sooner or later when he least expects. No matter what, you and Croix will be protected at all times. I promise."

"I trust you, Eli. And I love the way you love me, but we've got a lot going on in this relationship. Between Pandora and Satchel, I feel like I'm on a really bad roller coaster ride and I can't get off."

"Don't worry about my ex or yours. I'm not going to let either one of them tear us apart. The investigators are working around the clock to find proof of Pandora's infidelity, and I believe the police are going to catch up with Satchel soon enough. Until then, I'm going to love you and Croix endlessly and protect you at any cost. I'm your man, babe. I've got you."

"I know."

"Damn right, you do."

"Good morning, Mama Sadie. How are you?"

"I'm fine, sugar. How are you?"

"I feel great. What are you doing here on a Saturday? As pretty as it is outside today, you should be at home tending to your vegetable garden."

"I planted some squash, lima beans, and a few rows of collards last week. I'm expecting a mighty fine harvest in the spring."

I poured myself a tall glass of orange juice and filled my plate with cheese grits and bacon. When I turned around, Mama Sadie was smiling at me. I smiled back, but I was a little edgy. There was a knowing look in her eyes.

"Your secret is safe with me, chile. Don't you start to fret now. Mama Sadie minds her own business."

I walked to the table and placed my juice and plate of food down. "What are you talking about, Mama Sadie?" I asked, knowing damn well what the old woman was referring to.

"I'm not going to say it out loud. Just know that you can't hide some things from an old bird like me no matter how hard you try." She patted my shoulder tenderly. "I'm happy for y'all. Thank you so much, baby."

"What are you thanking me for?"

"Thank you for the gift you're about to give Eli. I'm sure he's about to burst wide open with pride and joy. I'm going to act surprised when he finally decides to tell me, so don't you worry none. My lips are locked tight."

Mama Sadie knew I was pregnant, and apparently, she thought Eli and I were keeping it a secret from her as a surprise to be revealed at a later date. I needed to think and think quickly. I didn't want to make a direct confession, but I sure as hell couldn't lie to the old woman about something that she already knew to be true. It wouldn't be right.

I closed my eyes and took a deep breath. "It wasn't planned, Mama Sadie."

"I figured it wasn't. That's how come I know it was meant to be. It's a blessing from God. Eli has always dreamed of becoming a father. He loves children. I guess you can tell that by the way he treats Croix. How did he react when you first told him you were pregnant?"

Oh shit! She just had to go there, didn't she? I swallowed hard, and when I did, the truth went down my throat with a big forkful of cheese grits. "He cried."

"I bet he did. When should I expect the little angel?"

"I have another five months to go, so around February the sixteenth, we'll all be knee deep in stinky diapers, formula, and baby powder."

"I can't wait."

"Mama Sadie?" I said softly because I was choking on guilt. "Can you keep the news about the baby to yourself, please? Eli and I want to make a big announcement to everyone at the right time. With all of the foolishness going on with Pandora and Croix's father, we decided to wait for a little while. You understand, right?"

"I understand, baby. I won't say a word."

Chapter Thirty

Pandora and Eli

"Okay, Pandora, you have exactly ten minutes to say whatever is on your mind. I'm a very busy man. I don't have time to leave my office and meet you in the middle of the day over any bullshit." Trapper sat down in the chair across from me with a deep frown on his face.

"My, my, my, aren't we testy today? What's gotten your boxer briefs in a bunch?" I leaned across the table and batted my eyes suggestively. "You do still wear those sexy cotton underpants, don't you?"

"Why don't you call Radiance and ask her? She can give you a very explicit description of what goes on down below."

I felt like throwing my glass of Armand De Brignac Brut Gold in his face, but I couldn't afford to. I was in financial distress at the moment due to carelessness. That's why I had called this impromptu meeting with my hubby. I needed some cash. My fingers were crossed, hoping that he was ready and willing to make a deal with me.

"I don't need to call your feisty chocolate Barbie doll to ask her anything about you. I know you better than anyone on earth. I'm your *wife*, darling. I know what you like. No one can make you feel the way Pandora can."

"You're right about that. No one else in the world is a bigger pain in my ass than *you*. What the hell do you want, Pandora? I have a company to run."

"I'm ready to get this nasty divorce over with."

"We didn't have to meet for you to tell me that. Your attorney has the papers. The only thing missing is your signature. Sign them, and in sixty days our three-year marriage will be behind us."

"We've been married five and a half years, Trapper," I corrected and took a sip of champagne.

"The last two and a half years don't count. We were separated, thanks to you."

"Are you still bitter about me leaving you to take a break, sweetheart?"

"Not at all." Eli shook his head, causing his long hair to fan over his broad shoulders.

I became instantly aroused. I would always be sexually enslaved to his good looks and raw masculinity. I would commit mass murder for just one more romp in the sack with him. I cleared my throat and dismissed my lustful thoughts. I needed to stay focused in order to present my appeal.

"I beg to differ, Trapper. I sense that you're still angry that I left. But I was suffocating in the marriage. You were putting an immeasurable amount of pressure on me to get pregnant. Life was good for us until you started whining about a baby. Why couldn't you have been satisfied with McKenzie and me?"

"I was content, Pandora, but I wanted a child of my own. Was that too much to ask my wife for? If I were to ask Radiance tonight to allow me to impregnate her with my child, she wouldn't hesitate to do it."

"Of course she wouldn't. Those people are totally obsessed with sex. It's like a hobby for them. And they breed babies by the pack like rabbits," I spat, wrinkling my nose."

"Watch your mouth, Pandora. I won't tolerate those kinds of remarks. I was raised by a sweet and beautiful black woman, and I'm in love with one now. You can't compare to either one of them." He pinned me to my chair with his dark mesmerizing eyes. "For the last time, why am I here?"

"Like I said, I think it's time to wrap this divorce up. I'll sign the papers today if you'll give me fifteen million dollars, which is ten million short of the amount I'm entitled to according to the compensation clause in our prenuptial agreement."

Trapper smiled, but it wasn't a pleasant smile. It was menacing, distant, and cold as ice. It caused me to shiver when his eyes slashed through me, piercing my soul like he hated my guts. My actions had turned him into a man I no longer recognized, but I didn't care at the moment. I needed money until I recovered from a string of bad investments and a dilemma that had recently been brought to my attention. Apparently, while I was off on my international adventure, my accountant helped himself to a hefty chunk of my money and failed to pay my taxes for two years. And to top it all off, every single cent of the money that had been transferred from my offshore accounts was now frozen while Uncle Sam went over all of my banking and investment records with a magnifying glass in a quest to collect my unpaid taxes. Trapper was my last hope. If he refused to settle with me on the fifteen million dollars, I didn't know how I would survive.

"So what do say you, my darling husband? Do we have a deal?"

"To get rid of you, I'm going to consider your proposal, Pandora. It'll be worth every damn dime to be free from our miserable marriage so I can take my relationship with Radiance to the next level. Give me a few days to discuss it with her. And naturally, I'll have to run it past Marlon, Thomas, and Mama Sadie. I'll get back with you as quickly as I can." Trapper stood and walked away.

I watched his smooth and measured gait until he was out of sight. He was the absolute perfect male specimen. God must've cracked the mold after He created him because there wasn't a man in the universe who could match his masculine beauty. And I, of all women, would definitely know because I had fucked men all over the world from the Equator to Antarctica and back again. I never ran across a man who was more gorgeous than Trapper. And he still reigned as the undisputed heavyweight champion of the world in the bedroom hands down. Radiance Alexander was one lucky bitch. She was now living the life that I had so foolishly given up all because I didn't want to ruin my teeny tiny body to bare my husband a little brat.

There was no use in me revisiting the past. I had made a terrible mistake that I would have to live with for the remainder of my existence. My season with Trapper had long since passed. Money was my main concern now. I needed my estranged husband to deliver on the settlement I'd proposed. If he would agree on the fifteen million, I might be able to push my luck and convince him to throw in one of his condos in Buckhead or a penthouse apartment at the top of the Diamond Tower on Peachtree as a bonus. Regardless, I would not leave our marriage as a broke woman.

"How did it go with Pandora, baby?"
"It didn't go *yet*."
"Huh?"
I reached a hand out to Radiance as she walked further into the great room. She hurried over and took the seat next to me on the couch. I patted my thighs when she kicked out of her shoes. She knew what the gesture

meant. I was about to massage her feet after she'd
walked around campus all day long. She slanted her body
sideways and placed her feet on my lap.

"Pandora *claims* that she's ready to sign the divorce
papers."

"Cool. When?"

"Babe, you know nothing is that simple with my ex-wife.
She's willing to set me free for fifteen million dollars. She
considers the decreased amount of money a favor to me.
I must admit that I'm actually considering paying her off
although Marlon and Thomas are completely against it.
What do you think?"

"I think this is a decision you'll have to make on your
own, Eli. Is your freedom from Pandora worth the
money? If so, give it to her. But if you want to fight her for
what's rightfully yours based on principle, don't give that
skinny skank one nickel."

"How did you get to be so wise?"

"I hang around wise people, sir. Every night I share a
bed with a super smart and sexy businessman with lots
of money. He used to be my professor." She winked and
leaned over to plant a sweet, juicy kiss on my lips. Then
she stood up. "It's Croix's bath time."

"I'll watch the news while you get him settled. I'll be up
by the time you finish."

"When you come upstairs, bring some extra energy
with you."

The sway of Radiance's hips was as sexy as sin even
with the few extra inches that she'd put on over the past
few months. All of the women I knew were sensitive
about their bodies. That's why I hadn't mentioned the
extra junk in Radiance's trunk or the increase in her
breast size. She still looked incredible despite the weight
gain. The situation with Pandora was affecting her more
than she cared to share with me. And I imagined the

possibility of having her child snatched again by his fugitive father didn't make life any easier for her either. Maybe tomorrow I would suggest that we start taking daily walks in the evening around the estate. Then she could burn some of the extra calories she'd been taking in recently.

~♥~

"Jihad, darling, who are all of these people?" I smiled at the eclectic group of strangers. At least twelve men and women were sitting casually on all four white leather sofas in the living room, sipping cocktails, and eating plates filled with heavy hors d'oeuvres. Rap music with X-rated lyrics was blasting from the state-of-the-art sound system.

"Oh, these are a few of my peeps I invited over for a li'l get together to celebrate the new contract my boy, Psycho, just signed with 9 Millimeter Records." He smacked me on my ass. "Go on over there and grab some food and a drink. Bring me a beer when you come back."

I walked toward the spread in the dining room where two uniformed servers were manning carving stations. One was slicing a massive prime cut of roast beef. The smell of greasy ham lingered in the air as the other guy sliced away. My appetite vanished instantly at the disgusting sight of the pork. So I walked over to the bartender in the corner of the room to get Jihad a beer.

"I'd like a Corona please."

"Yes, ma'am." The gentleman removed the top from the bottle and handed it to me with a smile filled with bright gold teeth.

"Thank you."

"No problem, baby girl."

As I exited the dining area, I noticed a group of men in the kitchen smoking what smelled like marijuana. They were standing in a circle passing the neatly-rolled, nameless cigarette around. Two other guys were sitting at the dinette snorting lines of cocaine from a small mirror. I hurried in Jihad's direction and shoved the beer in his hand.

"Thank you, baby." He leaned down and covered my mouth with his. "Where's your food, girl?"

"I'm not hungry. Actually, I have a headache. I'm going to lie down."

"Okay. I'll check on you in a few."

I couldn't make it down the hall fast enough. I was mentally drained after meeting with my financial advisor and Trapper before I finally ended up at Whitley's office. My head was spinning from learning that I had almost blown through fifty million dollars in just two years. I could've shot myself in the foot for being so careless with my finances. When Trapper and I were together, he took care of McKenzie and me. I only used my money for fashion and entertainment. But when I took off like a teenage runaway, I became responsible for my own welfare as well as my daughter's for the most part, especially in between lovers. During those periods when I didn't have a rich man to bankroll me, I had to secure my housing, transportation, food, wardrobe, and entertainment. And because I have ridiculously extravagant taste, I spent millions. Now I was damn near a pauper. If the IRS seized all of my money and Trapper refused my proposal, I was going to be totally screwed.

Chapter Thirty-one

Radiance and Eli

"Mommy, what are these?"

I glanced over my shoulder for a brief moment before I returned my eyes to the road. "Put those back in my purse right now, Croix."

"I didn't get them from your purse, Mommy. They were on the floor. What do you call these kinds of pictures? They look really, really weird."

"They're pictures of the inside of the human body. It's a woman's tummy. The doctor takes those kinds of pictures with a special camera. We call them sonogram images. Now put them in Mommy's purse please."

I smiled at the thought of giving Eli a daughter. I was going to tell him after dinner tonight. Time was up. It didn't matter about what was going on with Pandora, Satchel, or Barack Obama. I was going to tell my man he was about to become a father. Besides, I was having a difficult time trying to hide my small baby bump. And I had more hips and ass than Beyoncé, Nicki Minaj, and JLo altogether. I couldn't even fit into my cheetah getup anymore.

I had gone to the doctor alone to learn the sex of the baby while Mama and Mama Sadie prepared a special meal of Balsamic braised beef short ribs, sautéed kale, sweet potato soufflé, and wild rice. They were excited that I was going to finally tell Eli about the baby, but initially, I had to endure a lecture and the threat of fifty lashes from Mama Sadie for lying to her about my secret. However, after a tearful explanation and apology, she forgave me and agreed to assist with preparing the royal feast. She even promised to bake a deep-dish mixed berry cobbler, Eli's favorite dessert, for the occasion. And God bless my mama for volunteering to take Croix home with her for the entire weekend. There was going to be a whole lot of celebration sex going on at Diamond Estate. Since my cheetah ensemble was now too small, I had stopped by my favorite lingerie boutique and bought a sheer red baby doll negligee trimmed in faux fur of the same color and a matching thong. I had to get the red faux fur slippers to top it off. Eli loved to see me in heels and lingerie, but because I was now pregnant, I had to downgrade my spikes. I couldn't take any chances. I was carrying precious cargo in my womb. So instead of four-inch stiletto heels, I opted for the two-inch wedges. Regardless, Eli would be pleased.

I parked the SUV in the garage and hopped out. I grabbed my bags from the back seat and released Croix from his booster. "Let's go inside, baby. Mommy is going to give Eli a *big* surprise tonight."

"Will it be a party?"

"Well, it'll be sort of like a party for grownups. You're going to spend the weekend with Grandma. It's just going to be Eli and me when I give him his special gift."

"I want to give him a special gift too."

"You can, baby. What would you like to give Eli?"

"I'll give him a picture! I can draw a cool one for him."

"Okay, I'll get you settled in the great room with your sketch pad and markers *after* I give you a snack."

"Okay."

"While you draw your picture for Eli, Mommy will pack your overnight bag for your weekend with Grandma. And then I'll get fresh and pretty for the grownup party. Eli is going to be so happy about his special gift."

"He's going to like my picture too. I'll put it on his desk in his office when I'm done."

"That's a good idea, baby."

~♥~

The view of Radiance from the rear was exquisite. I swear her ass should've been on exhibit at the Smithsonian Institute among its finest American treasures. She had gained at least twenty pounds since we'd been together, but the extra weight had fallen in all the right places. My eyes were glued to her defined curves, teasing my masculine senses underneath the sheer red fabric of her lingerie. And damn it! She had on heels to set it off. After dinner, she was going to be my dessert. Her nipples and clit didn't stand a chance. They would be sucked and licked unmercifully.

"I'm home," I announced, walking up behind her sexy ass and wrapping my arms around her waist. I kissed her neck as she stood at the island placing fresh fruit on a serving plate. I knew I was in trouble the moment I smelled the passion fruit and maple fragrance rising from her soft skin. Better yet, *Radiance* was in trouble.

"Dinner will be served in ten minutes, sir."

"I'm not sure if we're going to make it through the meal because of this outfit you're wearing. Why do you have to look so damn delicious?"

"Tonight is all about *you*. I bought this ensemble with you in mind. Don't you like it?"

"Hell yeah, I do, but it's making me hungry for something other than food, babe.

She squirmed out of my embrace with the plate of fruit in her hands. She walked over to the refrigerator and placed it inside. "Go and take off that suit and wash up. By the time you get back, the food will be on the table. Then we can get this party started."

"When will I get my surprise?"

"Don't be so impatient, lover. Good things come to those who wait."

"Ugh! So you're going to make me suffer?"

"Yes," she said with a wink.

I hurried upstairs to do as I'd been told. My cell phone vibrated in my pocket. Sergio, Marlon, and the rest of my staff knew that I was not to be disturbed this weekend unless it was a matter of life or death. I checked the caller ID. It was Marlon. I waited until I was inside the master suite before I answered. "This better be important, bruh."

"I believe it is. Please tell me that you haven't had the cashier's check delivered to Pandora yet."

"The bank issued it, and the courier picked it up from Violet this afternoon along with the amended documents that Thomas drew up. Pandora should receive everything first thing Monday morning."

"Shit!"

"Why? What's going on, Marlon?"

"There's a young lady in Paris, a model by the name of Taziah. She claims that she and Pandora became friends some time last year. They spent a lot of time together partying, shopping, going to sporting events, and attending fashion shows. It seems that your ex got a little too chummy with the woman's husband, a restaurateur, and ended up having an affair with him."

"You don't say?" I sat down on the bed and removed my shoes.

"I do indeed say. According to Taziah, a friend of a friend gave her a head's up that her husband was creeping around with Pandora. So wifey followed hubby to a hotel in Chantilly one evening when he was supposed to have been going to his restaurant to orientate his new evening chef. Guess who was there waiting for him on the balcony of the hotel suite?"

"My guess is Pandora."

"Bingo," Marlon said. "The model made an ugly scene, and Pandora disappeared. The affair eventually destroyed the couple's marriage. They're currently in the middle of a very nasty divorce and custody battle over their young son."

"Where did this story come from?"

"Jake, your lead investigator followed a tip all the way to the model's apartment in Versailles. He scoped her out for a few days before he approached her at a bistro after a photo shoot. She thought he was cute. They went out on a few dates before he won her trust. When she felt comfortable enough, she told him her story."

"How can we get her to sign an affidavit or give us a recorded eyewitness statement?"

"That's the reason why I called you, bruh. Taziah will only hand over proof or provide an affidavit to *you*. She wants to face Pandora's husband and tell him and *only* him her story."

"Fuck! I can't go to France anytime soon!"

"Yes, you can, Trapper. We can't blow this. The woman is ready talk to you. The arrangements have already been made. You and I will be leaving for France in three hours."

"No, Marlon, you didn't see Radiance a few minutes ago. I mean she's got on this red see-through outfit and *heels*, man! The food smells scrumptious, and so does she. That passion fruit and maple scent is my aphrodisiac, dude. And she has a surprise for me. Her ass—"

"Stop it, Trapper! Put your dick on ice and get packed. Radiance will understand. Once you get rid of Pandora, you can wax that fine ass of hers every night in peace for the rest of your life. Get your shit together and be ready when Sergio gets there."

"I'll be ready, damn it," I grumbled. "You know I hate you, right?"

"Yeah, I know. You've told me that every time I've pissed you off since you were six and I was seven."

"But I really do mean it this time."

"I'm sure you do. Anyway, I'm going to call Violet to see if she can cancel the delivery on that cashier's check."

"Fine."

~♥~

The doorbell chimed, interrupting the quietness in the house.

"I'll get it. You finish eating."

I hurried to the door with the light fabric of my black caftan flowing with each step I made. I knew it was Sergio. He had exactly one hour and forty-five minutes to get Eli to Hartsfield-Jackson International Airport. He and Marlon were flying first class on a commercial airline because there hadn't been enough time to secure a pilot for the private plane on such a short notice.

"Come on in, Sergio." I stepped aside so he could enter the house after I received my customary hug from him. "Your boss is in the dining room eating. He needs to hurry."

When I reached the dining room, I smiled when I saw Sergio helping himself to what was supposed to have been a special candlelight dinner for Eli and me. The news about the baby and the celebration would have to wait for a few days. Getting the evidence from the French model to prove that Pandora was a low-class cheater was more important right now.

"Radiance, I need to speak with you in the kitchen for a moment before I leave, sweetheart."

I followed Eli into the kitchen and was immediately pulled into his arms. The hint of red wine on his breath mixed with the spicy scent of his cologne made me miss him already. He kissed me long and deeply, causing my heart to flutter.

"Since I can't make love to you all weekend long like I had planned, can an old man at least have his surprise before he takes off?"

I wanted to tell him. God knows I really did, but the time wasn't right. "You'll have to wait until you come back home. It'll be right here waiting for you. As a matter of fact, you may even enjoy it better once you have the evidence you need to get rid of Pandora."

"Well, can I have something to hold on to as a reminder of what I'll be missing because of this unexpected trip?"

"You sure can. Croix drew you a picture. It's in an envelope on your desk. I'll get it for you." I turned to exit the kitchen, en route to his home office.

"Radiance, sweetheart?" Eli crooned in a gravelly drawl.

"Yes?"

"I'll take the picture with me, but I wanted something a little more intimate from *you*."

"You can have whatever you'd like."

It happened so fast that I didn't have time to react. With speed and expertise, Eli walked over, snatched my caftan and negligee up, and yanked my thong down to my ankles. Then he lifted my feet one by one and removed the skimpy underwear completely from my body. I stood with my mouth wide open for a few seconds after he inhaled the thong's scent and stuffed it inside his pants pocket. Then I left to get the picture Croix had drawn for him from his office.

Chapter Thirty-two

Eli

"The woman is extremely wicked," the very stunning Taziah spat in her thick French accent. "I offered her my friendship and introduced her to my colleagues, my family, and friends. And what did she offer me in return? She fucked my husband! She's an evil bitch, and I hope she rots in hell for destroying my family."

Marlon and I stared at each other briefly. The gorgeous creature sitting across the table from us was very bitter. Her emerald eyes flashed with the contempt she harbored in her heart for Pandora. I could relate very much to her feelings. I despised my ex-wife. Her selfishness and greed exceeded all limits. She used the people in her life and manipulated them like pawns, draining them emotionally. And then when she no longer had use for them, she discarded them like common waste.

"I'm sorry for what my ex-wife did to you and your family," I finally said. "There's no excuse to justify her betrayal. All I can say is Pandora is Pandora, and she lives life by her own rules."

"I sympathize with you too, Taziah," Marlon offered. "And I believe you deserve some type of retribution for your misfortune. Don't allow Pandora to get away with her deviousness. Make her pay for her sins."

"How?"

"Help me prove that Pandora was unfaithful to me during our marriage. She was still my wife *legally* at the time she carried on an affair with your husband. If you'd be willing submit an official written statement or a recorded account, verifying Pandora's infidelity with your husband while she was married to me, you'll cause her to forfeit millions of dollars. And ultimately, my marriage to her would be dissolved without a hitch."

Taziah leaned back in the chair and crossed her arms over her bosom. "What's in it for *me*?"

"I'm not sure of what you're asking," Marlon rushed to say. "What do you wish to gain for your cooperation?"

"Monsieur Jamieson is a very wealthy and successful businessman. Pandora often boasted of his abundance of money and expensive possessions." Taziah licked her lips and bathed me with her emerald eyes as if she were undressing me. "Your wife was very fascinated by your good looks, and she described you as the consummate lover. Mmm . . . Je veux vas te faire encule."

"What the hell did she just say?" I asked.

"I don't know, bruh, but it sure did sound *nasty*."

"I said I want to *fuck you*, Monsieur Jamieson. Fuck me the same way Pandora fucked Gaël. *That* is what I want."

Her shamelessness threw me off my game. I literally flinched, but I quickly pulled it together because I needed resolution. "I must admit that I'm very flattered by your offer, Ms. Taziah, but um, I'm going to have to decline. I'm good in the *fucking* department. Thank you."

"What else can Mr. Jamieson do to persuade you to help him? This would be a golden opportunity to avenge yourself where Pandora is concerned. Don't let it slip through your fingers, Taziah. Tell us how we can convince you to provide us with the evidence we need."

"I will give Monsieur Jamieson a picture of my husband in a very compromising position with Pandora, credit card receipts from one of their many luxurious getaways, and an official written statement for ten million US dollars."

"Done."

"Hold up, Trapper," Marlon said, placing his hand firmly on my shoulder. "You can't do that. It's *illegal*. It's against the law to pay a witness for their testimony or for any evidence he or she may provide that'll influence the outcome of your case. I'm sorry I can't let you do that, bruh."

"Damn it! Why not? I'd rather pay her for the truth than to give Pandora a dead fly for my freedom. I'm going to give this woman the money, and that's final."

Marlon plastered a smile on his face and looked at Taziah head-on. "Will you excuse us for a moment? I need to speak with my client in private. Order another drink on him and an appetizer or two. We'll be right back." He stood and yanked me to my feet by my arm and led me away.

~♥~

"Give me that!" Marlon snapped and snatched the crystal glass from my hand. A few drops of brandy sprinkled my lap. "You've had enough to drink, bruh. I don't want you acting like a fool on the plane. You never could hold your liquor."

"We . . . came . . . all . . . the way . . . here . . . for . . . *nothing*," I slurred loudly. But I didn't give a damn.

I was inebriated and depressed. Other travelers in the VIP lounge at Paris Charles de Gaulle Airport stared at me in disgust. Marlon shifted in his seat. I think he was embarrassed.

He leaned in and whispered, "I'm sorry, but as your attorney, I couldn't allow you to pay Taziah to be a witness. That's considered bribery. Shit like that has the tendency to circle back around and bite you in the ass. That's why I had to put my foot down. Hey, but I would've let you fuck her. Radiance wouldn't have ever known." He laughed.

I didn't want to touch Taziah. The only woman I had eyes for was Radiance. I felt like crying when I thought about how sexy she'd looked before I left her home alone to chase down evidence for my divorce. I reached into my pocket and pulled out her thong and inhaled it. Her feminine scent intensified my already intoxicated state. Damn, I loved that woman! She was my heart. Neither Taziah nor Pandora or any other woman alive could compare to my Radiance. I inhaled her panties again.

"Man, put those away, you *freak*." Marlon snatched the thong from me and stuffed it back inside my pocket.

"I-I . . . want . . . to go . . . home . . . to . . . Radiance."

"You're going. Our flight is scheduled to leave in thirty minutes."

My phone vibrated in my pocket, and I struggled to remove it. I was a drunken mess. Marlon finally had to reach inside my pocket and get it for me. He pressed the power button and placed the phone to my ear.

"Hell-ooo?"

"Eli? Is that you? It's McKenzie. Did I call you at a bad time?"

Oh . . . hell-ooo . . . McKenzie . . . darrr-ling . . . "

Marlon quickly removed the phone from my ear.

The sound and impact of the plane's landing gear touching down on the tarmac jolted me from my sleep. I sat up and looked out the window. It was dark outside, but it didn't look like we were in Atlanta. The building and the layout of the airport's taxiway were unfamiliar.

I turned to Marlon who was flipping through a brown leather binder. "Where the hell are we?"

"I guess you don't remember the phone call from McKenzie, huh?"

I shook my head and instantly regretted it. I had a major headache and the cotton mouth. "What did McKenzie want?"

"Let's get off the plane. I'll fill you in once we get in the car. Grab your bag from the overhead compartment."

"Okay. Hey, you didn't answer my question. Where are we?"

"We're in Zurich, Trapper."

"Why the fuck are we in *Switzerland*?"

"McKenzie has some very important information she wants to give you. Don't ask me what it is because she didn't tell me. It's for *your* ears."

I followed Marlon down the plane's narrow aisle and into the airport with my overnight bag in tow. I felt like certified shit. My head was as heavy as lead on my shoulders, and it was throbbing. "I need to call Radiance to tell her where I am."

"I've already spoken to her. She knows everything, and so does Mama. I even took a picture of you sleeping in the airport in Paris with your mouth wide open and sent it to them." Marlon grinned and shook his head. "You never could hold your liquor, dude."

We quickly retrieved our luggage from baggage claim and stepped outside where we were greeted by chilly weather. In the distance, I could faintly see the peaks of the Üetliberg Mountains offering us their beauty. I was sluggish and slightly dizzy, but I forced myself to keep moving. I followed Marlon to a black limo where a stocky driver stood outside the back passenger's side door holding a sign with our last names scribbled on it.

"I'm Marlon Lawson, and this is my brother, Eli Jamieson."

"Welcome to Zurich, gentlemen." He opened the door and made sure we were seated comfortably before he closed it.

As the limo left the airport, I looked at Marlon. "What's going on, man?"

"McKenzie reached out to you after speaking with Pandora. She was upset when she found out that you and her mother were still married in light of what you'd told her about your relationship with Radiance. Apparently, Pandora wasn't very forthcoming with the child, so—"

"She called me to get the truth."

"Exactly."

I scratched my chin. "What did you tell her, Marlon? She's such a sweet girl. I hope you didn't hurt her feelings. No matter how terrible of a mother Pandora is, McKenzie adores her."

"I know. That's why I chose my words carefully. But by the end our conversation, she clearly understood that her mother was holding up the divorce, trying to be greedy. That's why the child begged for us to come here. She was in tears, Trapper. I couldn't tell her no, so here we are."

"When and where will we meet with McKenzie?"

"We'll be joining her for breakfast in a private dining area on her school's campus at eight o'clock in the morning."

Chapter Thirty-three

Eli and McKenzie

When Marlon woke me up the next morning, he was already fully dressed in a sharp brown suit with bronze and rust accessories. After he snatched the covers off of me, he sat down behind the desk in the hotel suite and took out his iPad. I had no idea what he was doing, but he seemed very busy.

"What time is it?"

"It's time for you to get your ass up and shower so we can make it to McKenzie's school on time. I believe today is your lucky day, bruh. I feel victory on the horizon. Hell, I feel like you're about to strike gold."

I shook my head and padded to the bathroom. As the warm spray of water pounded my weary body, a million thoughts came to mind. The first one was Radiance. I was too loopy to speak with her more than a few minutes after we checked in the hotel. Plus she sounded sleepy. I was grateful that Sergio had decided to spend the night at the house with her while I was away. She said they had watched a couple of action flicks and snacked on popcorn to pass time.

My thoughts drifted to McKenzie when I stepped out of the shower to dry off. I wondered what she had to say to me that was too important to discuss over the phone. What was the sense of urgency? It was weird. I had never known her to be an impulsive or demanding child. I couldn't wrap my mind around it. But I totally understood why Marlon had made the decision to come to Zurich. He told me that changing our travel arrangements at the last minute wasn't a hassle at all. Actually, we could've hopped on a train in Paris and arrived in Zurich six and a half hours later. But since we were already at the airport when McKenzie called, it only made sense to fly.

I hurried to the bedroom draped in a towel. Marlon had placed my charcoal gray suit on the bed with a crisp white dress shirt and a red paisley print tie. I smiled at his helpful gesture. We had been looking out for each other since we were young boys. I guess old habits were hard to break.

"I'm going downstairs to grab a cup of coffee from one of the restaurants. I'll be in the lobby waiting for you when you finish getting dressed."

"Cool. I'll be down in twenty minutes. I want to check in with Radiance."

"So your father's coming for a visit today? How exciting is that?"

"Well, he's not my father, actually. He's my mother's estranged husband, but while they were married, he treated me like I was his daughter. Sometimes I wish he was my father. I hardly even know my real dad. My mother left him when I was very young. I've only seen him a few times since."

My roommate, Ilsa, gave my hair one last stroke with the brush and tapped me on the shoulder. "I'm all done. I hope you like."

I walked to the dresser in our small dormitory room to take a look in the mirror. I smiled at my reflection. My hair was perfect. "I love it, Ilsa. Thank you."

"You're very welcome."

I turned from side to side to inspect my hairstyle from all angles. I looked so much like my mother although I didn't have her blue eyes and blonde hair. I had inherited my sandy brown curls and dark eyes from my father, but my lips, nose, and facial structure were features that my mom had passed along to me. I was even skinny just like her.

"Come on," Ilsa said. "I'll walk you to the cafeteria. It's only proper that you arrive before your stepfather does."

We left the room with our backpacks bearing our school's name, colors, and logo. And just like every other girl on campus, we had our cell phones in our hands. In silence, we rode the elevator down to the first floor and exited the building. I was very nervous. I hadn't seen Eli since my mother and I had left Diamond Estate early one morning two and a half years ago while he was away in the Cayman Islands on business. At the time, Mother told me that I'd only attend boarding school in Switzerland for a year while she established herself in the fashion world in London. She promised to return for me once she got settled and opened her design studio.

After a year, she came back and announced that things didn't work out for her in London after all, so she was moving to Madrid. More lies and disappointment followed in the months to come. Her visits became less frequent, so she started sending me pictures and emails instead. And each time she was with a different man in a different city around the world. Each was to become my new stepfather at some point, but that has yet to happen.

Each time in the past whenever I asked about her marriage to Eli, she told me that she would give him a divorce whenever she received the necessary documents, but it wasn't until my birthday last year that I learned she was avoiding the divorce. Eli told me. Months later, when he called and told me that he had fallen in love and was sharing Diamond Estate with his mistress named Radiance, I was happy for him. And when my mother finally visited me I begged her to set him free. But instead of going home to sign the divorce papers, she decided to try and cheat him out of twenty-five million dollars based on a scam. I felt awful and embarrassed when Marlon told me about my mother's plans. That's why I begged him to bring Eli to Switzerland for a visit. I wanted to talk to him in person.

"We're here."

I blinked a few times to clear my head when I realized we had reached the cafeteria. I followed Ilsa inside. My knees were knocking because of my nervousness.

"I'm going to go and join Malala, Chiyo, and Zahara at our regular table." Ilsa hugged me and pulled back to look into my eyes. "Enjoy your visit with your stepfather and his brother, my friend."

"I will."

~❤~

"McKenzie Isabella . . ." I opened my arms and walked further into the private dining area.

As lovely as a porcelain doll, she rose to her feet gracefully and walked over to meet me halfway. "Hello, stepfather. It's so good to see you."

I was too full to speak at the moment. I squeezed her tightly and basked in the joyous feeling of having her in her arms. I had always loved McKenzie because she was such a precious child. It was my dream to have a daughter as pretty and as kind as her someday.

I stepped back and took her in at an arm's length. "You're even more beautiful than I remember."

"Thank you. You don't look so bad yourself. How are you?"

"I'm fine. You look well, sweetheart."

"I am." She looked over my shoulder and spotted Marlon. "Uncle Marlon, how are you?"

He hugged her. "I'm great. It's been a long time."

"It has been much too long." McKenzie turned and waved toward the impeccably set table behind her. "Let's sit down."

As if on cue, a male server appeared, rolling a cart topped with a pitcher of orange juice and one filled with milk. There was a carafe of coffee too. We each told him our beverage preference, and he served us accordingly. Then he handed all three of us a menu.

"The eggs Florentine looks good. I'll have that please," Marlon said.

"Please bring me a southwestern omelet and spiced apple rings," I told the server.

The older gentleman smiled at McKenzie. "You'll have the French toast sprinkled lightly with confectioners sugar and Canadian bacon on the side."

She smiled brightly and nodded her head.

"McKenzie, I'm glad that you wanted to see me. I believe it was divine intervention that made my visit possible. How else can you explain the fact that I was in Europe so close by at the time that you called?"

"I can't explain it."

"Mama Sadie would say that God was stirring up something. Wouldn't she, Marlon?"

"Yeah, that's what she always says whenever something that she can't explain happens."

"So tell me why you insisted that I come to Zurich, sweetheart."

Without a word, McKenzie picked up her cell phone from the table and touched the screen. Then she offered it to me. There, in living color, was a picture of Pandora sitting on the lap of a man wearing a Brazilian soccer uniform. I scrolled to the next picture and saw her kissing a man, who appeared to be of Middle Eastern descent, fully on the mouth. I gasped at the picture of her lying on her stomach topless on a sandy beach while an older man applied sun screen to her back. Picture after picture illustrated the tale of a woman who had enjoyed a very extensive love life over the past two years with multiple men.

"I have emails, text messages, and letters too. I know most of the men's names, where they're from, and their professions. Every one of them is filthy rich or at least has the potential to be. She was supposed to have become the eighth wife of the Saudi sheik, but she sneaked out of the country two nights before the wedding."

I handed the cell phone to Marlon. "Why did you decide to do this for me, McKenzie? You're betraying Pandora. Why, darling?"

"You deserve to be happy. Every good person does. You're a wonderful man, Eli. I have nothing but good memories of you during the three years I lived on Diamond Estate. When you told me about Radiance, I could hear the happiness in your voice. You've made me smile many times, so I wanted to make you smile too. I'm ashamed of what my mother is trying to do to you. I won't let her get away with it because you don't deserve it."

I got up and rounded the table. McKenzie stood up and accepted a big hug from me. We separated when we heard the server enter the room with the food.

"There are more than a dozen emails tying Pandora to just as many men, Trapper. I can't even count the text messages. But everything has been printed out. Plus I faxed copies to Thomas. We have one hell of a file on that witch. How do you feel, man?"

"Words can't describe how I feel."

Marlon and I fell silent as the limo weaved its way through the afternoon traffic en route to Zurich Airport. We were on our way home. I couldn't wait to see Radiance and tell her the good news in person. I thought about Croix. The finalization of my divorce would affect him too. He had asked me to become his father, and I was going to do it. I planned to have a public notification issued to inform Satchel of the termination of his parental rights and my intent to adopt Croix. Because he was still on the run, I expected the process to be quick and easy.

I unzipped a compartment on my overnight bag and pulled out the envelope with the picture Croix had drawn for me inside. I opened it and pulled out the cutest and most colorful picture of a family of three. A name was written above each person's head. My heart jumped when I saw my name above a male stick figure with long black hair. I folded the picture and was about to place it back inside the envelope when I saw a black and white picture inside. I pulled it out and soon realized there were three pictures conjoined. I had never seen anything like the bizarre images before.

I studied the strange pictures more closely. The subject in each looked almost human. I could've sworn they were babies. Then I noticed Radiance's name and birth date at the bottom of each picture. The hairs on the back of my neck bristled. Suddenly, I had an out-of-body experience. The realization hit me like an avalanche. I was holding sonogram images in my hand. It didn't take my brain long to process it all. Radiance's weight gain and increased appetite in recent months along with her body's acute sensitivity all made sense now. She was *pregnant*. And according to the note typed on the last image, she was going to have a girl.

I wanted to be happy that I was going to be a father, but I was pissed too. I racked my brain for any sensible reason why Radiance hadn't told me she was carrying my child. Maybe that was the big surprise she'd planned to give me the night I had to fly to Paris. I'm sure it was. I would tuck my feelings and all speculations in until I reached Diamond Estate where we would discuss everything face to face.

Chapter Thirty-four

Radiance

"Where the hell are my sonograms pics?" I emptied everything out of my purse onto the bed for the second time, but they were nowhere to be found.

Totally frustrated, I stuffed everything back inside the purse. I sat on the bed trying to mentally retrace my steps. I hadn't been anywhere since I'd returned home Friday evening. I had searched every inch of the SUV I'd driven that day, but the images weren't in there. *Mmm . . . when did I last see them?* That was the prize-winning question tumbling through my head. Croix had found them on the floor in back of the truck and asked me what they were. That was the last time I'd laid eyes on them before he put them back in my purse. I had no idea how they had disappeared.

Eli had called and said that he was on his way home from the airport. His flight had landed thirty minutes ago, and he'd already cleared customs. I expected him any minute. That's why I needed those damn sonogram images. I wanted to give them to him to top off my surprise news. I was going to tell Eli about the baby the moment he crossed the threshold, I was tired of waiting for the perfect time and the unnecessary hoopla. I just wanted to kick back and shoot it to him straight. Whatever he wanted to tell me about his last-minute trip to Switzerland to visit McKenzie would have to wait.

I hurried downstairs to the kitchen to pour Eli a glass of red wine to go along with a snack I had prepared for him just in case he was hungry when he arrived. It was after nine on a quiet Sunday night. Croix had been asleep for about an hour, so there would be no interruptions from him. My baby had enjoyed his weekend with his grandma and all of her silver-fox home girls in her apartment building. They always made a fuss over Croix whenever he spent the night with Mama. I imagined he had thoroughly entertained the ladies over the weekend, but he was too exhausted to give me a full report when Sergio brought him home earlier. After his bath, he fell asleep on the sofa in the great room watching TV. Sergio carried him upstairs for me before he left to pick up Eli from the airport.

My heart started racing when I heard the security system chirp. I had no worries because I knew it wasn't Pandora with another one of her surprise visits because Eli had ordered the locks changed as well as the security code. Plus he'd increased the number of surveillance cameras that monitored the exterior of the house since Satchel was out there somewhere running loose.

"Radiance . . ." His voice was so arousing.

I turned around, and for the first time ever, my baby kicked in my womb. Like her mommy, she was excited that her daddy was home safe and sound. My baby girl couldn't see what I could see, and she wouldn't be able to appreciate the sight the way I did anyway. Eli was an erotic vision dressed in a pair of well-worn jeans and a black turtleneck sweater. His five o'clock shadow and the gold hoops in his earlobes set me on fire. I would never grow tired of the rugged appeal his long loose hair gave him. It never ceased to make me lust for him like a horny nun.

"I'm glad you're home."

"If I'd had my way, I never would've left you."

I walked toward him with the glass of wine in my hand. "You can make it up to me."

Eli reached for me and pulled me into his arms. Much too caught up in the rapture to think straight, I wrapped my arms around his neck with the wineglass still in my hand. It slipped from my grasp when he lifted me off my feet. The sound of glass crashing to the floor sounded faint in the background when he captured my lips in a kiss so soft and sweet that it felt like time was standing still. I wrapped my legs around his waist when he started walking across the room.

Eli placed me on top of the center island and broke the kiss. When he pulled back, I saw fiery passion in his eyes. He had missed me just as much as I'd missed him. I had a feeling that whatever we'd been robbed of Friday night was about to be recovered five times over. And I had no problems with it. Eli quickly stripped off my leggings, over-sized t-shirt, and pink lace boy shorts. Then he got rid of his sweater and jeans, leaving only a pair of red cotton boxer briefs between us.

"I would've died if I'd had to spend one more day away from you. I was miserable, babe."

"I was so lonely, Eli. I almost lost my mind."

He pulled me to the edge of the island and leaned in to cover my right nipple with his mouth. I threw my head back and cooed like a baby. My breasts were extra sensitive now that I was expecting and my clit was too. That's why it was hard and thumping out of control. And there was a small puddle of my feminine moisture on the island. I was ready for the main event, so I tugged on the waistband of Eli's underwear. He didn't disappoint me when he stepped back and removed them and his jeans completely after he kicked out of his loafers. The sight of his beautiful penis, long, thick, and hard pushed me closer to the edge. My expanding hips started thrusting forward on their own.

I enjoyed a smooth and slow entry that was more satisfying than I'd expected. Oooh! Eli knew how to hit my spot every damn time. His eyes bore into mine as he slid in and out of my wet goodness. I bucked and rotated my hips in response to his even thrusts. Our movements were perfectly coordinated. I was giving my lover as good as I got. My walls were filled with his hard dick stroking me to the stars. I squeezed my muscles around him and released him repeatedly. I loved to make him growl out his pleasure and sing my name.

When I grabbed his butt, I got the reaction I'd expected. He went in deeper and picked up his pace. And like always, his grunts and moans grew louder. I stayed with him, gyrating and throwing my pussy back at him with force. The onset of an orgasm was creeping up on me. My toes curled as the wave began to rise. I closed my eyes and held on. My walls contracted around Eli's magic penis, and I felt the earth move.

"Ah, baby, you hit my spot! Wooo!"

I knew the very second Eli came because I felt the heavy stream of warm semen rush into my body. It was a good thing that my womb was already filled with his baby because I would've been a sure candidate for conception tonight. We held on to each other in the aftermath of our homecoming sex, panting and struggling for air. I wanted Eli to catch his breath before I finally gave him his long overdue surprise. I needed a moment to recover too.

"Oh shit! I hope I didn't hurt the baby." He took a step back and placed his hand on my tiny baby bump. "Do you think she's okay?"

I pushed Eli and hopped down off the island. "You knew I was pregnant all this time and didn't say anything?"

"Of course not! Radiance, you know me better than that. I just found out about the baby before I boarded my flight home." He raked his fingers through his hair. "Make me understand why you didn't tell me we were expecting a child. Don't you think I had the right to know?"

"I was waiting for the right time. You were going through all of that bullshit with Pandora, and then we found out that Satchel was still out there dodging the law. And honestly, I wasn't sure when I first found out if you even wanted a baby with me or not. I didn't plan it, Eli. I swear I didn't."

He wrapped me in his arms. "Take a deep breath, sweetheart. It doesn't matter if you planned it or not. I believe it was meant to be."

"You think so?"

"Absolutely." He kissed my forehead. "I understand that you were afraid to tell me you were expecting, but that's still no excuse. You should've told me the moment you found out."

"I know. Are you mad that I'm pregnant?"

"Why would I be mad, Radiance?"

"I don't know," I said, sniffling on his shoulder. I was buried deeply under my hormones.

"Truthfully, I'm very happy about the baby. I don't appreciate the way that I find out, but I'm over that now."

"I'm sorry, Eli. I really mess up, didn't I?"

"It's okay, love. All's forgiven." He picked me up and spun me around. "I'm going to be a daddy! Wooo hooo!"

I laughed like crazy, feeling dizzy and relieved all at once. Then it dawned on me that Eli didn't tell me how he'd found out that I was pregnant. "Wait a minute. Put me down, Eli."

He placed me on my feet. "Are you okay, babe?"

"Yeah, I'm fine. But I need to know something. Who told you about the baby? Was it my Mama?"

"Nope." He smiled slyly. "It was *Croix*."

"*Croix*? How the hell did he know I was pregnant? He probably doesn't even know what that word means."

"Wait right here." Eli ran from the kitchen butt-ass naked and returned with something in his hand. He gave it to me.

"My sonogram pictures!" I laughed. "I've been looking everywhere for these. How did you get them?"

"For some strange reason, Croix put them in the envelope with the picture he drew for me. I didn't get a chance to open it until we were on our way to the airport in Zurich to catch our flight home. I didn't even know what the damn pictures were at first. It took me a minute to figure it out."

"Well, I'll be damned." I started laughing all over again. "I'm glad that you're okay with this. I don't know what I would've done if you'd been upset. You *are* still married. This could cause more problems."

"Yeah, I'm still *legally* married, but not for long."

"I thought the situation with the French model flopped."

"It did. *McKenzie* turned out to be my saving grace."

"What did she do?"

"Let's go upstairs and take a hot bubble bath, and I'll tell you all about it. Come on." Eli offered me his hand.

I laced my fingers through his and allowed him to lead me away.

Chapter Thirty-five

Eli

"My client has already deposited the check in a brand new bank account, gentlemen," a visibly flustered Attorney Warren argued.

"She just received it this morning. There's no way she could've spent fifteen million dollars already. Where is your client, anyway?" Marlon asked.

"She'll be here shortly. It's not like you gave us an advance notice for this meeting, Mr. Lawson."

"We notified you as soon as we could. This evidence just fell into our laps over the weekend. But make no mistake about it. Everything is certified and admissible in a court of law. And we expect more pictures any day now," Thomas said, exuding confidence.

I sat there as cool as an icicle and allowed my brother and his partner to do their thing. I was still on a natural high because I had a child on the way with the love of my life, and I wanted the buzz to last as long as possible. Plus I was getting a major kick out of watching Pandora's snooty-ass attorney squirm and squabble with my legal duo. She saw the writing on the wall. Pandora was about to lose her royal crown as international queen. And who would've ever thought that her one and only child would be responsible for her fall from grace?

"What the hell is going on?" Pandora asked, bursting through the door out of breath. She paused abruptly when she noticed me seated between Marlon and Thomas facing her at the conference table.

I'm sure she didn't wake up this morning expecting to come face to face with me. She turned as pale as a ghost. She stomped toward the table and took the seat opposite me right next to her attorney. I watched them closely as they indulged in a hushed conversation. Pandora's facial expressions were all over the place. I saw anger, shock, and sadness in a matter of seconds.

"Let me see the pictures!" she finally demanded loud enough for everyone in the room to hear.

Marlon slid the file to the other side of the table, and it stopped directly below Pandora's chest. I couldn't help but compare her boobs to Radiance's. It amazed me how significantly my taste in creatures of the opposite sex had changed in two years. It was hard to believe that I had once been attracted to a woman like Pandora. She was the total opposite of Radiance in every way. Physically, my love registered off the chart. She was a perfect 10 plus. Pandora didn't even come close. And when it came to character, there was no comparison. Radiance actually had a heart. She was sweet and generous. Nothing and no one meant more to her than her son. And her love and commitment to me were uncompromising. She was my soul mate, and I loved her more than I loved myself.

Pandora, on the flip side, was selfish, arrogant, and greedy. In her mind, the world revolved around her. Everyone else, including McKenzie, were insignificant players that she used at her disposal in her attempt to have her way in life. The woman was a cold piece of work.

I leaned back in my chair with my eyes still focused on Pandora. She was flipping through the dozen or so pictures over and over again like the images would somehow magically disappear. I couldn't wait to hear her explanation. I anticipated a list of very creative lies and excuses.

"We live in the age of advanced technology," she offered, replacing the stack of pictures in the file. She shoved it hard back across the table in Marlon's direction. "Someone obviously went through a lot of trouble to Photoshop me into those pictures. Trapper is a multimillionaire. He could've hired the best of the best in photography and imagery editing to produce pictures that make me look guilty. I'll admit that the woman in the pictures is me, but I didn't pose for a single one. I was never with any of those men."

"I suppose these emails and text messages that originated from your current email address and cell phone are fake too. Perhaps someone else sent them." Thomas stood up, and like a real Southern gentleman, he offered Pandora another file. "Handwriting experts have already verified that you wrote the letters you'll find inside, so don't waste our time denying their authenticity."

Pandora jumped to her feet. "Where did you get these? Who gave you these? Damn it, tell me!" Pandora screamed, skimming through the pile of printed emails, text messages, and letters. "I demand to know how you got your hands on this! Surely McKenzie would *never* have given you these."

Attorney Warren pulled Pandora by the arm, forcing her to sit down. "Gentlemen, may I please have a minute to speak with Mrs. Jamieson alone? You all can wait in my outer office. My assistant, Phyllis, will be more than happy to serve you coffee or tea while you wait."

Marlon, Thomas, and I stood and left the room quietly.

~♥~

"I don't have time for this, Marlon," I complained, pacing the floor. "Pandora and her pompous lawyer have been in there concocting lies for thirty minutes now.

What the hell could they be talking about? The evidence is clear. Pandora cheated on me first. Case closed."

"You're right, and Pandora and her attorney are aware of that. We have nothing to worry about, so sit down, Trapper. Let's give them all the time they need to come up with a strategy. No matter how they try to spin it, in the end, you're going to walk away a free man with all of your assets intact."

I sat down quietly, engrossed in my thoughts. A moment later, Attorney Warren appeared before us looking like she wanted to puke. Marlon and Thomas stood up, but I didn't. I was so over the whole mess already. I wanted to go home and spend the rest of my day off with Radiance.

"Gentlemen, against my professional advice, Mrs. Jamieson wishes to speak with Mr. Jamieson alone. Are you willing to allow your client to have a conversation with his wife without either of you present?"

"I don't see a need to—"

"Hell, I'm not a baby!" I snapped, cutting Marlon off. "I don't need to be protected from Pandora. I'll talk to her alone."

"Very well. Come with me, sir. I've made arrangements for you and your wife to meet in one of our lounging areas. You'll have all the *privacy* you need."

The smirk on the snob's face wasn't lost on me, and neither was the emphasis she'd placed on the word, privacy. I smelled a rat. Attorney Warren and Pandora were up to something. Even with their britches caught on a hook, they were still determined to put up a fight. I was interested to find out what they had up their sleeves, so I would indulge Pandora in a private conversation. But in less than sixty days, I would walk away a divorced man with every penny I had worked hard for.

"Are you sure about this, Mr. Jamieson?" Thomas asked with genuine concern in his voice.

"I've come across ladybugs tougher and smarter than Pandora. Stay put. I'll see you two soon."

~♥~

I was already seated when Pandora entered the small room. I had chosen a recliner in the corner, leaving her the entire loveseat to herself. No matter how in control she attempted to appear, she was frazzled out of her mind. She sat down on the end of the loveseat closest to me.

"Trapper, I feel that we can come to some type of agreement so we can dissolve our marriage quickly and amicably. I'm willing to sign the papers today if you'll allow me to keep ten million dollars of the money you gave me."

I shook my head. "I don't owe you any money, Pandora. My suggestion is that you sign the papers today to expedite the divorce, return the fifteen million dollars I gave you, and then I won't seek the twenty-five million-dollar compensatory award that I'm entitled to because of your *proven* infidelity. Take it or leave it because my attorneys and I are ready and willing to duke it out in court before a judge."

"Trapper the truth is I'm almost broke and in desperate need of money."

I was completely taken aback. "How is that possible, Pandora? Your grandfather and your father left you well off. And while we lived together as husband and wife, I took good care of you and McKenzie."

"I know, but I lived extravagantly while I was away. I spent money like it grows on trees. I also made some terrible investments that set me further back than I realized. And on top of all of that, my accountant stole from me and failed to pay my taxes for two years."

"I'm sorry, Pandora, but those are problems that you're going to have to deal with. You made choices, and unfortunately, they were bad ones."

"Trapper, I'm your *wife!*" she shouted. "No matter how you may feel about me today, you once loved and cherished me. Can you find an ounce of compassion somewhere in your heart for me now?"

I seriously pondered her question. I wasn't angry with Pandora anymore for leaving me. I now considered our separation a blessing from God because if we had still been together, I never would've met Radiance. My life took on new meaning the night I carried her out of the Pleasure Palace. Because of her, I was a better man. I was looking forward to the birth of my daughter in February, and I already had an adorable son. I felt like I was king of the world. So maybe I did owe Pandora some type of reward for abandoning our marriage. Although she'd had ill intentions, her disappearing act was the best thing that had ever happen to me. It had freed me to find the woman I was meant to spend the rest of my life with.

"Trapper, did you hear anything I just said?" Pandora asked with tears streaming down her face. "I'm at your mercy. Please help me. I'll sign the papers today so you won't have to wait sixty days to be rid of me."

"All right. I will pay McKenzie's tuition in full upfront for the remainder of her years in boarding school. I'll cover her college education all the way through even if she wants to be a neurosurgeon. It doesn't matter. I'll foot the bill. And I'll set up a trust fund for her that she'll have access to at the age of twenty-five. If she needs a car anytime soon, I'll buy one for her and maintain it. Just consider McKenzie my financial responsibility until she turns thirty."

"Thank you so much, Trapper." She wiped her eyes with her fingertips. "I appreciate your commitment to McKenzie. It's very kind of you. But what about *me*? I'm still financially vulnerable."

"By taking care of McKenzie, I'm helping you, Pandora. Now it's time for you to help yourself and stop depending on others to take care of you." I stood from the recliner. "I'll expect you to return the fifteen million dollars within seventy-two hours. If not, the deal is off, and I'll see you in court. Good luck."

"Trapper, wait!" She tugged at my arm frantically. "Listen, if you will let me keep the money, I *swear* I'll give you a baby. Radiance's son is not your son. Let me give you a son to carry on your legacy. I know I should've done it when we were together, but I was selfish. Let me make it up to you. I'm willing to conceive right away. I'm ovulating right now, and this room is *private*."

I snatched my arm free from her grip. "Thanks, but no thanks. Radiance has already taken care of my baby business. We're expecting a daughter in February. I'll make sure we send you a birth announcement."

Chapter Thirty-six

Radiance

"Whew!" I rubbed my growing belly. "Why is that she moves and kicks every time you or Croix is anywhere near me. It's like she knows who you are."

"My daughter is a daddy's girl already. I pamper you, but I'm going to spoil her rotten." Eli reached for the moisturizer on the nightstand and squeezed a generous amount in his hand. "Relax and let your man take care of you."

His warm hands caressing smoothly over my skin felt like he was casting a magic spell on me. When he reached my stomach, he kissed it and whispered softly to our daughter. And like she never failed to do whenever he spoke to her, she kicked.

"I don't know who's more excited about the baby—you or Croix. He refuses to give me back those sonogram images. He's fascinated with them. That's why he sneaked and gave them to you in the first place. He knew the weird pictures were special. Now he keeps them under his pillow."

"Be grateful that he wants a younger sibling because Mama Sadie once told me that my sister, Eunice, pitched a fit when she found out my mother was pregnant with me. And the day I came home from the hospital, she cried and told everybody I looked like a prune."

"I saw your baby pictures. You were a cutie pie."

"I agree. Eunice was just a mean brat."

I rolled over onto my side so Eli could apply moisturizer to my back. "I've been thinking about names for the baby. Have you?"

"No. I'll leave that up to you, babe. I trust you."

"Okay. I'll surprise you. I'm going to keep the name a secret until the day she's born."

"Are you sure about that? Ms. Gloria and Mama Sadie might tickle it out of you before then. Those two are a pair of characters. They want to know *everything*."

"I won't tell them no matter how much they torture me."

Eli helped me sit up on the bed and put my nightgown on. He walked across the bedroom and stood in front of the window. It was a beautiful fall night with a bright full moon hanging in the sky. I studied his posture. Something was on his mind.

"What is it, Eli? You're stiff and robotic, which means your mind is working overtime. Come and sit down. Let's talk."

"You sure do know your man." He walked to the armoire and opened the double doors. Then he bent down, opened the bottom drawer, and removed a small black box.

"What is that?" I asked, rubbing my belly. Our little angel was kicking up a storm. "Eli?"

He sat on the bed next to me and looked into my eyes. "Radiance, I love you so much. Sometimes I feel like pinching myself to make sure that this life I have with you and Croix isn't a dream. You're beautiful and smart and sassy. You could have any guy you want, but you settled for me, an older man, and all of my drama. I don't deserve you, but I sure as hell want to keep you for a lifetime." He opened the black velvet box and revealed its contents. "Stay with me forever, Radiance. Be my wife."

I covered my mouth with my hands as a fresh flow of tears fell from my eyes. I couldn't speak because the brilliant oval-shaped diamond had snatched all words out of my mouth. The huge stone was set high in a platinum setting and flanked by a trio of vertical baguettes on each side. The only thing I could do was nod my answer as my baby flipped and kicked like hell.

"I need to hear you say it, babe. Tell me that you'll marry me so that you, Croix, our little girl, and I can be an official family."

I sniffed and swiped at my tears. I couldn't stop them from falling. "Yes, Eli, I'll marry you."

"Thank you, babe." He pecked my lips.

"Why are you thanking me?"

"Because you just made me the happiest man alive." He kissed me again. "Now let's see how this thing looks on your finger."

I gladly gave him my left hand, and he slid that fat diamond on my ring finger with ease. I just sat there admiring it with more tears of joy sliding down my face. I felt my heart falling in love with Eli all over again.

"It's a perfect fit, babe. Do you like it? I told my jeweler everything about you, and he designed it to fit your likeness and your personality. Are you satisfied with the design? If not, I can have him—"

"Are you crazy? I *love* my ring, Eli, and I'm never going to take it off. How many carats is it? It looks like a giant iceberg on my finger."

"It's only ten and a half carats," he said, grinning. "And it's *flawless*. That center stone came all the way from Sierra Leone, West Africa, but I was assured that it's not one of those blood diamonds."

"Well, it's the most beautiful ring I've ever seen in my life. You did a good job, sweetie. Now I wonder how I can show you my appreciation for my proposal and this lovely diamond."

Eli pulled his t-shirt over his head and tossed it away carelessly. "I have an idea," he told me in a low and sexy voice as he unzipped his jeans. The imprint of his erection was humongous.

"Mmm . . . I'm listening, sir."

"My idea doesn't require me to talk. It's more of an *action* thing."

I relaxed on the bed and opened my arms to him. "I like that. Come and show me, baby."

Shopping for the baby was so much fun! Sergio followed me all around the swanky boutique carrying little girls' dresses, rompers, blankets, jewelry, and stuffed animals. I cut my eye at Eli occasionally. He was sitting in the daddy's corner sipping champagne and eating hors d'oeuvres with a few other men who all looked bored out of their minds. He had insisted that he tag along for my impromptu shopping spree. It was our third stop of the day, and he hadn't complained a single time although I was sure that he wasn't enjoying shopping as much as I was. Sergio was a trooper, and he had great taste. Surprisingly, he'd done an excellent job helping me select the baby's furniture and linen pattern. We had decided on an angel theme for the nursery. It was going to be heavenly.

"Wow! Look at that, Sergio!" I squealed. "I've got to have it!"

A miniature bear claw bathtub had grabbed my full attention. I waddled toward it as fast as my baby weight would allow me to. As I got closer, I realized it was equipped with a soft padded headrest, a drainage component, and a tiny compartment to store soaps and shampoo. The entire thing would fit inside the bathtub in the nursery's adjoining bathroom. It was perfect for a little princess.

"I want it, Sergio," I announced, running my hand over the smooth, white porcelain.

He laughed. "Boss said you could have anything your heart desires, so it's as good as yours."

The thing cost fifteen hundred dollars, and the matching training potty next to it was a grand. I didn't care. Both pieces were going home with me for my baby girl.

"You see something you like, ma'am?"

My body jerked at the sound of Eli's rich voice in my ear. He'd startled me. I turned around and smiled. "I want the baby to have this bathtub and potty. Aren't they fabulous?"

"I suppose they are," he mumbled, inspecting the items. "Nothing is too good for my daughter or her mom."

"Thank you, sweetheart. Now I need to find a rocking chair to put in the great room, a high chair, a hamper, towels, and wash cloths. After that, we'll have to take a break for lunch because I'm starving. I've been craving Houston's spinach dip since yesterday. I want a banana split from Bruster's too. Then we can start looking for a stroller, car seat, and a swing."

"So it's official. November the twenty-sixth, two days after Thanksgiving, is the date. Everyone raise your glasses in a toast to my pending nuptials to this extraordinary woman sitting next to me. She has agreed to relieve me of my misery. As pretty and clever as she is, she has a soft spot for this old dude."

The group seated at the dining room table laughed and touched glasses with the person closest to them. I smiled shyly and rubbed Eli's free hand before I took a sip of sparkling apple cider. Croix giggled next to me with a glass of milk in his hand, but I wasn't sure if he even got the gist of the joke. I think my son was just happy that I was pregnant with his little sister and Eli and I were going be married soon. I had explained everything that was about happen to Croix in the simplest terms possible, and at the end of our many conversations, my son always concluded that he, Eli, his baby sister and I were going to be a family. That's all that mattered to him.

I was excited and grateful that I had been blessed with the perfect man to love Croix and me. As I looked around the table at our family, I felt God smiling down on me. Mama, Mama Sadie, Marlon, Golden, and Sergio were celebrating my upcoming wedding to Eli, and in a few months, they would welcome our daughter. Pandora had finally returned the money that she had accepted from Eli without cause, and the countdown to the finalization of the divorce was on. She had refused to sign the divorce papers, adamantly arguing that she wasn't willing to give Eli the satisfaction. It didn't matter, though, because the divorce was still very much in progress.

Eli had chosen November the twenty-sixth as our wedding date because he would officially be a free man four days before. He didn't want to waste any time making me Mrs. T. Eli Jamieson. And he had already begun Croix's adoption process. My man was busy preparing for our future, and I couldn't have been happier.

Chapter Thirty-seven

Satchel

I felt naked without my locs. I had been rockin' them since my last year in high school before I moved to Atlanta with Janelda for college. They were gone now, and I had a beard and a mustache that I hated, to replace them. But when you were living life on the run and trying to stay a free man, changes had to be made. My life had undergone several adjustments just so I could survive. The bullshit job I was working in a strange land was far different from the way I usually earned money. Yeah, when I was a kid I had learned how to fish. I was actually pretty good at it, but I had never imagined fishing for a living. But that's exactly what I was doing. I had been hired as the last man in a crew on a fisherman's ship off of the coast of the Bahamas. We fished off of the coasts of other islands in the Western Caribbean sometimes too, but the Atlantic Ocean near the Bahamas was our main spot.

The other eighteen guys and I had been out to sea for three weeks straight, fishing with gigantic nets and trapping lobsters on the ocean's floor in cages. It wasn't the flashiest job in the world, but it was the best I could do under the circumstances. The pay was decent for a fugitive, so I couldn't complain. My girl, a Haitian chick named Nova, who I had hooked up with when I was on the run down in the Florida Keys, had helped me get on with the fishing crew. Her cousin, Rick, was a veteran on the small ship, so he had juice. Most of the guys I worked with were undocumented immigrants, or they had criminal records, so I felt right at home. But I kept my business to myself. I didn't need them to know that I was a wanted man. I worked hard and spent most of my down time in my small cabin in the lower deck that I shared with this older cat named Alejandro. He was from the Dominican Republic. He spoke minimum English, which was cool with me because I didn't do too much talking.

The only dude on the ship that I hung out with from time to time was Rick. He and I would fire up a blunt and drink vodka up on the top deck sometimes late at night. He was a cool guy, and he was very protective of Nova. Rick liked me because I treated her right even though I wasn't in love with her. He once told me he almost had to kill her last boyfriend for putting his hands on her. I wouldn't ever hit a woman. It wasn't in my DNA. Plus Nova was good to a nigga. She was a few years older than me with no kids, and she worked hard as a janitorial supervisor for a cleaning company. We got along fine because she knew how to treat a man. Every time I reported back to Key Largo after weeks on the sea, she fed me good every day, kept my clothes clean, and gave me plenty of good loving. And although she knew I was on the run, she had my back.

Nova was gonna help me get to Atlanta on my next break from the ship. She and I had been keeping in touch with my boys, Nuevo and Pete. They had been looking out for a nigga while he was dodging the badges. They'd wired Nova money to help us out, and they'd been keeping up with the news on my case. The buzz had died down 'cause I had covered my ass good thanks to my pretty little Haitian lover. I don't know what would've happened to me if it hadn't been for her. That's why I was gonna take care of her. I just needed to get to Atlanta to collect my money from Janelda.

Nuevo and Pete had told me that the police had finally allowed her to clear out my shit from my townhouse. She had sold whatever furniture she didn't want for her crib, and I knew she had gotten my money out of the safe. She was the only person who knew it existed and she knew the combination. I needed that money bad, so I hoped Janelda hadn't gotten greedy and spent it all. She shouldn't have spent a dime. If she had a conscience, she should have given most of it to Ray for Croix, but I doubted that she had done that. Pete said that his baby mama had told him that Bambi said Janelda was gonna put the money in the bank so whenever I finally got caught, I could hire myself a lawyer. I didn't know if that was true or not. That's why I needed to get to the A to see what was going on for myself, and Nova was gonna help me.

We had been working on a plan for a minute. Nuevo and Pete were in on it too. They had volunteered to watch Janelda and Bambi on the regular and check up on them occasionally, asking if they had heard from me. I was surprised at how sour they said my sister acted whenever they asked her about me. Nuevo said it was almost like she had written me off. How could my one and only sister feel that way about me? She was real short with me when I called her from Nassau a month ago right before I boarded the ship. It hurt me, but I understood that she was still kinda pissed with me for snatching Croix and running with him. But I believed if I could see Janelda and talk to her, she would have a change of heart.

I would see my sister soon enough 'cause once I returned to Key Largo on my next break, I was gonna rest for a few days before Nova and I made the trip to Atlanta. I was gonna collect my money so that I could take better care of Nova and myself. I also wanted to wire some money to Ray for Croix. Man, I missed my son like crazy! My boys said they hadn't seen him or Ray anywhere. They had no idea where that cracker, Eli, lived. Maybe it was for the best 'cause if they did, I probably would end up doing something really stupid during my visit to the A. I didn't need to do anything that would cause me to get caught. I wanted to stay free. I refused to go back to prison. I didn't give a damn what I had to do to stay on the outside. I would rather die than go back to the pen.

"Hello? Hello?" Ray sucked her teeth and hung up the phone.

Just the sound of her voice made my dick jump. She would have that effect on me for the rest of my life. I wanted to say something to her so bad, but I knew it wouldn't be smart. That rich cracker she was living with would probably hunt me down all the way to the bottom of Florida. I couldn't have that. A nigga was enjoying his freedom. So whenever I called Ray just to hear her voice, hoping that by chance I could hear my son say something in the background, I kept my mouth shut. I didn't call her very often, but a month never passed by without me ringing her phone at least once. I had a Tracfone, so I wasn't worried about the call being traced.

I grabbed my duffle bag from the ground and ran to catch up with Rick. Nova was coming to the dock to pick us up. I was excited about seeing my girl 'cause she was good to me, and hearing Ray's sexy-ass voice had a nigga horny as hell. I was looking forward to a home-cooked meal and a hot shower. Then I would ride Nova for a while with visions of Ray in my head before I fell asleep. That would be my routine for the next few days. Then we would rent a car and travel to the A. Hopefully, I would be able to have a civilized conversation with Janelda. And I prayed to God that she would give me my money.

"Somebody missed me." I smiled at Nova and kissed her again. "Are those spicy oxtails I smell, girl?"

"Yes. I always cook your favorite meal the day you return home from the sea. Wash up while I fix your plate and get you a couple of beers."

I smacked Nova on her fat ass before I headed down the hall toward the bathroom. Only a woman in love would go through all the trouble she went through for me. She was taking a big risk having me in her life. She had secured me a fake ID and passport. The girl had single-handedly given me a brand new identity. I owed her my life. I scrubbed my hands as I thought about how she never flinched when I first told her about my situation. Most women would've put me out or even turned me in to the authorities, but Nova didn't. She got behind me and held me down. I was lucky to have her.

I headed to the kitchen and took a seat at the table. Nova placed a plate of spicy oxtail stew over steamed Jasmine rice with sweet fried plantains on the side in front of me. Then she went to the fridge and pulled out two ice-cold bottles of Budweiser beer. She removed the tops and placed them on the table.

"Thanks, Ma. Fix yourself a plate and sit down. We need to talk about the trip to Atlanta."

"I'm not hungry." She sat down across from me. "Your friends have reserved a hotel room for us to stay in while we're there. It's right outside of the city limits. They said we should be safe. I reserved the rental car in my name. It's a Ford Explorer. Is that okay?"

I finished chewing a mouthful of food and swallowed it. "That's fine. Remember if anything goes wrong, you should get with Pete and Nuevo right away. They'll make sure you get back home safely. Don't worry about me, Nova. Just get the hell outta Atlanta."

"I won't leave you no matter what, baby. I can't."

"Listen to me," I snapped, grabbing her by the wrist. "I ain't gonna let you go to prison behind my bullshit! You don't deserve that, Nova. You've been good to me. Plus Rick will never forgive me if I were to let something happen to you. Do what I say. Promise me."

"I promise to do whatever you say, Satchel."

"That's my girl. Don't worry, though, baby. Nothing is gonna go wrong."

I continued eating the good food that Nova had cooked for me. She was a rider if I'd ever met one, but I wasn't a selfish nigga. Just like I had protected Ray when drugs were found in our apartment, I would protect Nova if something bad were to go down in Atlanta. I would go to my grave claiming that she didn't know I was running from the law. I would take full responsibility for the fake ID and passport and anything else that could be used to incriminate her. I was a real man, and at the end of the day, all of my sins belonged to *me*.

Chapter Thirty-eight

Radiance

"You have got to be kidding me, Radiance. Are you seriously going to make me wait until our wedding day to see your dress?"

"Yes. It's bad luck, Eli. Haven't you ever heard that before?"

"Yeah, I have, and I think it's the most ridiculous thing I've ever heard in my life. Now let me see the dress, damn it!"

"No! And if you try any funny business I know of something else that I'll make you wait for until our wedding day. Do you feel me?"

"Don't threaten me, Radiance," he challenged, spinning me around to face him.

"I don't make threats, sweetheart. That's a *promise*." I left the room with the garment bag draped over my arm and headed for the stairs. I heard Eli grumbling behind me, but I ignored him.

"Is that the top-secret wedding dress?" Mama asked when I reached the great room.

"Yes, it is. It's going home with you, because your future son-in-law is determined to see it before the wedding."

"Oh nooo, we can't have that."

"That's why you're going to take it home and keep it there until the day of the wedding. I don't trust Eli to behave."

"Okay, baby, I'll take the dress home. Is everything else in order?"

I nodded my head as I went over my mental checklist. "Everything has been taken care of. Pastor Kelly has agreed to officiate. We've scheduled a meeting with him for Monday to go over the details. Other than Eli's family and Uncle Walter and Auntie Joyce, we expect only twenty other guests. We like the idea of a small and intimate ceremony with just our family and closest friends. Eli invited a few of his longtime business associates, and McKenzie is coming from Switzerland. And I sent Janelda and Bambi an invitation so they can see Croix give me away in his tuxedo. Like I told you, the four of us have met for lunch a couple of times recently. Croix and I enjoyed their company both times."

"Has Janelda heard from her evil brother?"

"No, ma'am, she hasn't."

"Good. Now tell me more about the wedding. What's the menu for the reception?"

"You already know the ceremony will take place in the formal parlor, and we chose a whimsical contemporary theme. Everything will be snow white and splattered with silver. The florist and decorator have promised to turn the dining room into a five-star supper club for the reception. The next two weeks will be the longest of my life."

"They'll pass by quickly, Ray."

"I hope so. Anyway, Eli insisted that we hire the head chef from Montiff's in London because they're personal friends. Chef Vincent is going to prepare a five-course feast consisting of leg of lamb, stuffed blue crab, and orange-glazed duck with a variety of vegetables, soups, and salads."

"Will he do the cake too?"

"No, ma'am. I found an award-winning cake designer right here in Atlanta. Her name is Kathryn Kruggs. She's the premier wedding cake designer to the stars on the east coast. I decided on a four-tier, heart-shaped cake with each tier a different flavor all covered in her famous cream cheese icing. She's going to cover the entire thing with tiny pearls of confection."

"Oh my . . ."

"I said the same thing, Mama," I gushed, smiling from ear to ear. "And there's this five-piece jazz ensemble from Seattle that Eli fell in love with last year that's going to fly in and provide the music for the evening. Heck, I would've settled for a deejay."

"What about the honeymoon?"

"We're going to Cayo Espanto. It's a private island off of the coast of Belize. A staff, including an obstetrician highly recommended by Dr. Wexler, is coming with us. He'll be close by at all times to make sure the baby and I are fine. Sergio will be here to look after you and Croix."

"It sounds like Eli is going to give you the wedding and honeymoon of the century, honey."

"He is. He promised me I could have anything I wanted. I just wish that Daddy was here to give me away."

"I imagine he'll be looking down from heaven with a smile on his face. You were his pride and joy, Ray."

"I know."

Just then, Sergio entered the great room with Croix trailing close behind him. They had been outside tending to the dogs. "Are you ready to go home, ma'am?" he asked Mama.

"I sure am." She walked over and removed my wedding dress from my arms.

"Thank you, Mama."

"You're welcome." She pecked my cheek. "I'll call you later, baby."

"Okay. I'll be right here." I stared at Croix. "It's bath time, little boy. Come on."

"Wait, Mommy. I've got to give Grandma a goodbye kiss first."

I watched my little man wrap my mama in a big bear and kiss her cheek before he ran over to me and smiled brightly. "Let's go and get clean, baby."

"By the power vested in me by the state of Georgia, I hereby pronounce you husband and wife. Eli, my man, you may kiss your lovely bride."

When Eli took me in his arms and joined his lips with mine, my soul soared to the heavens. It was like kissing him for the very first time. He got greedy and pulled my tongue into a slow dance, twirling and tasting it thoroughly. I heard a loud cough from someone sitting in the first row of chairs in the parlor when his hands slid below my waist and rested on my ass. I knew it was Mama expressing her disapproval. I gave Eli's chest a subtle push to end the long kiss.

"Family and friends," Pastor Kelly said with his hands raised in the air. "I present to you Mr. and Mrs. Trapper Eli Jamieson in the name of the Father, the Son, and the Holy Ghost."

Golden, my matron of honor, handed me my gorgeous bouquet of snow white, cascading calla lilies wrapped in silver ribbon seconds before Eli whisked me up the aisle to the sound of boisterous applause. Instead of our guests tossing rice at us, white flower petals and bubbles filled the air.

After the traditional photo shoot, my husband and I joined our family and guests in the formal dining room. The place looked like a dream with white linen table clothes on each round table. The chair covers accented with sheer, silver sashes added a regal touch to the scene. Beautiful white roses in large crystal vases shaped like swans surrounded by candles sat atop each table. I couldn't believe my eyes. The sound of smooth jazz and jovial voices greeted us followed by cheers and applause. Croix left the table he shared with Mama, Mama Sadie, Eli's siblings, and their spouses. He ran over to us, and Eli scooped him up in his arms. Their midnight Tudor-style tuxedos were identical.

"Now that we got married, we're a *family*! I have a mommy and a new daddy. I'm going to have a baby sister soon too. I'll feed her, change her diaper, and rock her to sleep. Then I'll get a baby brother and—"

"Whoa, little buddy! Slow down. Let's just enjoy tonight. We're going to eat lots of good food and cake. Then we'll dance until we get tired. It's time to celebrate. We'll talk about that baby brother you want later."

"That's one discussion I'm not looking forward to," I mumbled.

The three of us made our way around the room greeting our guests. Everyone wore a smile and seemed genuinely happy for us. Croix couldn't contain his excitement. He soon forgot about Eli and me and hit the dance floor with McKenzie. They had been spending lots of time together since she'd arrived at our home the day before Thanksgiving. Now they were bosom buddies. Unfortunately, Pandora didn't feel the same way about her daughter as Croix did. She refused to even speak to the child because of what she'd done for Eli. It was fine, though, because our family was committed to McKenzie, and she was working on building a relationship with her biological father.

Our wedding coordinator rushed us to the elegant table for two at the front of the room, and the maître d' announced that dinner was about to be served. The serving staff of ten immediately went to work.

"I *love* your dress, Mrs. Jamieson," Eli leaned in and whispered in my ear. "It was worth the wait."

"I'm glad you approve. I feel sexy and pure at the same time. I chose white because I'm not a traditionalist. The form fit and sweetheart neckline was to show off my new cleavage and curves. And you know how much I hate sleeves. That's why I picked a dress without them."

"You did well, darling, but I'm more interested in what's underneath all of the lace, beads, and crystals."

"Be patient. The best is yet to come."

"Really?"

"Oh, yeah, baby, you ain't seen nothin' yet."

Chapter Thirty-nine

Satchel and Janelda

My plan was to wait fifteen minutes to enter the house once Bambi went inside, but my patience was slipping away from me. Apparently, Janelda wasn't home. Her car was nowhere to be found. I figured if I spoke to Bambi first and softened her up, she would help me to break down the brick wall my sister had around her heart for me.

I ran around to the back of the house and took out my key. It was a good thing that I'd had a mind to hold on to it. I didn't want to scare Bambi, but knocking on the door didn't seem to be the smart thing to do. I had no other choice but to sneak up on her. I inserted the key into the backdoor's lock and turned. I guess my sister hadn't changed the locks on the house because she figured I would never return to the A with the law hunting for me. I entered the laundry room and stood perfectly still. I heard water running from the kitchen sink's tap and Bambi singing Rihanna's song, "Rockstar" like she could really sing.

It was now or never, so I took a deep breath and walked slowly into the kitchen. "What's up, Bambi?"

"Uggghhh!" She screamed and turned toward me. "Get away from me! Get away from me right now!"

I rushed toward her with speed and grabbed her, placing my hand over her mouth. "It's me, *Satchel*. I ain't here to hurt you, girl."

Her eyes popped out like an alien as tears rolled down her cheeks. I could tell she was having a hard time believing it was me because of the beard and mustache. Plus my locs were gone, and I had lost about twenty pounds of muscle.

"I need to talk to Janelda. You've got to help me explain to her that I made a bad mistake by taking Croix to Miami without Ray's permission. It was stupid of me. But I ain't no bad person, Bambi. You know that. I just do dumb shit sometimes, but that's all in the past."

I removed my hand from her mouth slowly, hoping she wouldn't scream again.

"Please leave, Satchel," she begged softly through tears. "Janelda and I don't want any trouble. Just go back to wherever you were and leave us alone."

"I ain't going nowhere until I see Janelda and get my money. That's all I want, Bambi. What did my sister do with the money she got out of the safe in my townhouse?"

"I don't know."

"You're lyin'! You've been running your mouth around town, telling folks she's got my money. These streets talk, girl. Where is my money?"

"It's in the bank. Janelda put in there to save it for you just in case the cops finally caught you. You're going to need a lawyer when they find you, Satchel. You can hire a good one with that money."

"They ain't gonna ever catch me, so I won't be needing no damn lawyer. I need that money *now* so I can stay free. And I want to give some of it to Ray for Croix. That's how come I need to holla at Janelda and make her understand my situation. Where is she, Bambi?"

"I don't know. She went to hang out at Big Harry's Bar with Tater and them while I went grocery shopping. We only have your truck now because Janelda wrecked her car last month. She told me she would get a ride home later."

"Well, I'm gonna wait right here until she gets home 'cause she and I need to have a conversation. Go ahead and do whatever you were doing. Don't mind me, but don't try no sneaky shit, Bambi. I don't want to have to gag you and tie your chunky ass up."

~♥~

What my stupid brother didn't know was that I had already made it back to the crib from the bar. And I had witnessed his entire conversation with Bambi from the moment she screamed. She woke me up, so I peeped out of our bedroom door and saw Satch. I recognized my brother right away even with his new look. At first, I felt like getting my 9 millimeter handgun from my closet and blowing his fucking head off for terrorizing my woman over his bullshit. But I did something better instead. I called Detective Washington and reported his ass. Any minute an army of Atlanta's finest would arrive without the use of sirens or flashing lights. They didn't want to give that motherfucker any warning that his days as a free man were about to come to an end. All they asked me to do was go into the kitchen calmly and engage him in a normal brother-sister conversation about his money until they arrived to haul his ignorant ass away.

I slipped on my bedroom shoes and walked coolly into the kitchen. "What the hell is going on in here?"

"What's up, sis? I didn't hear you come in." Satch got up and threw his arms around me.

I hugged him back. "You shouldn't be here, li'l bruh. If the police catch you, the judge is going to stack mad time on your ass. Bambi and I don't want to be a part of your mess, man."

"Okay, I understand, Janelda. Damn! Just tell me how I can get my hands on the money you took from the safe in my townhouse, and I'll be out for good."

"I put that money in the bank. It's after five. How the hell are we supposed to withdraw a hundred grand from an ATM, fool?"

He nodded and stroked his raggedy beard as my words sunk in. "So it looks like I'm gonna have to spend the night here with you ladies so we can get up in the morning and go to the bank."

"Oh, hell nah, nigga! Your ass can't stay here! I refuse to hide a fugitive of the law in my crib! You better go and spend the night with one of your homies!"

"Janelda, stop acting like a bitch! I'm your *brother*. I was slangin' dope and sliding you money back in the day just because. Now when I need you, you wanna turn your back on a nigga? Fuck that!"

My eyes caught movement outside of the window behind Satch. He was too deep in his selfishness to even realize the house was being surrounded by cops. I figured Bambi was too damn scared to notice anything.

"Yeah, you're my brother, but you're selfish as hell. Look what you did to Ray and Croix. You were selling drugs from your apartment where your family lived. That girl could've caught a case and lost her son behind your bullshit."

"I protected her, didn't I? She wasn't charged with anything, and she didn't lose Croix!"

"You're right, but you put Ray through more drama when you got out. You snatched your son after she trusted you enough to have visits with the boy at your spot. And the worst thing you could've ever done was bring trouble to Auntie Lois' doorstep, Satch. She didn't deserve that shit. Just admit it. You're a selfish, troublesome motherfucker who only cares about Satchel Dewayne Young."

"That ain't true! I love Croix and Ray! I love you and Bambi. I'm just in a bad situation right now."

"You're right, li'l bruh. Your situation is all fucked up. Take a look out the window."

Satch turned and looked out the window above the sink. He ran to the other side of the kitchen and looked out of another window where three police cruisers were parked outside, and at least six uniformed law enforcement officers were facing the house with weapons drawn. "You threw me under the bus, sis? You actually called five-oh on your own fuckin' brother?"

"Hell yeah!"

That fool had the nerve to rush to the butcher block on the counter and pull out a big knife. He grabbed a hysterical Bambi from behind and placed the blade to her throat. "I'll kill her, damn it! I swear to God I will, Janelda! I'm not going back to prison. Call them off or I'll slit her damn throat!"

Bambi's soft whimpers and nonstop tears added fuel to my fire. She was horrified, and I felt helpless because there was nothing I could do about it. I was pissed that I had left my burner in my room. My anger had spiked off the fucking chart. I could actually envision myself busting a cap in Satch's dumb ass.

"Put that fucking knife down and let Bambi go, Satch," I said calmly although my blood was boiling. "Your punk ass ain't no killer. Hell, you're scared of blood."

"You don't know shit about me! I'll do whatever it takes to stay out of the pen!"

I laughed because he sounded crazy. "How is killing Bambi supposed to keep you from going to prison, huh? If you kill her, they'll hit you with murder charges on top of everything else they already have on you. There're only two ways out of here. Either you surrender or you'll leave in a body bag. Your time is up, bruh. You can't escape this time. Let her go and surrender before you do something stupid." I paused when my cell phone rang in my pocket. I checked the caller ID. It was Detective Washington. "It's the police. What should I tell them?"

"I can't go back to prison, Janelda!" Satch screamed with his nostrils flaring. My brother was crying like a frightened child.

"Put the knife down, let Bambi go, and go outside with your hands up. We won't tell the police about what happened in here. Just face your parole violations and the child abduction charges. I'll help you, Satch. You'll have a lawyer by tomorrow morning. I swear."

Satch dropped the knife in the sink after a while and broke down in sobs that pierced my heart. Bambi ran over to me, and I wrapped my arms around her briefly. Then I removed the cell phone from my pocket again and dialed Detective Washington's number.

"This is Washington. What the hell is going on in there, Ms. Young?"

"I've convinced my brother to surrender. He's about to come out the front door with his hands in the air. He's not armed, so please don't let any of the officers shoot him. I'm begging you. He ain't got no weapons, so there's no need for anybody to fire. Got that?"

"Yeah. Tell him to walk out slowly with his hands on his head. I need him on the ground after that. I mean it, Ms. Young. Do you understand?"

"Yes, sir, I understand. I'll tell him what you said. He's on his way out."

I sat there staring at the phone unsure of who I should call. Janelda had promised to retain me an attorney, so I didn't need to call one. I appreciated her for buying me the extra time I needed to call Nova and my boys before I surrendered. Pete and Nuevo had promised me that they would get my girl back to Key Largo after my first appearance in court. I was gonna man up and take responsibility

for my actions for once in life. It would be foolish of me
not to 'cause I was guilty as sin. Plus I didn't want to use
all of that money on an attorney to fight charges that I
couldn't beat. So after I entered my guilty plea with an
attorney by my side, the remainder of the money would
go to Ray for Croix.

Tears filled my eyes and threatened to spill when I
thought about my son and his mother. We could've had a
good life together if I hadn't fallen so deep into the drug
game and quit school like a damn fool. And even after
God gave me a second chance, I blew it when I snatched
my li'l man and took off. I had made a mess of my life.
I would probably never see Croix again, and Ray had
already put me in the wind for Eli.

I picked up the phone and dialed the familiar number.
I waited to hear the voice that always soothed me. The
phone rang several times. I was afraid that she wasn't
going to pick up.

"Hi! Who is this?"

"Croix, is that you, son?"

"Yes, this is Croix. What's *your* name?"

"This is your daddy."

"No, it's not. My daddy's name is *Eli*, and he's not here.
He and Mommy went on a honeymoon to the beach. The
three of us got married, and we're a family now. They're
going to give me a baby sister in February."

If my boys could see me crying like a li'l bitch, they
would disown me. But my heart was aching 'cause I
had lost my son, and I was about to lose my freedom
for a long time. I sniffed and wiped my eyes. "Kiss your
mommy and take good care of her and your little sister.
And always remember that your father, Satchel, loves
you." I hung up and broke down in a full-bitch cry before
Croix had a chance to respond.

Chapter Forty

Radiance and Eli

"Oh, why does the magic have to end, Eli? Why can't we send for Croix and live here forever? This island is so beautiful and peaceful. It's paradise."

"All good things must come to an end, darling. It's time for us to return to the real world. We'll come back next year in the summertime with both of our children. Who knows? We may conceive that little brother Croix is hoping for right here on the tropical paradise of Cayo Espanto."

"Unh-unh," I said, shaking my head. "I'm going to retire from the baby-making business after I drop this one. We'll have a boy and a girl, one of each. There's no third option."

"You're still young and energetic. I know you can handle one more pregnancy."

"But you're older. I don't want you to die and leave me with three children to raise by myself," she teased as always about his age.

Eli laughed at their private ongoing joke. "I'm not going to leave you, sweetheart. You and the kids will keep me young and on my toes for another fifty years. I promise."

I smiled at the thought of growing old with Eli. I imagined us surrounded by our children and grandchildren on Diamond Estate. I looked forward to making lasting memories with him. My life was perfect because of this amazing man. He completed me. I never would've thought I'd be living such a fabulous life with the kind of husband that any woman would die for. His smile alone gave me life.

"I'm glad you carried me out of the Pleasure Palace that night. I wanted to kill you at the time, but now I realize it was the beginning of our destiny."

"I think you're right." He pointed to the sun slowly making its descent over the ocean. It was a magnificent sight. "Look at that sunset, babe."

"It's awesome. I told you we were in paradise."

Eli laced his fingers through mine as we continued our last evening stroll on the beach. I would never forget our time on Cayo Espanto. It was the most amazing honeymoon any girl could ask for and so much more. But in the morning, we would board Eli's private plane back to our life on Diamond Estate where we would live happily ever after as husband and wife.

As promised, I didn't turn on my cell phone until after we had landed in Atlanta. I'd given my wife my word that we would enjoy six nights and seven days of uninterrupted honeymoon bliss. Marlon, Mama Sadie, Ms. Gloria, and Sergio knew how to contact me in the event of an emergency. Apparently, there hadn't been one while we were away because my head of security on the island didn't receive a call from any of them. However, Radiance and I did call home a few times to check on Croix and Ms. Gloria.

My cell phone chimed several times back to back a few seconds after I turned it on, alerting me that I had some text messages coming in."

"Yep, we're home all right," Radiance complained with annoyance in her voice.

I scrolled through my messages to see who was trying to reach me. All with the exception of three were from Marlon. Two were from Sergio, and Ms. Gloria had sent the other one. I decided to read Marlon's messages first. He wanted to let me know that Satchel had been arrested by the police in Atlanta at Janelda's house yesterday. She had blown the whistle on him when he sneaked into her house. Ms. Gloria and Sergio had sent similar messages.

"I guess those messages are business related."

"No." I shook my head. "They were all about your ex."

Radiance lifted her head from my shoulder as the limo cruised toward Diamond Estate. "What happened? Did the authorities finally catch him?"

"Yes, they did. Janelda called the police when he entered her house with a key he'd obviously kept from his brief stay with her. He'll appear before a judge in three days to enter a guilty plea *supposedly*. Marlon said it's all over the news."

"I'm glad they caught him. I can rest easier at night knowing he's exactly where he belongs—in a cage like an animal. I never want to lay eyes on him again."

"Well, I'm sorry to tell you that you most definitely will see him again, babe."

"No, I won't. By the time Satchel gets out of prison, Croix will be your son officially, and he would've forgotten all about that fool. Plus, my baby will probably be a grown man. My link to Satchel will be a thing of the past."

"All of that may be true, but the DA's office attempted to reach you this morning. They want you to appear at Satchel's plea hearing. More than likely, the judge will go ahead and sentence him at that time, so the DA plans to subpoena you to testify on Croix's behalf about the abduction charges."

"I don't want to see Satchel, Eli. Just the thought of being in the same room with him makes me sick."

"I'm sorry, but you don't have a choice, sweetheart. You can't disregard a subpoena. Besides, the judge needs to hear the devastation you experienced when Satchel took Croix to Miami without asking you. You trusted him, and he betrayed you at your weakest moment."

"I guess I can face that loser one more time. Maybe if the judge hears what I have to say, he'll throw the book at Satchel. Will you be there with me, Eli?"

"Of course I will. I wouldn't dare let you face your ex alone after what he did to you and Croix."

"I'm so blessed to have you." She wrapped her arms around me and squeezed.

"No, babe, I'm the one who's blessed. I have *you* for the rest of my life."

~♥~

"Mrs. Jamieson, did it ever cross your mind during the many hours that your son was in the *unauthorized* physical custody of Mr. Young that you might never see him again?"

"Yes, that scary thought was on my mind constantly the entire time Croix was away from me. I couldn't shake it."

Mr. Dunbar, the assistant district attorney, walked closer to the witness stand, his gaze boring directly into mine. "Did you think that Mr. Young would harm your son or maybe even kill him?"

"No, sir, I never entertained that thought," I answered honestly, looking at my husband. "I believe that Satchel loves Croix, but what he did by taking him endangered his life. It traumatized him. And since then, he's had the audacity to call my child, which confused him terribly."

A stream of whispers and gasps filled the courtroom following my revelation.

"Order in the court," Judge Lynmore demanded, banging his gavel.

"Please continue, Mrs. Jamieson," Mr. Dunbar encouraged after the room was silent again.

"Satchel called Croix on my cell phone the evening he was finally arrested. I was out of the country. He identified himself as his father, which confused him. Ever since Croix was abducted by Satchel, he has considered my husband, Eli Jamieson, as his father. He's afraid of Satchel."

After a few more questions from Mr. Dunbar, he yielded the floor to Satchel's defense attorney, but he declined to question me. So I left the witness stand and took a seat between Eli and Mama amongst the other hearing observers. Janelda and Bambi were present as were Sergio and Marlon. I saw raggedy-ass Nuevo and Pete in the back of the courtroom. There was a very attractive woman with cocoa skin and long braids sitting between them. I'd never seen her before. I was curious to know which one of those fools she was dealing with.

I sat quietly for the rest of the hearing as Satchel's attorney pleaded to the judge for leniency on his client's behalf. Judge Lynmore was attentive throughout the very passionate appeal. Satchel, on the other hand, appeared aloof and emotionless. I wondered what kinds of thoughts were floating through his mind. When all was said and done, Satchel was sentenced to fifteen years in federal prison for multiple charges, ranging from a list of parole violations to child endangerment to abduction of a minor.

I whispered a prayer of thanksgiving to heaven because now Croix and I could move past the nightmare that Satchel had cast on her lives. Hopefully, he would use the time during his long incarceration to work on whatever issues he had that caused him to do the crazy things he often did.

After the hearing, Mama and I waited for Eli while he went to shake Mr. Dunbar's hand for a job well done. Sergio followed him, and so did Marlon. I glanced at Janelda and Bambi as they made their way out of the courtroom. Both of them waved and smiled at me, and I felt immediate relief. I didn't want bad blood between us for Croix's sake. He loved his auntie, and I wasn't going to discourage his feelings toward her.

"Aaaggghhh, fuck, nah!" A deep and demonic voice shattered the calmness in the courtroom."

The first gunshot elicited blood-curdling screams from the slowly dispersing crowd all around me. Mama yanked me by my hand, trying to pull me down to the floor along with her. But before I lowered my head all the way down, I looked toward the front of the courtroom. Satchel had a gun in his hand, firing shots in rapid succession toward the prosecutor's table where Eli, Marlon, and Sergio were standing talking to Assistant District Attorney Dunbar. A bailiff was trying his best to get the gun away from Satchel and restrain him, but he was throwing punches with one arm and shooting aimlessly like a deranged terrorist with the other. My heart dropped, and I screamed from deep down in my belly when I saw my husband's body jerk violently as Sergio lunged to cover him. They both collapsed to the floor seconds after Marlon dropped down low.

One last shot crackled above the screams and sound of bodies scrambling in all directions. Women were crying and pleading for mercy, and I saw men crawling around on the floor attempting to comfort them. The scene was insane and chaotic. I raised my head slightly with my heart pounding like a jackhammer in my chest. I saw a group of bailiffs huddled above someone lying on the floor where Satchel had stood firing off shots.

I struggled to my feet when I saw Sergio walking stiffly toward me with blood oozing from his left shoulder, drenching his beige suit coat. I hurried in his direction even though a bailiff tried to hold me back.

"Where is Eli?" I asked, already knowing the answer to my question. I could feel it in my gut. My man had been hit with at least one bullet. Otherwise, I would've been in his protective arms instead of facing Sergio.

"He's been shot, Mrs. Jamieson. I'm so sorry. I tried my damnedest to protect him, but it happened too fast. Stay calm, though. An ambulance is on its way."

I pushed past him and forced my way through the crowd. I didn't stop until I reached my husband. I kneeled down and touched his pale face. He looked at me and attempted to smile. He must've been shot in the stomach because his lower body was saturated with bright red blood.

"Eli, please don't leave me. You promised me fifty more years."

He tried to speak, but blood bubbled from his throat and spilled from his mouth before his eyes rolled to the back of his head and closed. This was not supposed to be happening! Had God suddenly forsaken me? And if He had, I wanted to know why. No, I *demanded* to know why as a seizure ripped through every muscle in Eli's anatomy.

"*Noooo, Eliiii, noooo!*"

Chapter Forty-one

Eli and Radiance

"Trapper! Oh, my baby boy . . . I can't believe it's you. Come on, sweetheart. Take my hand. We'll be together again at last. I never wanted to leave you or Homer Junior and Eunice. The three of you were the reason why I lived. I'm sorry that I left you all too soon. But you're about to join me now. Come closer. I want to hug you."

My mother was so beautiful. She looked just like she did when I was a little boy. Her smile was bright, and there was a sparkle in her eyes. I loved the soothing sound of her voice. It had always comforted me when I was a kid. I wondered if her scent was still the same. She used to smell like rose petals all the time.

"Is that you, Trapper?" I heard my dad ask before he appeared next to my mother out of the blue. He wrapped his arm lovingly around her shoulders and smiled at me.

I tried to speak to let him know it was me, but I couldn't. I didn't understand why I couldn't talk to them. What the hell had happened to my voice?

"Come here, Trapper. All you have to do is reach out your hand. Come on, son. It's time for you to join us."

I looked around and noticed the beautiful scenery. There were stunning flowers of all colors and huge trees everywhere. I saw a rolling stream beyond the garden. The sun was shining brilliantly above the crystal clear *water. I wanted to know where I was and how I'd gotten there. Maybe I was dreaming, but it all seemed so real.*

"Come to me, son."

"Do as your mother said, Trapper. Hurry. Give her your hand."

I reached out with both arms and closed my eyes, anticipating the warmth of my mother's embrace. Then all of a sudden, I heard a baby crying in the distance. I turned around quickly and saw Radiance sitting in a rocking chair under a tree, holding a baby. Croix was standing next to the chair. They looked sad. My heart crumbled when I noticed tears streaming down Radiance's pretty face. Croix was weeping pitifully too. I started walking toward them. The baby's cries swelled, piercing through the tranquility, and Radiance's tears and Croix's continued to fall.

"Where are you going, son?" my father asked. "Come back."

I looked over my shoulder to stare at him and my mother, emotionally torn. Then I turned and laid compassionate eyes on Radiance and the children—my children. I couldn't leave them. They needed me. I had to stay and take care of them. I turned and waved goodbye to my parents. I wanted to explain why I couldn't come with them, but I still couldn't speak.

"Trapper, come back!" my mother yelled as I made my way toward Radiance and our children. "Please come back!"

"Don't go, Trapper!" I heard my dad plead.

I started running when Radiance looked up from our crying daughter and smiled at me. She stood from the rocking chair and started walking in my direction with Croix close behind her. She was a portrait of beauty. The love in my heart wouldn't let me leave her. I reached out and stroked her cheek, and she smiled with tears in her eyes.

"You didn't leave us."
I shook my head. *"I never will because I love you."*
"We love you more."
"We've got a heartbeat and a faint blood pressure! He's back! Let's start the transfusion *now*!"
"You heard him! Stat!"

I was beyond shocked. There were no words to describe the dull pain in my heart or the emptiness in my soul. I was numb from crown to sole, yet I felt everything from my baby girl kicking restlessly inside of me to the grittiness of Eli's dried blood on my palms and wrists. As I struggled to digest the reality that my husband of a few days was in grave danger, our daughter continued kicking and flipping fiercely in my womb. She sensed that something in the world that she would soon become an inhabitant of wasn't quite right. And she was on point. Her daddy was on the brink of death. I wasn't a physician or a nurse or any type of medical professional. Hell, could barely read a thermometer, but I knew that Eli had lost a crazy amount of blood. His body had gone into shock because of it right before my very eyes. I was horrified when I watched him seize, jerking violently and uncontrollably as blood poured from his stomach and mouth. Marlon had to *literally* fight with me to pry my hands away from his body.

With tears streaming down both of our faces, we'd actually tussled and argued before he picked me up from my kneeling position and hauled me away from Eli so that the emergency medics could attend to him. By the grace of God, the trio of trained trauma experts was able to stabilize him and suppress the bleeding to a minimum before they placed him on the gurney and rushed him into the ambulance. Marlon was their shadow, running merely steps behind them with me crying hysterically in his arms. Sergio, who'd taken one of Satchel's random bullets to his left shoulder, had refused medical treatment. He chose to take care of my frantic mother and drive her to the hospital to meet Marlon and me there. Only then did he request to see a doctor.

It was eerily quiet in the waiting room located on the other side of a set of double doors just beyond the operating room. I was all cried out. There were no more tears in my ducts. I was filled with anger to the max. Hate was a word that I'd been taught to never use or welcome into my heart, but every fiber of my being was dispensing hatred toward Satchel. In the moment, I considered him below the scum of the earth. He was lower than the lowest on the food chain. His actions, and no one else's, had landed him in front of a judge once again, yet he had taken his rage out on the innocent. Three other people besides Eli and Sergio had been wounded in Satchel's shooting spree. A female reporter, a veteran bailiff, and a law school student had all fallen victim to gunshots. I wasn't an insensitive person, but my husband was my only concern. While I sat praying and waiting for the surgeon and God to perform a life-saving miracle on Eli's behalf, I'd heard snippets of the conditions of the other victims as the doctors spoke to their loved ones.

The reporter was expected to survive a bullet to the leg while the bailiff, whose gun Satchel had somehow managed to swipe in his foolery, was struggling to survive a chest wound. Mercy had fallen on the young law school student. A bullet had grazed his left temple, causing only a minor flesh laceration. Satchel had been shot too, but his ass had deserved it. Only a bullet to the back had stopped him from shooting more people. A young bailiff had done all of us the honor. The man deserved a gold medal and a million bucks.

"Radiance, your mother and Sergio have gone to the cafeteria for a bite to eat. Don't you think we should do the same? I'm starving."

"Then you should go and eat, Marlon. I'm not going anywhere until the surgeon or someone in that operating room comes out here and tells me that my man is okay."

Marlon sat down next to me and wrapped his arm around my shoulders. "Trapper is going to be fine, sis. Mama said God told her so. You know she and the Lord are BFF's," he said with a hint of humor in his voice.

"My mama believes Eli will pull through too, but what if—"

"I refuse to go there," he interrupted. "My brother is a fighter. He will cheat death and live. I heard everything the doctor said about the severity of his internal injuries, but I know Trapper like no one else does. I mean no disrespect to you because I'm sure you know him even better. That's why you should know that his ass is too damn stubborn to die."

We shared a light laugh before we fell silent. My thoughts quickly wandered back to the possibility of a life without Eli, which brought on a new stream of tears. I had no idea what was going through Marlon's mind, but he looked scared. I wondered if he truly believed that Eli was going to live. We knew he was in bad shape. The doctor had explained that the bullet had ruptured his spleen and nicked his liver. It had also shattered his lower ribs, and the bone fragments had punctured his right lung. The excessive blood loss was the doctor's main concern upon Eli's arrival. He'd required a blood transfusion before the surgeon could even begin to repair the internal damage and remove the bullet.

"Let's make a deal, Radiance," Marlon suggested, snatching me from my thoughts.

I faced him without uttering a word. I wasn't about to allow him to talk me into leaving my seat in the red vinyl chair, no matter how uncomfortable it was. I needed to be as close to my husband as possible.

"I'm going to join your mother and Sergio in the cafeteria. I'll gobble down a burger or two and hurry back here. Then *you'll* go down to the cafeteria and eat while I keep watch."

"I can't do—"

Marlon waved his hand and shook his head. "Before you refuse, please hear me out. If I allow you to sit here and starve and deny my niece proper nourishment, Trapper will kick my ass when he gets back on his feet. You need to eat and hydrate for the *baby's sake*, Radiance. Please don't fight me on this. Haven't we already fought enough today?"

I sighed heavily. Marlon was right. Eli would slit his throat if he allowed the baby and me to starve. And I *was* hungry. "I do need to feed the baby. It's not fair to starve her. I'll hurry to the cafeteria and grab a sandwich as soon as you get back."

"Thank you," he said and stood up. "I'll return in a few. Text me if there's an update on Trapper before I make it back."

"I will."

I removed my cell phone from my purse as soon as Marlon turned to leave. I wanted to call Mama Sadie to check on Croix. He was clueless about the shooting, and I wanted him to remain that way. Right as I began to dial the number, the double doors swung open, and Dr. Wang emerged with Marlon trailing him. I got up from the chair as fast as I could and met them in the middle of the corridor. My heartbeat accelerated three times its normal rhythm.

"How is my husband?"

"Can we sit?" the doctor asked, motioning toward the row of chairs.

Marlon grabbed my hand and led me over to retake my seat. He draped his arm over my shoulders after he sat down next to me.

"It was touch and go in the beginning because of the excessive bleeding. Mr. Jamieson stopped breathing, and he didn't have a heartbeat for a few seconds before the blood transfusion. He had to be resuscitated. But once he stabilized, we were able to get some fresh blood inside of him so that he could undergo surgery."

"Oh my God," I whispered as Marlon rubbed my back.

"I was able to remove the bullet and stop the internal bleeding. I removed his badly damaged spleen too, but he can live without it. The puncture to his lung was more severe than we'd initially thought, so he's on oxygen, and we had to insert a chest tube."

"Is Eli going to be okay?"

"He's stable but *critical*, Mrs. Jamieson. Although the liver was only grazed, it bled profusely and swelled. Because the liver is a regenerative organ, it has the ability to grow back or regenerate after some forms of damage. I believe once the swelling goes down we'll be better able to assess its condition. Dr. Kaplan, Atlanta's most renowned gastroenterologist, will examine Mr. Jamieson in the morning and take some ultra sound images of his liver."

"Just give us an honest prognosis, Doc," Marlon requested. "Do you expect him to make it?"

"He will live, but he has a long road to recovery ahead of him."

"I want to see him."

"He's in the recovery room right now, ma'am. Give our personnel there time to update his vital signs and get him situated. Then they'll allow you to see him before they transfer him to the critical care unit."

"Thanks so much, Dr. Wang."

"You're welcome."

Marlon and I hugged the moment Dr. Wang stood and walked away. Even though he'd told us Eli would recover, I was still an emotional mess. I allowed my tears to fall as I silently thanked God for allowing my husband to live.

Chapter Forty-two

Radiance

I would've collapsed at first glance if Marlon hadn't been there to hold me up. Eli was hooked up to four different monitoring devices, all of which made annoying beeping sounds and displayed lighted graphics. The tube inserted down his throat looked painful. My heart ached for my sweet husband.

My legs found new energy as I made steps toward the bed. I reached out and rubbed Eli's cheek before I placed a kiss on his forehead. Even sedated under powerful medication, he still looked strong and rugged. Not even a bullet to the stomach could rob him of his raw manliness. He was one hundred percent pure male.

"I wish you would open your eyes so that you can know I'm here." I kissed him again. "I love you so much. I don't know what I would do without you."

"You won't have to worry about that anytime soon, Radiance. Trapper will be around to annoy the hell out of you and me for a very long time." He touched his brother's arm. "Ain't that right, bruh?"

Marlon pulled a chair from the corner of the room and placed it right next to Eli's bed. I sat down and took his hand into mine. I closed my eyes and reflected on every memory—good and bad—that Eli and I had shared. Yes, our relationship could be considered unconventional and much too rushed by most, but it worked for *us*. I had no regrets. I could even look back and find the humor in his crazy, over-the-top caveman antics that had landed me over his shoulder that night at the Pleasure Palace. He hadn't kidnapped me from my job that night all. He had *rescued* me and soon introduced me to more love, passion, and happiness than I could've ever imagined.

He was arrogant and bossy to a fault. And he was the most stubborn person that I'd ever met. Some may even describe him as a bully. But in my eyes and in Croix's, Eli was the most loving and caring man in the world. That's why I was going to be by his side every waking moment of the day, encouraging him and nursing him back to health no matter how long his recovery process would take. I had pledged to love and honor him forever, and that's exactly what I was going to do.

Marlon moved closer to the bed when one of the monitoring devices began to beep loudly. The lighted graphics started to flash quickly and change colors. Fear gripped my heart until the hand that I was holding squeezed mine. It was a weak squeeze, but a squeeze nonetheless. I looked at Eli's face just as a doctor entered the small glassed-in room followed by a nurse. The nurse immediately pushed buttons on the machine while the doctor checked Eli's heartbeat with his stethoscope.

Much to my surprise, the hold on my hand tightened, and Eli's eyes fluttered open slowly. Tears like a waterfall poured heavily down my face. A quick glance at Marlon confirmed that I wasn't the only emotional person in the room. He wiped the lone teardrop from his cheek and smiled.

"He's a strong man," the doctor told us as he aimed a penlight at Eli's eyes one at a time.

Slowly but surely, his orbs followed the light as the doctor moved the object from side to side in front of his face. He then turned his head slightly and stared at me. I felt born again as Eli caressed my face with the eyes that had lit my fire with passion on many mornings, afternoons, and late nights. I saw the love he nurtured in his heart for me. The deep soul-binding connection we shared required no verbal communication. Eli's eyes were telling me not to worry because he was going to be just fine. We would share many happy years together in marital bliss with our children at Diamond Estate.

"I'm here, baby," I whispered through sniffles. "The doctors say that you're going to make a full recovery."

Eli blinked slowly a few times but maintained his focus on me. He gently rubbed my palm with his thumb, and I squeezed his hand in response. I watched his eyelids lower gradually as we held each other's gaze. Seconds later, his brief encounter with consciousness dissipated under the influence of the powerful medication.

Epilogue

Eli

Six months later . . .

Cayo Espanto Island, Belize

My heart danced at the sight of my sexy wife and our adorable children frolicking in the ocean. The joy they brought me every day was often more than my heart could accommodate. Never a religious man, I had learned the meaning of the words, miracle and blessing, over the past six months. After spending three dreadful weeks in the hospital recovering from my gunshot wound, I returned home to Radiance and Croix with newfound gratitude and a fresh outlook on life. All of those days that I'd laid up in a hospital bed, helpless to perform even my very basic daily activities humbled me greatly. Every day that Radiance had to bathe me, brush my teeth, comb my hair, and feed me, among other tasks, had confirmed that I'd indeed married my soul mate. She alone was my greatest blessing.

Even with her belly protruding with our daughter and on swollen feet, she'd stayed by my side day in and day out. I was fortunate to have such a wonderful wife, and my heart was filled with gratitude for her. The thought that I had almost died and left her to raise our children as a widow still caused me to become emotional sometimes. Satchel's insanity had nearly cost me my life. It was a miracle that I had survived. I often relived the scene in my head, entertaining different outcomes. Thankfully, I had escaped death and was almost one hundred percent again. I was only eleven pounds shy of my normal weight, and I seldom needed breathing treatments to clear my lungs. I had a hideous scar for life on my stomach, but I felt great.

Satchel, on the other hand, was now a paraplegic, serving out the first phase of his fifteen-year sentence in a wheelchair at the Augusta State Medical Prison in Augusta, Georgia. The gunshot wound to his back had severed his spinal cord, leaving him paralyzed from the waist down. But even in his debilitated state behind prison bars, he continued to torture Radiance. As was his legal right, he was fighting Croix's adoption with determination. We were in a heated custody battle like no other. However, Marlon believed that when all was said and done, Croix would become my legal son. Radiance and I would just have to continue fighting tenaciously until the end.

I dismissed Satchel from my mind when Radiance dipped our infant daughter's tiny feet into the ocean, and she began to kick against the low waves. I slid on my sunglasses and left the comfort of my hammock nestled under the shade of two huge palm trees. The white sand felt warm underneath my bare feet as I trekked over to Radiance and the children. Her post-pregnancy body was perfect in a classic red bikini as she waded waist-deep in the ocean with our four-month-old daughter, Teigen Eliah, in her arms. Croix noticed me and ran to meet me halfway with a large conch shell in his hands.

"This is for you, Daddy. I want you to put it on your desk in your office at the Diamond Tower right next to our family picture."

I scooped my son up into my arms. "I'll do that, buddy."

"Look at Teigen!" he squealed excitedly, pointing at his baby sister. "She's kicking in the water."

I took in my wife and our beautiful daughter and was immediately reminded of just how blessed I was. Life couldn't be sweeter. "She likes the ocean. Do you?"

"Yes, Daddy, I *love* the ocean. I love the sand too. Can we build a sand castle now?"

"Sure. Let's get your mommy and baby sister to help us. Get your bucket, the molds, and the shovels. Bring the blanket too." I placed him on his feet.

"Okay."

Croix took off running a few yards down the shore to get his toys and the blanket. I walked into the ocean with the sun kissing the bare skin on my shoulders and back. Embracing my wife around her waist from behind, I brushed my lips softly across her neck.

"Excuse me, sir," she said with laughter in her voice. "Although being in your arms feels wonderful, if my husband catches you groping me, he'll be highly pissed. He's the jealous type. He'll punch you to sleep."

I pressed my body closer to hers and kissed her neck again. "He won't catch me. I guarantee it. He's too damn old and slow."

Radiance turned around in my arms, laughing, and looked into my eyes. Her smile was so bright that it competed easily with the Caribbean sun. She was an exquisite woman inside and out. Teigen was just as pretty with a head full of long, thick curls and pouty lips. Her flawless skin reminded me of creamy caramel. She had my dark eyes and straight nose, but all of her other features had come from her mommy.

Radiance handed me our daughter, and she started cooing and kicking in my arms. I kissed her chubby cheek, my heart melting with each passing second. I cradled Teigen in the crook of my left arm and wrapped my free one around Radiance's waist. Together we waded through the water and joined Croix on the sand. Once we were comfortable on the blanket, our family started building a sand castle.

JUN 2018

About the Author

Germaine Solomon is a native of Macon, Georgia who now resides in McDonough, just south of Atlanta with her husband of 11 years and their 10-year-old son. Germaine writes and edits fulltime.

Contact Germaine

Website: www.germainesolomon.com
Email: iamgermainesolomon@gmail.com
Twitter: @iamgermainesol1
Facebook Profile Page | Facebook Fan Page
Tumblr: http://romanticstoryteller.tumblr.com/